Hunting Adventures, From Father to Son

By

Kimber L. Shoop, Jr.

authorHOUSE

AuthorHouse™
1663 Liberty Drive
Bloomington, IN 47403
www.authorhouse.com
Phone: 833-262-8899

Published by AuthorHouse 08/17/2020

ISBN: 978-1-4184-5266-7 (sc)
ISBN: 978-1-4184-6955-9 (e)

Table of Contents

Acknowledgments

- To my Dad for introducing me to the world of hunting and to the quality of time together it provided until his death in 1985.

- To my other deer, duck, and goose hunting companions through the years, including Louie Argentina, Tim Arner, Tom Arnold, Wes Blackwell, Charlie Brown, Jay Crowell, Dennis Donnelly, Charlie Eskridge, Maurice Grillon, Bill Henderson, Tom Herlihy, Tony Kerbs, Dave McHeffey, Jim Parent, Alex Petrovich, Ray Poulke, Paul Reif, Tim Shaheen, Frank Utermehle, and brothers George and Roger.

- To all the fellow hunters, guides, and outfitters I met on my guided hunts, and for the experiences we shared.

- To the North American Hunting Club whose files of "hunting reports" helped me greatly in choosing the highly qualified outfitters and guides who made all my hunts so enjoyable and successful.

- To the many friends and professionals who gave their helpful input and suggestions, with a special "Thank You" to my sister, Marian, for her ongoing encouragement and support.

- Lastly, to the glorious bond market of the 1980's which enabled me to afford many of the guided big-game hunts summarized in this book!

Forward

This book is dedicated to my beloved son, Kimber III, as a gift for his graduation from the University of Virginia on May 19, 1996.

In determining an appropriate graduation gift, I wanted one that was meaningful, personal, and unique, yet something that would endure and be cherished long after I take leave of this life. It occurred to me that authoring a book about my numerous hunting experiences would satisfy all the gift criteria and intentions.

The chronological format used, beginning with my first duck hunt in the 1950's and concluding with my mule deer bow hunt in 2000, provides an overview of my metamorphosis as a hunter. My growth and maturation as a hunter has been an interesting, long-term process evolving from my youthful emphasis on bag limits and kill count to my current fascination for and enjoyment of the *total* hunting experience. As a result, I regard harvesting game as a bonus, and *not* a required or necessary measure of hunting satisfaction or success. I now understand and share the feelings and opinion of former President and notable hunter, Theodore Roosevelt, when he stated, "I know that as far as I am concerned, I have long gone past the stage when the chief end of a hunting trip is the bag."

The wonderful experiences and memories that hunting has given me are similar to those treasured by thousands of others who venture forth with bow or gun to spend endless hours in woods, fields, blinds, and tree stands pursuing their favorite game. Companions and places differ, but the sights and sounds are the same for all! Members of the hunting fraternity enjoy reading about each other's experiences, both for pure enjoyment, relaxation, and amusement, and as a learning tool to help eliminate past mistakes and promote future successes.

From such thoughts, *Hunting Adventures, From Father to Son* was born. Enjoy these readings, fellow hunters, and while doing so, I hope you'll imagine being at my side during each experience.

Introduction

In truth, I have always been an outdoor writer, having recorded in diary form all the details and aspects of my hunting adventures, which now span nearly 50 years. From the beginning of my learning curve as a 12-year-old neophyte to my current status as a wiser, more experienced, *seasoned* hunter, I have benefited from each trip afield, but still feel my "curve" has yet to peak.

As a fledgling outdoor writer, my preference centers on the "outdoor" part of that title. When I began this literary venture from my Conifer, Colorado study, with its breathtaking mountain and valley views, I yearned to be on the other side of the window, hiking through the pines, breathing the crisp clean air, scouting for rubs, scrapes, and bedding areas; in general, to be a part of the wilderness I so love. However, since I greatly admire and appreciate those fellow writers who share their experiences, I decided to provide a **verbal** "window" for viewing my own adventures.

Many fascinating, exhilarating, **and** frustrating hunting incidents have occurred to me over the years. I am hopeful these chapters have captured the excitement and will interest and entertain you, especially during those long, antsy off-season months.

Go now to that favorite chair, get comfortable, and let your mind's eye join me while I relate some of my most memorable hunting moments.

Reliving my adventures brings back many fond and cherished memories, which, along with a few mounts and photos, are all any of us will have left when our days in the field, marsh, and woods are over. Enjoy.

Chapter 1:   Ducking In Delaware (1955-1961)

I was born in Wilmington, Delaware on October 12, 1943. Soon afterward, my mom, sister, and I moved to Shamokin, Pennsylvania to live with relatives while waiting out the war and hoping for Dad's safe return from his stint with the Big Red One in Germany. After two years in the trenches he did come back to us alive **and** whole with a Purple Heart and other decorations. He was ready to start a new life. Ironically, Dad's brother, Walter, was killed at a train crossing near Wilmington while tending Dad's business while he was away dodging enemy bullets. Go figure that death thing!

The reunited Shoop family returned to Delaware and our first home at 121 Stahl Ave., Wilmington Manor, Delaware. In 1949 we moved a short distance away to a community named Llangollen Estates, a suburb of New Castle, Delaware. It was there that my hunting experiences took root.

My earliest memory of hunting was when I was eight years old, of Dad returning from a hunt dressed in his usual black and red plaid Woolrich shirt and tan canvas ducking hat. He had spent the morning either sitting in a duck blind or walking the fields searching for cottontails and ringnecks, but he would invariably have a full game bag upon his return. I relished seeing and handling the rewards of his effort and skill. It didn't matter to me if it was a brace of fat mallard drakes with their green heads and bright orange feet, or a cockbird with its multi-colored, iridescent plumage. All the game and the stories behind their demise fascinated me. I didn't know where Dad had been, with whom, or how he did it, but I *did* know my curiosity was building with each return trip. I wanted to be a hunter, too.

Looking back, I'm sure more than one discussion transpired between Dad and Mom about **when** I would be old enough to go on my first hunt. I don't think many non-hunting mothers, as mine was, feel very comfortable having their young children near loaded guns. It may have been a contributing factor to Mom's prematurely white hair, but she finally hedged her confidence in Dad's care, safety, and supervision by negotiating an additional four years before I could venture afield.

1

Those intervening years were spent reading every hunting magazine I could get my hands on and accompanying Dad to the local gun club, where I learned to handle an autoloader at its skeet and trap ranges. My first shooting thrill occurred at one of the club's "turkey" shoots when I won two frozen turkeys. That was accomplished by breaking six of ten clays and then having one of my birdshot penetrate closest to the intersection of an "x" drawn on a target at 40 yards. Although the second win was more luck than skill, I was equally proud of both prizes and beamed all the way home. Dad was one of the adults I had successfully competed against, but I could tell from the twinkle in his eye and pat on my back that he wouldn't have changed the outcome for anything in the world. The gun club, north of Frenchtown Road just off of the Dupont Highway, is long gone, but the memory of that day will last forever.

Another vivid memory of my prehunting years is from the fall of 1953 when Dad rushed excitedly into the house and told me to "jump in the car" so he could show me a sight "I wouldn't see again in my lifetime". Boy, was he right!

As we drove through Llangollen toward the bordering farm fields owned by Buck Shaffer, I became fully aware of the source of Dad's excitement. Pouring into Buck's newly-cut cornfields were literally thousands of ducks; blacks, mallards, and pintails, among other species, which had begun arriving from their Canadian breeding grounds. The sight from our concealed lookout along a hedgerow was breathtaking and the noise, deafening. It seemed the equivalent of 5,000 accomplished duck callers trying in unison to win a "feed" call competition! Wave after wave of various-sized flocks of "puddlers" and "divers" descended on that field, and I'm certain not a single stray kernel remained when the assault ended.

Dad and I stayed until well after dark, since illumination from the full moon kept the spectacle alive. It was an unforgetable event in my young life, and if I'm ever asked when my enthusiasm for waterfowl and desire to duck hunt began, I'd reply without hesitation, "One crisp fall day when I was 10 years old and my dad took me to Buck Shaffer's field to watch a *million* ducks feeding!"

The hunting seed had been planted, but it still needed two more years of water and sunshine! However, my time was coming, and I started counting down the days to my first hunt. I longed for the day when I could finally start to learn how to become a hunter, but that dream would remain so until I could accompany Dad. In the meantime, I kept reading my magazines.

Finally, the big day arrived! Before I opened my eyes I heard Dad's voice whisper, "Time to get up. It's three o'clock. I'll be in the kitchen." I gave a tired but excited, "OK, Dad, I'm awake!" It seemed like only minutes before that we had laid out our clothes in the kitchen, but I didn't need a second call.

My first hunting wardrobe consisted mostly of Dad's extras, which gave me plenty of "spinning" room inside, but as Dad explained, "You want to be warm 'cause it can get pretty cold sitting in the blind. Nobody will see you anyway." As it turned out, I did stay warm. However, I remember feeling embarrassed when introduced to some of Dad's hunting buddies at the boat landing wearing a lined coat, canvas pants, and hip boots, all several sizes too big. I mean, part of hunting is *looking* like a hunter, isn't it? If Dad's design was to see if I liked duck hunting before spending the money to outfit me, then by the end of the day he realized it would be money well spent.

I am pleased to report that before my second trip to the marsh, I had received several early Christmas presents, including a set of red thermal underwear, a dark green down vest, canvas hunting pants, and my first pair of hip boots, size seven, with separate gray insulated rubber booties to wear inside.

My first hunt **was** the adventure I had anticipated and hoped for, with one exception: I didn't have a gun! Dad wanted to break me in slowly and felt there was enough for me to observe and learn before and after the shooting to keep me busy. In retrospect, I realize Dad's game plan was for me to understand and appreciate the total hunting experience of which shooting was a part, and not the end-all. Hunting, especially duck hunting, can be a lot of hard work, which I came to realize once we finished our hunters' breakfast of eggs "over light", ham, home fries, and coffee at the Crossroads Diner near home. There were many other "duckers" at the diner, and I remember trying to act and look older than my 12 years. If "clothes make the man", then I had a lot of work to do!

After the diner, our next stop was at George Trivet's Texaco station, where Dad boarded our retriever; a six-year-old female Chesapeake Bay named Strawberry. I don't recall how the name came about, but Dad had bought her as a puppy to train exclusively as a ducking dog. I do remember clearly her excitement when we drove up to the pen that morning, her jumps and barks giving full evidence that she knew she was about to "get after some ducks"! Just the

thought of making repeated plunges into the frigid Delaware River - let alone actually doing it - made me shiver! Better her than me, that's for sure!

All of Dad's ducking buddies owned Chesapeake Bays. Even though they could be a bit pig-headed and difficult to train, you couldn't ask for a stronger, more reliable, or durable "best friend" in any blind.

Dad taught Strawberry to sit in her compartment inside the blind until the first shot was fired. At the sound, she'd leap into the water through the reed-covered front opening to retrieve each downed bird. I marveled at how carefully she swam around the decoys to avoid dragging or tangling them, then drop each bird on the shore until all were retrieved. Some pursuits covered 200 yards or more through the fast-moving tidal waters.

The final phase of Strawberry's ritual was to shake off and walk triumphantly from shore to blind with each duck or goose. She happily accepted the pats and praises from all inside. Then, back in her box, she'd eagerly await the next barrage; shivering, yet content. Years later, I remember Dad complaining more out of heartache than annoyance that Strawberry's days in the marsh were drawing to a close. Age was catching up with her; she had started to take short cuts through the decoys! We eventually gave her to our garbage man, George, who wanted a companion. She became his special friend and rode next to him in his truck. He took good care of Strawberry until her death at the age of 14 - a dog's life, but not a bad one at that!

Dad had invited a friend, Judd Dimling, to hunt with us and serve as official witness to my first ducking adventure. Judd joined us after breakfast, and, with Strawberry aboard, the four of us headed south on Route 13 toward the town of Odessa. There, we turned east and followed some county roads past the Daniel's farm to the river, where Dad kept his sturdy 14-foot duck boat near the landing's parking area. After dragging the three seater 30 yards to the water's edge, attaching the 10 HP Evinrude motor, and loading the guns, ammo boxes, lunches, thermos bottles, and a pair of oars ("just in case something happens to the motor"), we were ready for the 20-minute ride to the blind. Dad was part of a marsh lease in the Taylor's Bridge area, and four shore blinds had been built using 4 by 10-foot metal "Coke" boxes for their foundations, which were anchored firmly into the mud to prevent flood tides from washing them away. Their upper wooden frameworks included compartments on both ends to hide dogs and gear, and each structure was completed with a plank seat along the back, an ammo shelf in front, and an overhang above our heads to conceal us from birds passing directly overhead. Wood floor slats kept our boots dry and feet warmer on extremely cold days. "Reeding" the blinds added the final touch, and cut myrtle branches stuck in the mud around the structures broke up their outlines. The blinds were aptly designated the north, south, east, and west blinds, and were so located to take advantage of any prevailing wind condition. The west blind was the most productive, since the winds blew predominantly out of the west or northwest and caused the birds to "pitch" directly into the calm, inviting waters of its lee shore. However, when a "nor'eastern" blew in, **all** the blinds were productive, with ducks coming off the choppy river seeking sanctuary in the calmer inland ditches. Those big winds brought wonderful hunting, but also created dangerous flood tides well above normal levels. Dad told me of one incident when he got caught in a howling northeastern storm and the water rose **above** the blind. His only chance to keep from being swept out to the main body of the white-capped river was to tie the boat's anchor rope to the blind's frame and ride out the storm. It was a harrowing experience that he never forgot!

Dad had an uncanny and unfailing ability to locate each blind in the pre-dawn darkness. With only the stars as his guide, he'd navigate through the maze of channels and ditches for 20 or more minutes and, then, instinctively shine his flashlight shoreward. Presto, instant duck blind! I guess it was a function of his having covered those routes so often over the years that he could have done it blindfolded. Still, it never ceased to amaze me.

That morning of my first hunt was no navigational exception as we arrived at the west blind. A light wind was blowing from the northwest and promised to increase with the change of tide in a few hours. The tide was low when we arrived, and a 15-yard stretch of black, thick, oozy mud separated us from the blind. Dad kept his decoys in a locked box sunk in the mud near the blind, but before attending to that chore, we first had to push the boat through the mud, unload the gear, and carry it to the blind along narrow board walkways. While Judd helped Dad unravel the weighted decoy cords and arrange the "blocks" in an alluring pattern, I stayed with Strawberry in the blind and observed their work. However, I had successfully passed my first test: getting through the mud without becoming stuck up to my waist!

That peaceful time before sunup enabled me to fully absorb the distinctive sights and sounds of my surroundings; shooting stars and bright constellations, the moon's reflection on the water, and ghostlike flocks of mallards and teal coming off the river, among other observations. My overall feeling was one of excitement and anticipation. What was going to happen when the sun came up?

As it turned out, anticipation of a "top 10" day was quickly replaced with the reality of a "blue bird" day. The expected pickup in wind never materialized, and once the early migration of ducks found their resting places, few flocks were spotted. Those that were sighted definitely had plans other than to visit our "spread". The decoys looked real, but due to the lack of wind, they didn't *act* real.

Thousands of blackbirds kept passing overhead, partaking in their annual fall migration, and I accepted as gospel Dad's statement, "When you see blackbirds, you'll usually see ducks flying." That day was obviously an exception! By 10:00 a.m. Dad's great overhead shot on a fast-flying, blue-winged teal was all we had to show for our endeavor.

Dad finally suggested that we take the boat out to the river to stir up some of the contently resting flocks. What did we have to lose? Hopefully, they would continue trading long enough for us to return to the blind and be rewarded with some good shooting! After securing Strawberry, the three of us got into the boat and headed towards the big water. Fortunately, the tide had come in, so we didn't have to negotiate the mud again!

The trip to the river started innocently enough, but by the time we emerged from the last slough, the wind had started to pick up. The calm, even swells rose in height quite rapidly. We had spotted a sizeable raft of ducks about 200 yards farther out in the open water, and our goal was to get them flying.

Two hundred yards doesn't sound very far, but in an increasingly turbulent expanse of water the size of the Delaware River, it seemed like a mile. The boat rose and dipped in the waves with enough force to engulf us in spray with each sequence. The uneven weight distribution of the occupants, coupled with the sudden look of concern in Dad's eyes, convinced me that our plan was in serious trouble and that the possibility of capsizing was real. I think my cry, "I'm scared, Dad!", confirmed the adults' thinking as well, and "Captain" Shoop quickly turned the boat around and headed back to the blind. Since it was close to noon, we decided to call it a day, our satisfaction being that we had diverted a potential disaster and survived to hunt another day. The sun had broken through a spotty cloud cover and few ducks were in the air, so it made our decision to quit an easy and unanimous one. The bobbing waterfowl we had seen on the river were holding their place, unaware of the near tragedy they could have been witness to only moments before. Strawberry didn't have a hint.

I watched as Dad and Judd collected the decoys, which consisted mostly of blacks and mallards. Those were the two preferred species for filling the four ducks per hunter limit. Before point systems and certain species restrictions became the rule, you could shoot any type of duck. Teal, redheads, and scaup were reserved for calmer days when selectivity was not an option!

Since Dad and his buddies made their own decoys, shooting **over** them was the unwritten rule. Not only was wing shooting more sporting, but it also minimized shot damage to one's labor of love. It wasn't until I reached my mid twenties and started making my own decoys that I fully appreciated the satisfaction and thrill of having ducks cup their wings and confidently glide into a "rig" made with my own hands. It was confirmation that I had crafted them well enough to fool their live counterparts.

Dad loved to make and repair his decoys during the off-season. Starting with one by eight-inch pine planks, he cut the needed number of oval bases and similarly shaped body forms from compressed sheets of dark brown six-inch thick cork. Once glued together, clamped, and allowed to dry, the rough body was ready for refinement and shaping with a wood rasp. A solid wooden head was held in place with a section of half-inch doweling that ran through the cork and attached to the base. A tapered one-inch thick rudder ran lengthwise along the bottom, and soft lead was nailed wherever balance was needed. After a little paint on the head and base, those "working" decoys were ready for action. The total weight of the materials used prevented the unnatural bobbing and rolling that is so prevalent in many of today's lighter, plastic models. I'm certain the natural movement of our handmade variety contributed to the high success rate we experienced. When I later made my own dozen black duck decoys, I copied Dad's design and materials for the base, body, and rudder, but chose to buy prepainted, durable plastic screw-on heads from *Herters*. Even so, my enjoyment, satisfaction, and success were the same!

After each hunt, the decoys were carefully collected, and their 15-foot nylon cords were wound tightly around the bodies. The end of each cord was tied to a lead anchor and wrapped around the decoy's neck. Dad also used a half dozen Canada geese decoys, which he liked to place to one side of the spread. Not only did that arrangement attract an occasional "honker", but, as Dad explained, they also added a sense of safety and security to the entire rig. Geese decoys also helped pull in some shot-wary ducks that otherwise may not have given us a second look. That's what I was told, and it seemed to make sense!

With the hunt over, we headed back to the landing, unloaded the gear, and secured the boat. I was introduced to some of Dad's cronies who had also completed their day's hunt. Walt Miner and "Ricey" always hunted together, and both were excellent shots. They always seemed to get their limit **regardless** of weather conditions or which blind they used. They didn't waste many shells is what I'm trying to say! They had scored on some "greenheads" at daybreak, and I listened intently to their recollections, while at the same time trying to hide my oversized hip boots behind an overturned boat! Strawberry and Walt's dog, Duke, played along the water's edge.

Brothers George and Bob Trivets were also there with equally interesting stories to absorb. Until my graduation from high school, I enjoyed many exciting days in the marsh with both of them, their sons, and other family guests.

When I later reflected back on that first duck hunt, I realized I had enjoyed every minute of it - fun, danger, and excitement all wrapped into one big adventure. I felt like Tom Sawyer and couldn't wait to do it again.

Even though Dad had bagged the only duck, I tied with Judd for second place and didn't even have a gun! However, my weaponless plight ended the following Christmas when Dad surprised me with my first shotgun; a three-piece, single-shot, full-choke, .410-gauge Winchester model 37! On December 25, 1955, it became the most cherished gun in the whole world. Shortly thereafter, I shot my first duck with it; a fat mallard drake.

Many fond memories of those early waterfowl hunts and the quality time spent with my Dad come flooding back every time I look at that little .410 inside my gun cabinet. I remember him teaching me how to wingshoot by pointing and swinging through as I pulled the trigger and telling me to keep my head down when ducks passed directly overhead. He also taught me how to use his old black P.S. Olt duck call to attract and lure them in via a combination of greeting, come-back, and feeding calls, and, more importantly, when **not** to call! He showed me how to distinguish the various species of ducks by their flight patterns, speed, size, and coloration and how to properly space the decoys and set them within effective shooting distance of the blind.

Also, when ducks appeared overly weary or flared abruptly as they neared the blind, Dad would immediately check for spent shells outside our enclosure to be sure their brass wasn't reflecting the sun! In addition, many wonderful stories about past hunts and other unusual occurrences were told and retold, such as when Dad thought he saw a clump of brush drifting toward the blind only to have that "brush" materialize into the eight-point rack of a whitetail buck swimming past the decoys!

Dad's own trusty duck gun, a 12-gauge Remington model 11 occupies the next position in my cabinet, and in my mind's eye I can still see him using it to make one great shot after another. He rarely missed, and I used to pity the poor duck or goose that flew within his range. With Dad's death, his favorite shotgun was silenced as well. In deference to his memory and shooting prowess, I intend to keep it that way.

The
Hunting
Shoops:
(L to R) George,
Kim Sr., Kim Jr.,
and Roger

A Delaware
Duck Hunt:
(L to R) Roger,
Kim Sr., and
Kim Jr.

(Above) handmade black duck decoys of Kim Sr. (top left and right) and Kim Jr. (bottom left and right)
(Below) black duck decoys made by Kim Sr. (left) and Kim Jr.

Kimber L. Shoop, Jr.

Chapter 2: Bowhunting for Bucks at Buck's (1957-1961)

I was introduced to "bows and arrows" while attending Camp Matahoon during the summer of 1957. My lifelong pals, Bill and Paul Reif, had attended the camp, sponsored by The Boys Club of America, the previous summer. I was determined to do the same, even though our family cottage on Shallcross Lake near Middletown, Delaware had all the amenities of a camp. Of course, being "like" a camp versus actually being a camp are two entirely different things. So, after receiving the required Boys Club membership as a 13th birthday present, off to camp I went. I participated in all the usual camp activities, including shooting .22-caliber rifles at the range, riding horseback, fishing in White Clay Creek, making lanyards in craft shop, and swimming laps at dawn as a member of the Polar Bear Club. However, the one activity that I enjoyed the most was archery. The straight-limbed 30-pound wooden bows and cedar arrows with real turkey feather fletching were a threat only to the round straw targets with their white, black, blue, red, and bullseye-yellow facings supported on wooden tripods. I remember how thrilling it was to hit any part of the 25-yard target face, especially with "instinctive" aiming and shooting being the order of the day. Compared to today's high-tech cam compounds, aluminum or carbon arrows with plastic fletching, stabilizers, bowsights, and release devices, things were on a rather primitive level at Matahoon's range. But it was enough to peak my interest and get me involved in a sport that would bring me my most satisfying deer harvests many years hence.

Back in the mid 1950's, bowhunting was still in its infancy, and Bear Archery reigned supreme over all equipment manufacturers. Luckily for me, Dad got the archery bug one summer, and soon our cottage had a range of its own. I then divided my time between bass fishing and honing my skills with the bow; not bad choices for a youngster to have, especially with three long years before I'd be eligible for my driver's license. If I had just an inkling back then of bowhunting's potential growth in popularity, and the tremendous advancements in archery equipment over the next 40 years, "Shoop" would now be synonymous with Bear, Jennings, Hoyt, and Easton! Oh well, Mom threw out my baseball cards too!

After three months of rigorous practice at the cottage, I looked forward to taking my new skills afield during the fall archery season. Buck Shaffer's farm was less than a mile's walk from our winter home, and Dad told me he had seen a lot of deer tracks in that area while hunting small game the previous year. Since there were very few bowhunting books available then, and even fewer magazines devoted to the sport, I was about to begin my whitetail bowhunting career close to base "0". My knowledge of deer habits, scouting for bedding and feeding areas, the significance of rubs and scrapes, camo, scents, tree stands, and anything else needed to be successful had to be learned haphazardly. My learning curve had nowhere to go but up, and it was time to get started.

Among the factors contributing to my early interest in deer hunting were my visits to a local deer "check-in" station during Delaware's brief either-sex shotgun seasons. The Division of Fish and Wildlife began keeping harvest records when deer hunting was reintroduced during the early 1950's. Information about deers' sex, estimated age, weight, and kill site was collected by division personnel as hunters brought their newly-tagged bucks and does to the officially designated scale locations. One was just up the highway from Dad's Esso station at the intersection of Routes 13 and 40, and I remember as a wide-eyed 12-14 year old how exciting it was to spend entire days watching carloads of successful hunters pull in to have their deer "checked in". I was full of questions as to where and how they had scored, and also what gauge shotgun and type of ammo were used—slugs ("pumpkin balls") or buckshot. Since I had seen very few deer in the wild up to that time, I was awed and inspired by those who did fill their tags. There was a certain mystique connected with such accomplishments that was separate and distinct from bagging a duck or rabbit. My curiosity went into overdrive as I became determined to try my hand.

I clearly remember my feelings of fear and apprehension whenever I walked through our neighborhood in the predawn darkness to the bordering farmland owned by "Buck" Shaffer. Part of that apprehension was probably due to the fact that I hadn't asked Mr. Shaffer for permission to hunt on his land, and because of Buck's reclusive, unfriendly nature, I was afraid to do so anyway! He would be seen occasionally by the neighborhood kids as he drove the half-mile dirt lane to and from his farmhouse. Never a smile or wave was cast our way. This bald, ruddy-faced land baron was a bit short for his weight, and as far as could be determined, he had never married and lived alone. His only known regular human contact was with Mrs. Fox, his housekeeper, who visited twice a week. She was a friendly person according to feedback from the neighborhood girls, who would occasionally pay her a visit. But Buck remained a mystery. It was easier and more fun to paint him as a mean, grumpy, nasty character versus the quiet, introverted personality of a lonely man, which was probably closer to the truth! I wonder now whether his unfriendliness towards us boys may possibly have been caused by his suspecting that we were the culprits who visited his barn on occasion to rearrange his hay bales by riding them from the loft to the floor below! Of course we first had to cut a *few* bales and spread their contents to a liberal depth to cushion our 15-plus foot drop! It was "kicks" and fun for us boys, but only a source of irritation and work for Buck to clean up the mess we left behind. No wonder he always seemed stewed! Is it possible that without our devilish, irresponsible behavior Buck could have had a successful career as a stand-up comedian? ....Nah!

Such thoughts were in mind on one particular fall afternoon when I made my way towards "the farm". With my green and tan two-piece camouflage outfit, rubber- soled boots, hip quiver of feather-fletched wooden arrows, 45-pound straight-limbed long bow, three-fingered glove, and arm guard, I pushed through the hedgerow bordering Buck's farm lane. I intended to proceed down the lane toward the farmhouse before crossing over to the other side, where a series of cut cornfields, hedgerows, and woodlots awaited my unseasoned skills. However, within steps I heard the truck coming behind me. I knew I had been seen, and I ***knew*** the driver of the old green Ford pickup could be only one person! My first instinct was to run, but I decided to hold my ground, come what may. Buck stopped alongside me, rolled down his window, and asked without any trace of humor, "Where are you going?" Trying to think on my feet as fast as any trespassing 14-year-old boy could, I told him my name - knowing that Dad was one of the few people Buck allowed to hunt small game on his land - and that I hoped he wouldn't mind if I bowhunted. After a big "please", he relented. However, it wasn't until years later that I realized his permission surely included his judgement that I and my primitive weapon posed little, if any, threat to his deer population!

With a sigh of relief, I proceeded across one cut cornfield towards another that marked my destination. It was near an old oak tree on the edge of that second field that I had spotted my first "racked" buck a couple of weeks before. I was walking along the edge of that field at daybreak looking for deer tracks in the soft mud, when I happened to glance over the adjoining hedgerow and saw him staring at me 20 yards away. Caught by surprise, I instinctively ducked down with the faint hope that he hadn't seen me, and at the same time praying he wouldn't run off. I shifted my position to prepare for a shot and tried to keep my heart from jumping out of my chest! As I slowly rose, my knees were shaking harder than when I exchanged "I do's" for the first time in June 1965. Needless to say, the buck was long gone, and only his widely-splayed tracks at 15-foot intervals convinced me he **had** been there and wasn't a figment of my imagination. That confrontation was both exciting and disappointing. My dream of parading back home with a deer in tow would have to wait for another day. However, the hunting bug had taken another big bite!

But I digress. I still had to negotiate a thick hedgerow to get to the second cut cornfield where the old oak, "buck-spotting" tree stood. Since the hedge was too high to climb over, I got down on my hands and knees and crawled along until I found a large enough opening to squeeze through **under** the tangle. I remember thinking how clever that move was as I clutched my bow and quiver close to my side and inched my way through. Once clear, I rose to my feet and started toward the oak approximately 30 yards away. Abruptly, I froze in my tracks! Along the nearside of the hedgerow by the oak stood a large doe facing me with front legs spread and a look of, "You're the largest hedgehog I've ever seen," combined with "I'm not sticking around long enough to ask questions either!" At the same time, I was slowly pulling my bow up and trying to nock the arrow I had already drawn from my quiver. While trying to keep one eye on the doe and one on my work, I quickly realized to my complete horror and consternation that my bow was upside down with the arrow rest on the bottom - an inadvertent **turn** of events, literally, resulting from my under-the-hedge crawl. I'm not sure if I heard a laugh as the doe leaped across the field, but I think she at least smiled and winked as she went by! My internal cry of, "Stop! Please, stop!" had no effect on her hasty retreat. Being caught off guard and unprepared had cost me again!

During another excursion to Buck's farm, I stood behind a hedgerow where I could watch an area of heavy ground cover, thorn bushes, small saplings, and weeds on the opposite side. There was a game trail that cut through the middle of that 40-yards wide growth which connected a woods and cornfield. Ahah, bedding and feeding areas! I was beginning to get the picture and had, in fact, spotted a pair of does there during a previous visit. This time I'd be ready for a shot. However, what I hadn't counted on was a small herd of deer, including a "racked" buck, entering the upper end of the field I was **standing** in! It didn't take long for 20-plus eyes to stare my way and conclude that I didn't belong there.

Their exit began with quick, stiff-legged gaits followed shortly by long bounds, while I tried to intercept them via a diagonal crawl across the field. To my dismay, not only had they seen me, but the wind was carrying my scent directly towards them! As the last white "flag" disappeared over a distant hedgerow, I cursed my bad luck and wondered what I needed to do to avoid the mistakes that were preventing me from getting close enough to my quarry for a decent shot. It wasn't as if I could go home and discuss my failings with Dad, since he didn't have much bowhunting savvy either, and, as I mentioned earlier, reference material was scant. It looked like trial and error was going to be my teacher.

With each trip to Buck's farm, I kept hoping for the right circumstances to prevail, ending with a triumphant march home, dragging a big eight pointer. I was just then beginning to understand a deer's distinct advantage over man via its ears, eyes, and, most notably, **nose**. Unfortunately, I didn't know how to counter those senses by using effective camo, masking scents, downwind tree stands, et al. Little did I realize at the time that I was at the bottom of my bowhunting learning curve with many more blunders and disappointments to follow before I'd accomplish my first harvest - an ongoing, often painful, yet necessary process most seasoned bowhunters can attest to and must go through. "Lady Luck" does play a part in any successful hunt, but to have **consistently** favorable results over time, no bowhunter can ignore or minimize the importance of knowledge, experience, and learning from one's mistakes. There are no short cuts.

Unfortunately, before I could gain such knowledge and experience, a high school friend, Drew Foster, killed a big eight pointer near Buck's farm during the shotgun season. I was certain it was the same buck that had spotted me on the wrong side of the hedgerow a month earlier. I can't tell you how far my heart sank when I heard the news. How dare he kill *my* buck!

Kimber L. Shoop, Jr.

Chapter 3: Pennsylvania Bowhunt – A Tough Lesson Learned (1958)

There is nothing in life more important than friendships, especially those deep-rooted alliances formed before age hits double figures, and which seem to survive and grow in strength even without constant contact in the years that follow. Such was the friendship that existed between Dad and Donald "Turp" Kline. They had grown up together in Shamokin, Pennsylvania, played basketball and football together for Shamokin High School, and enjoyed lazy summer days catching native brook trout in nearby mountain streams. They were like brothers, and, as adults, deer hunting forays with both bow and rifle kept their bond of friendship as strong as ever.

I remember Turp as a gentle giant, fond of butter, eggs, bacon, sausage, and any other food that clogged the arteries and added the pounds! Heavy jowls underscored his bald head, but a heavy, dark mustache added to his total hair count. Turp captured perfectly the speech pattern I can only label as "Shamokinese", almost melodic in deliverance with word emphasis given early in most sentences and volume decreasing from beginning to end. Meanings were freely substituted and subject to one's own interpretation. Typically, a fall phone call from Turp to Dad would be, "Heh, Sheebs" (Dad's nickname from high school), "*Are* you planning on comin' "down" to deer hunt with me?", even though his home in Elysburg, Pennsylvania was decidedly *north* of our home near New Castle, Delaware! Turp had settled there after marrying his high school sweetheart and operated a successful electrical contracting business. Don had two daughters and his homegrown hunting buddy, Donald, Jr.

In the fall of 1958, Dad received his annual invitation from Turp to come "down" for a whitetail bowhunt. The only difference from past years was that I was invited, too! Two weeks later, in early October, Dad and I loaded our gear and headed up Route 202 North out of Wilmington for our four-hour drive to Elysburg. It was a beautiful clear day, and the changing foliage was worth the trip alone. Greens, oranges, reds, and yellows blanketed the landscape.

After our arrival, with many hugs, handshakes, and introductions exchanged, Turp outlined plans for our two-day hunt. We'd be hunting with C.Q. McWilliams, our official host, and his brother, Doug. Their dad had acquired several thousand acres of prime whitetail land back in the 1920's and 1930's, and the boys inherited it when he died. The parcel was located in Liberty, Pennsylvania, a small town in Tioga County and only a short drive from Turp's home.

Several other friends and acquaintances of C.Q. joined the hunt, which was as much a requirement as a reunion, since their preferred hunting method was to "drive" the large mature woodland. By having four to six "drivers" move the deer ahead towards an equal number of "standers" posted about 50 yards apart, it was a time-tested way of harvesting deer. It was a new method of hunting for me, and I recall during that first morning's hunt how my heartbeat increased in speed and sound as the drivers' voices increased in volume when the distance narrowed between us. With a limited number of men to cover such a large expanse of woods, the drivers were encouraged to make a lot of noise, both vocally and by striking tree trunks with branches. I witnessed the hunter next to me make a clean miss at a doe from his perch atop a six-foot high boulder. She was moving at full speed! A "silent" drive, where drivers walk slowly and quietly towards the standers, may have produced better results, since deer tend to "sneak" rather than run ahead of the drivers when that method is used.

After three fruitless drives, we all gathered at the cars to exchange stories of sightings and misses. There was only empathy and encouragement from everyone when I explained how a small doe zipped past me before I could even raise my bow!

On Saturday morning we tried the same method, with the same results. Turp then suggested a new strategy for that afternoon which he felt could produce venison. His idea was to post along the estate's main road near crossings that deer used in the late afternoon on their way from bedding to feeding areas. After Dad was dropped off at his designated spot with an exchange of "good luck", Turp drove me several hundred yards farther to a spot he *assured* me would produce deer! He guided me to a spot five feet off the dirt road, and only 15 yards to the right of a well-worn deer trail that started at the road and curved behind me at a point about 20 yards inside the woods. The trail then maintained a parallel path with the road for several hundred yards. Turp explained that the deer would approach on the trail behind me and, if they stayed on course, would eventually appear at the edge of the road 45 feet away. He said they would almost certainly pause at the road to be sure the coast was clear before crossing, giving me time to choose my target and make a close, unhurried shot. I would have to stand, but the spot he picked for me afforded good concealment via two small pine trees. By facing the road I would be in good position to make a comfortable shot to the left. It sounded almost too easy, but coming from Turp, you just took it as gospel! As it turned out, if I hadn't altered his script, everything would have worked perfectly.

As any antsy 15-year-old boy whose patience had been tested to its limit after only an hour's wait, I decided to move to my right and sit on a pine stump I had spotted. However, by rearranging my priorities to meet my need for comfort, I situated myself beyond the high-percentage shooting range chosen for me! Sure enough, at approximately 4:30 p.m., I heard the first sound of hooves behind me! Enough leaves had fallen on the trail to easily follow the auditory progression of several deer as they headed around the trail's curve toward the road. At the first sound, I slowly turned my head to the left, and, within seconds, five does appeared in single file. If the mental butt kicking I gave myself had been real, I wouldn't have been able to walk for a week! Turp's game plan was right on target, only his "player" had added 10 yards to the challenge.

Well, there was nothing I could do at that point but prepare for as good a shot as I could make. The lead doe followed Turp's predicted route, cautiously emerged from the new growth, and stopped at the road's edge to check both ways. I froze as she looked my way. Then when she looked left, I raised my straight-limbed 45-pound wooden Bear bow and simultaneously drew back the 29-inch cedar shaft tipped with a single blade Bear broadhead with razor insert. As the doe moved onto the road, I raised the broadhead to a point behind her shoulder that I felt would allow for sufficient arrow drop during its flight. I remember thinking, "Well, here goes." My release was smooth, but the arrow's flight was slow and wobbly. As it struck its intended spot, my initial elation was soon replaced with an expletive! The bowstring had struck the sleeve of my hunting jacket! I had forgotten to put on my armguard. My heart sank as I watched the doe bolt across the road with my arrow sticking loosely from her side, its fletching almost touching the ground. At the sight of my arrow's superficial penetration, my thoughts turned to whether some quirk of fate, luck, or even divine intervention would come to my rescue, void my mistakes, and help me harvest my first deer with a bow!

21

Unfortunately, reality won out over hope. After the other deer retraced their path behind me, I went to where I had connected and found only the splayed hoofprints indicating her quick exit. There was no blood.

From his position, Dad had seen the doe dash across the road and saw me emerge from my ambush spot. Within minutes he joined me. After I explained the sequence of events, we started searching for my deer in the fading light. Turp soon drove up and joined us in our futile search on the other side of the road.

We found two small drops of blood about 20 yards inside the tree line and, then, my arrow along the escape route she had used. There were traces of blood on the broadhead, but none on the shaft. At that moment, I knew any further search was useless, and that the doe would make a complete recovery. I was very disheartened, and the words of hope and encouragement from Dad and Mr. Kline didn't help. Darkness soon enveloped us, and we decided to resume the search early Sunday morning. Our follow-up effort was unsuccessful.

I hadn't followed Turp's advice, founded on his local knowledge and years of experience, and I had to suffer the consequences. I made a promise to myself right then and there to listen and follow directions a lot better in the future. However, that didn't make the ride home any easier, and nothing Dad said relieved my disappointment. I just had to let time heal my mental wound.

A few years later, Dad received one of the most painful phone calls of his life. Turp's pickup truck had been broadsided by a speeding, drunk driver while he was taking Don Jr. to their cabin. Both were killed instantly. Don Jr. was only 12 years old and had just recovered from successful open-heart surgery when the tragedy occurred.

It was a loss and sorrow that Dad would carry for the rest of his life. His grief was ***real***, and it certainly put my ***grieving*** over that missed doe in its proper perspective.

Chapter 4: Duck Hunting on the Navesink River
(1966 - 1980)

Except for an occasional family goose hunt during the Christmas holidays back home in Delaware, I did very little waterfowl hunting during my four undergraduate college years, which ended in 1965 with a B.S. degree in Business Administration from The American University in Washington, D.C. I married immediately after graduation and moved to Matawan, New Jersey, a shorter commute to my banking job in New York City than from my wife's hometown on the Jersey Shore.

My parents-in-law owned a home on the Navesink River in Rumson, and during fall and winter visits during 1965, I'd often walk down to their bulkhead to watch large flocks of ducks trading back and forth or rafting on the river. I observed a wide variety of "puddlers" and "divers" on that wide tributary of tidal water that emptied into the Atlantic Ocean a few miles to the east. The sight of so many waterfowl, especially greater scaup and black ducks, conjured up memories of my early ducking days in Delaware. Suddenly, I felt a renewed interest in and enthusiasm for duck hunting and decided to get fully involved when the fall 1966 season rolled around.

My equipment and gear was wanting during that renaissance season. Since I didn't have a boat and had only five of Dad's old black duck decoys, I was forced to hunt from the shore, crouched down behind some reeds in front of the in-law's bulkhead, or similar areas. I also had to be careful not to throw the decoys beyond where I could retrieve them in my hip boots when the tide came in! My duck gun was a 16-gauge Savage model 720 semi-automatic fitted with a Polychoke, which enabled me to switch from improved cylinder to modified or full choke. I generally used #4 lead shot shells, since steel shot wasn't yet the subject of discussion let alone the required ammunition that it would later become.

The only success I can recall from that first season was a mallard hen I shot one late afternoon on Barley Point, a narrow peninsula that jutted out into the river, and located only a short drive and walk east of the in-laws. It was a good wing shot just as the sun was setting, a time when ducks flew inland to feed and rest in the protected coves and inlets that pocketed the

Navesink's shoreline. I had to use an old abandoned boat and push pole to retrieve it in the outgoing tide, but the effort was well worth it to me. It was my first New Jersey duck!

Before the 1967 season opened, I made a concerted effort to upgrade my equipment in order to increase my enjoyment and improve my success. First, I made a dozen "working" black duck decoys from six-inch thick sheets of dark brown Armstrong cork. I used one-inch pine for the bases and molded both cork and wood with a wood rasp to achieve a proportionate neck, wing, and tail configuration. I ordered heavy plastic, prepainted heads from *Herters* and nailed a 1½-inch pine rudder along the entire length of the bottom for balance. I was pleased with the finished product, especially when they passed the water test for floatability and stability!

My next project was a bit more ambitious, but as equally rewarding as my decoy making. I realized a duck boat was an absolute necessity if I hoped to improve my mobility and ability to get to more advantageous locations depending on weather and wind conditions. A boat would also enable me to place my growing decoy spread farther from shore and in patterns more enticing to passing ducks. I already had purchased three *Wildfowler* mallard drake decoys and three hand-carved Canada geese decoys to add variety and drawing power. I remembered Dad's early advice that a few geese decoys set off to one side of the main body of ducks added a sense of security to live ducks contemplating a visit. Who was I to argue with success!

My duck boat was a 12-foot wooden Pram with pointed bow for which I designed a burlap canopy nailed to a hinged frame screwed to the middle seat. When not in use as my attached portable blind, I rolled up the burlap, tied it to the top of the frame, and lowered the entire unit towards the stern where it fit snugly against the transom. When in the "up" position, heavy cord attached to metal springs on the top trim of the bow and stern kept the frame solidly in place, and a series of hooks and rings held the burlap firmly in place along the gunnels when draped over the heavy cord. To prevent the boat from shifting during high tides, I secured heavy metal rings to the top corners of the stern and one on the bow point, through which I sank long wooden broom handles into the mud. Those three poles held the boat in position and allowed it to rise and fall with the tide. I used a separate burlap bag slit up one seam to cover my outboard motor and painted the hull to match the drab brown of the burlap cover and canopy. The paint/cloth combination blended in well with the dead reeds wherever I placed my "boat-blind".

I was quite pleased with my ingenious, yet practical design. It gave me the flexibility I needed to set up my "spread" on any lee shore and move whenever warranted by the weather and/or wind. A single, permanent shore blind doesn't offer the same advantage or comfort, since my feet never got wet, and I kept warm via a catalytic heater placed behind me as I faced the stern to shoot!

With my new mobile blind and larger decoy spread came a noticeable increase in the number of ducks I harvested; notably, but not surprisingly, blacks and mallards. On the one hand, I was thrilled that my handmade "blocks" actually worked and drew the wary blacks within "scattergun" range. However, New Jersey's 100-point system for regulating bag limits designated blacks and hen mallards as 90-point birds, which meant once a hunter reached or exceeded 100 points with his last duck he was finished for the day. Since mallard drakes were 20 pointers, I concentrated on them to prolong my hunting time. The most generous point total was for greater or lesser scaup, a.k.a. "broadbills", and those 10-point ducks were by far the most abundant species on the river. I didn't need a degree in mathematics to figure out how I could increase my hunting time, bag limit, and fun; however, first I needed to buy several dozen broadbill drake and hen decoys to have any hope of pulling in that smaller, fast-flying species. They generally flew and congregated in large groups and preferred large expanses of open water. On many occasions I observed "rafts" of broadbills numbering in the thousands and extending for hundreds of yards in the middle of the Navesink River. To attract numbers you had to have numbers, so I ordered five dozen of *Herter's* over-sized "broadies" for starters!

It was always thrilling to call in a small flock of mallards with a combination of high ball, attractor, and feed calls and to watch them "lock up" and glide into range after circling the decoys several times. Just as thrilling was watching a group of high-flying greater scaup break off from a larger flock and turn almost inside out in their effort to lose altitude as quickly as possible to land among the "stool".

Such antics are what gave "diving" ducks their name! Their twisting and turning movements called for exacting wing shots, and it was always tempting to shoot at the whole flock instead of concentrating on one bird at a time. It's hard to believe you can shoot into a large, tightly- bunched group of broadbills and not touch a feather - until you've done it! It

25

doesn't take too many such occurrences - when your jaw drops open in disbelief after three clean misses! - to start zeroing in and narrowing your focus. I can speak from experience!

Attracting the attention of broadbills flying and sitting far out in the river not only called for large **numbers** of decoys, but also the right **pattern**. The "pipe" was one such formation that worked effectively, with the curved bowl of the pipe closest to shore and the opening inside the curve serving as the landing area for incoming birds. The stem of the pipe consisted of single decoys placed at increasing intervals and extending for up to 200 yards towards the middle of the river. The theory behind that pattern was that once the farthest decoy caught the attention of broadbills in flight, they would follow the stem to the main cluster of decoys forming the bowl and "pitch" into the open area in the middle. I must report that it was as effective in practice as it was in theory, and I used it consistently with terrific results, especially on days when fog or mist kept the ducks flying "low to the deck". At such times, broadbills would appear out of nowhere and literally explode onto the scene for some fast and furious shooting!

My enthusiasm for duck hunting occasionally went to extremes such as the time I couldn't wait for Saturday and decided to go on a weekday hunt before work. I got up at 4:00 a.m., had the boat loaded by 4:30, rowed (preoutboard days) across the river to my spot by 5:00, set out the decoys and grassed-in the boat by 5:30, hunted until 7:15 (shot one mallard drake), picked up the decoys and rowed back to the bulkhead by 8:00, drove home, showered, dressed, then drove to the train station in time to make the 9:15 train to Newark! I was a little late for work, but you know how difficult it is to get those "dental appointments" after work or on the weekends! Needless to say, that first prework duck hunt was my last; too much exertion with too little time to enjoy the fruits of one's labor. And besides, how long would the early dental appointment excuse work at the office?

Another time I was determined to duck hunt even though a mid-winter freeze had turned the entire river into a solid ice field. Not to be deterred, I chopped through the ice 15 yards from shore and kept removing large chunks until I had created an open circle 20 feet in diameter. That open water was the only available for miles, and within an hour I shot two fat mallard drakes! My effort had been rewarded. Thinking back to that day, I am still amazed at how that small pool of water had such a magnetic effect on those hungry ducks.

The little 3½ HP Sears outboard I had obtained provided adequate power to transport me, a buddy, and all our gear to and from my favorite hot spots along the Navesink. However, wear and tear from heavy use, pounding from the river's whitecaps on rough days, and general weather exposure from being outside and uncovered year-round took its toll on my customized boat/blind. By the end of the 1971 season, leaks and dry rot rendered it unsafe. I was in the market for a new boat.

During the summer of 1972, I first met my good friend Maurice Grillon, who owned a landscaping business and just happened to be an ardent duck hunter. My first thought was how much Maurice's physical appearance resembled Jack Palance, the actor. Going one step further, assuming Jack Palance was the nicest and biggest-hearted guy in the world, after meeting Maurice, Jack would rank #2! There is nothing Maurice won't do to help a friend, and if hard work were the sole criteria for wealth, "Mo" would be a multi-billionaire.

Mo grew up on the Navesink and had hunted ducks with his dad and brother for years. They hunted from Barnegat Bay Sneakboxes, a duck boat originally designed by craftsmen for hunters using the salt marshes of Barnegat Bay located along the southern coast of New Jersey. The basic dimensions of the one-man craft are a 12-foot length and 4-foot maximum width at the stern, tapering to a narrow, rounded bow. Its top is fully-decked with a two-foot wide by four-foot long open hatch in the middle, which enables the hunter to recline inside with his legs under the front deck and his back resting against a contoured cushion. Just his head is exposed above the opening. The hunter sits on a removable frame of wooden slats that fits above the bottom ribs below the hatch opening. (The raised frame enables the hunter to keep his butt dry during days when precipitation is falling.) Built-in shelves on both sides of the removable floor mat hold everything from shell boxes to lunch and are within easy reach of the hunter. A curved canvas "spray shield" is attached to the deck just in front of the hatch opening. When braced with a piece of sturdy doweling, the shield's center height reaches two feet above the deck, then narrows and curves back to its anchor point along each side of the hatch. The spray shield not only keeps water from entering the open hatch when traveling through choppy water, but also provides concealment from incoming birds and hides the hunter until he sits up to shoot. Hinged decoy racks stand about 10 inches above the deck and can extend along the boat's entire perimeter, although generally, they're secured to the stern half. Since a sneakbox's deck has a convex shape, the raised decoy racks keep any gear placed on top from sliding into the water. Their original and intended purpose was to stack rows of decoys inside the wooden frame, enabling hunters to make fast retrievals of large numbers of decoys without the necessity of wrapping each anchor rope first.

This type of boat is designed with a very shallow draft and, when occupied, has a visible height above the water line of less than one foot! By applying fiberglass to the bottom and drying it out after each use, a well-built sneakbox can last a lifetime. Cedar is the preferred wood to use in construction, and brass screws and fittings withstand the corrosion from salt water. Three evenly-spaced runners cover the entire length of the bottom, and they not only protect the fiberglass underside from constant scraping and sliding along coarse river bottoms, but also serve as excellent icebreakers. Including its removable hatch cover, the boat weighs a couple of hundred pounds, which is light enough for two men to lift comfortably, but heavy enough to provide a stable ride through turbulent water. For adaptability, comfort, concealment, and stability, nothing can top a Barnegat Bay Sneakbox!

As soon as Mo showed me his sneakbox, I knew that was the style of boat for me! I put all my ducking buddies on notice that I was in the market for a good "box" and placed ads in the local papers with the hope of attracting a seller. It wasn't long before my friend Timmy Shaheen alerted me to an ad in the *New Jersey Waterfowler* newsletter about a sneakbox for sale. I immediately contacted the seller, who promised to give me the right of first refusal; however, as soon as I saw it, I couldn't get my checkbook out fast enough. The seller was a carpenter by trade, and he had built the boat out of cedar, giving special attention to every detail, including interior shelves and a custom-made cushioned back support! The 12 footer was fiberglassed and had a new hatch cover, three-section decoy racks, and a canvas spray shield. Although built in 1960, the boat was in excellent shape inside and out. The seller wanted to buy one of the new molded fiberglass sneakboxes on the market at the time, and, luckily for me, he couldn't afford the new one without selling his cedar "box" first. For $175, I felt I had made the steal of the year and was convinced that after one ride in rough water with his lighter fiberglass model, the seller would regret his decision! (As it turned out, I owned that boat for thirty-two years. I finally sold it in 2004 for five times my original cost, and, as a result of proper care and normal repair and maintenance, its condition was as good as the day I bought it!)

With the heavier boat, I needed a more powerful outboard motor, something in the 10-horsepower range. I told Mo about my need, and he promised to be on the lookout. Before long we were on our way to visit an elderly gentleman who had placed an ad to sell his large 14-foot wooden "Johnboat", trailer, 9.5 HP Mercury outboard with 5-gallon gas tank, and a 50-gallon drum to be used to run fresh water through the engine - a must for avoiding saltwater corrosion and prolonging engine life. The seller was interested in selling the whole lot - all or none - at a firm price of $275. That's a laughable amount by today's standards, but even then it seemed like a bargain, so we sealed the deal. Mo had been looking for a sturdy fishing boat and trailer and the mint condition motor and tanks were exactly what I needed. My share of the total was $100!

With my new sneakbox and motor, I looked forward to the 1972 duck season with eager anticipation. Adding to the excitement was Mo's purchase of an additional five-dozen broadbill decoys. We were sure to have the best drawing power on the Navesink!

There was something special about putting out our decoy spread in the predawn hours on those crisp fall mornings. Having chosen a promising location, attention turned to determining the tide's flow and placing the "blocks" so they wouldn't cluster or tangle when it changed. Utmost care was taken to be sure the spacing between individual decoys and their distance from shore gave a natural appearance, yet were still within range. Shooting distance and wind direction determined where we left inviting, open landing areas both inside and outside the spread. It took only a couple of hunts together for Mo and me to get our decoy routine down to a science.

Most of our duck hunting was done from "The Sedges", a group of small reed-covered islands in the middle of the Navesink River. The broken shorelines of those narrow strips of land and availability of protected lees, regardless of wind direction, offered ideal choices for "setting up" and concealing our boats. There were several "points" of land where we could place our broadbill decoys in rough open water and still have protected coves within shooting range to put our mallard, black duck, and geese decoys. When heavy winds blew in from the northeast, ducks headed inland from Sandy Hook along the Atlantic shore and constantly traded back and forth looking for the kind of protected pockets of water that The Sedges offered. On such days the shooting was continuous, volley after volley, and occasionally we'd run out of shells before reaching our limit!

There was another day when my then brother-in-law, Tom Herlihy, and I hunted from nearby Starvation Island and got caught in a blizzard. Ice quickly encased the decoys and caused them to flip over. The wind was so strong that the snow blew parallel to the land and water, and one flock of brant was held in their locked position by the force of the wind and never did make the landing they had planned. The ferocity of the wind also kept the tide from going out, and the water rose to flood levels that covered the entire island. When our cover disappeared, we had no choice but to retrieve our decoys from the dangerous, white-capped river and pound our way to safety. Wind of that velocity made it almost impossible to judge proper lead and created more frustration and misses than it was worth. Besides, most of the waterfowl stayed put and didn't even attempt to fly under such conditions!

Those kinds of days were the extremes; otherwise, we relished the cold, overcast, windy weather that put birds in the air and brought great shooting opportunities.

For Christmas 1973, Dad surprised me with a new shotgun; a 12-gauge Remington model 1100 full-choke magnum! Its 34-inch barrel and higher muzzle velocity produced greater knockdown power at longer ranges, and more "shot" vis-`a-vis three-inch shells created denser patterns that resulted in more clean kills and less crippling. Those were vast improvements over my less potent 16-gauge Savage, and with my new firearm came increased confidence and better performance!

I have great memories of many enjoyable duck hunts on the Navesink River; fun days with many friends, including Jim Parent, Dave McHeffey, Tony Kerbs, Tom Herlihy, Charlie Brown, and Jay Crowell, and special days with my Dad, who on more than one occasion used my sneakbox for his mid-morning nap. I can still picture him tucked down inside, oblivious to the howling winds above!

Collectively, we harvested every legal species of duck imaginable; mallard, black, widgeon, shoveler, teal, scaup, rudy, redhead, pintail and canvasback. On occasion, sea ducks would venture too far inland, and we'd add a greater eider or scooter to our bag. I never shot a goose of any variety on that river, but we saw Canadas and Snows regularly. Hearing their respective melodic *honks* and high-pitched *cackles* added to the suspense and excitement!

Gradually, my hunting interest shifted from ducks to deer, and in 1980 I pulled my sneakbox out of the Navesink for the last time. I can't remember that final hunt exactly (and maybe it's better that way), but I do remember that Mo's workload stole his hunting time and caused him to give up ducking. When that happened, I lost my best duck-hunting buddy, and his absence made my decision to "retire" a lot easier.

(Top left) Kim's Barnegut Bay Sneakbox "grassed up" along "The Sedges" on the Navesink River (Top right) Kim takes aim on incoming broadbills with Maurice Grillon's "box" alongside, during November 1972 hunt (Bottom) Kim's sneakbox with spray shield up and decoy racks full

Raymond (left) and Maurice Grillon in their sneakboxes during November 1972 duck hunt on the Navesink River

December 1973: Maurice waiting for the next Navesink flight in his sneakbox, camouflaged with dead reeds

With Jay Crowell amid Kim's handmade black duck decoys on the Navesink River

December 1969: Kim Jr. and Sr. with our
broadbill "bag" taken on the Navesink River

Chapter 5: New Jersey Whitetail Adventures
with Bow and Shotgun (1971-1991)

From 1971 through 1991, I harvested 22 whitetail deer; 5 by rifle, 6 with shotgun, and 11 via bow. Eighteen of that total were bucks, ranging in size from a "button" buck to my big Alberta 10 pointer (see Chapter 11), and 16 of the 22 were taken during the liberal bow and shotgun seasons in New Jersey.

I have my former hunting buddy, Charlie Brown, to thank for introducing me to whitetail deer hunting in New Jersey. Charlie and I met while working as retail stockbrokers for Merrill Lynch during the late 1960's. At the time, my total hunting effort was directed towards limiting out on ducks on the Navesink River, and, since the deer and duck seasons overlapped, I couldn't be in two places at once! Besides, I enjoyed my waterfowl adventures with "Mo" Grillon and company.

The turning point came in the fall of 1970 when Charlie told me about his first bow kill, a doe in Hunterdon County. Hunterdon is **the** top whitetail- producing county in New Jersey year after year, and Charlie had obtained permission to hunt on a farm near Voorhees State Park in Clinton. I remember how fascinated I was to actually know someone who had killed a deer with a bow, and his account intrigued me. To me, any deer harvested by bow is the ultimate test of a hunter's ability to outwit "The King of Wary" when it comes to big game, and I admired Charlie's accomplishment. My enthusiastic response led to an invitation to join him and his hunting partners on their next hunt.

The hour and a quarter ride to our hunting area via the Garden State Parkway, Routes 287 North, 78 West, and 31 North gave plenty of time for the adrenaline to surge in anticipation of the days' events. Charlie and his buddies had befriended an old couple, the Irlings, who owned the apple farm we hunted on and sold their harvest each fall from a converted garage on their property. We frequently stopped to say hello and make purchases after our hunts, and the cantankerous "Pop" Irling would inevitably bend our collective ears with his views and opinions about local and national political issues or anything else that happened to be annoying him that day! However, we regarded those venting sessions as a small price to pay for his and Mrs. Irling's kindness for granting us exclusive bowhunting rights to their 100-plus acre spread.

Irling's huge orchard and surrounding woods backed-up to Voorhees State Park, which had vast acres of mature oak and pine trees, thickets, and ravines. All such cover was used by deer to funnel into the orchard, since apples were their prime food source during the fall months.

A county road separated the acreage, with the farmhouse, garage, apple stand, and orchard on one side and an open field and more woods on the other. We parked in the corner of the open field and planned our strategy depending on the wind. If the wind was blowing towards us from the orchard side, we could either make a cautious approach to the near side of the orchard for possible shots at the feeding deer or circle around the orchard and position ourselves in permanent tree stands along the opposite edge and wait for deer funneling through from the park. Such strategies were usually more effective during the late afternoon hours as the deer left their bedding areas to feed in the orchard and made their upwind approach toward our waiting arrows in the "holding" areas along its edge.

There was one morning, however, when I positioned myself on the far side of the orchard in a ground blind along its edge. I had just bought my first compound, a Bear Whitetail Hunter, and hadn't had time to attach all the accessories such as a stabilizer, string silencers, bow quiver, or bow sight! I had shot a few arrows at home during the previous week and felt fairly confident that my accuracy up to 20 yards could bring home some venison. I had chosen the ground blind because that location was exactly 20 paces from the first row of apple trees, and I could judge other distances, shorter or longer, from that known measurement.

At daybreak, I heard several deer behind me and to my left making their way through the woods towards the orchard. Since I was facing away from them and couldn't identify exactly where they would enter the orchard, I froze in my standing position hoping not to be seen or scented. I could feel the breeze on the back of my neck, so as long as it stayed that way I knew I might get a shot. I soon caught movement out of the corner of my left eye and slowly turned my head to get a better look. Six does stood 15 feet away at the edge of the open orchard. They exhibited a nervous demeanor as they scanned the rows of apple trees, with heads and ears moving back and forth. Eventually they left the edge cover and slowly made their way towards the first row of apple trees. So far, so good!

I waited for all six deer to enter the field and for their mindset to be fixed entirely on apples before I shifted into shooting position. The lead doe was the largest of the group, and once I was satisfied that a buck wouldn't be following, I locked into making a good shot on the big "flathead". As soon as she was in a broadside stance near the closest apple tree, I drew on my instinctive shooting ability, aimed the tip of the broadhead high on her shoulder, and released. With the muted *thump* of the bowstring she raised her head just as my arrow passed over her back and imbedded in the soft grass beyond. All six heads turned my way, but none of the females were alarmed into flight. I immediately nocked another Easton aluminum Autumn Orange XX75 and waited for the group to settle back to their feeding routine. My second shot flew an inch under her belly, and she jumped forward at the sound of the impact. The others appeared a bit unnerved, but it seemed obvious they relied on my intended target for their marching orders. Once again she held her ground and continued munching the fallen fruit. I couldn't believe my luck, both the bad and the good for giving me yet another opportunity. I should have realized that my two misses were an omen for the eventual outcome; that instinctive shooting was definitely not my shtick! My patient doe posed for two more errant shots before bounding off with the others close behind. She probably realized she was safe where she was, but just wanted to save me further embarrassment!

After that experience, I quickly equipped my bow with the necessary accessories which, when combined with much practice, eventually contributed to my first bow kill. Little did I know at the time that my first bow harvest wouldn't occur until 1977, a frustrating wait of six years! In the meantime, I was gaining some experience and success during the shotgun deer seasons.

In December 1971, I scored my first whitetail success with any weapon; a doe felled by "00" buckshot from my Remington 1100. My first whitetail buck, a four pointer, was taken with the same combination on opening day 1973 in Hunterdon County. That morning was particularly interesting in that my buck, accompanied by two does, ran across an open field and into the narrow patch of woods close to my tree stand location. Aware that my first whitetail buck kill was about to become a reality, my full attention was directed towards him, unaware that a larger buck was approaching from the hill behind me. I thought I caught a glimpse of that second buck's rack just as I touched off on the first one. At the report, my buck fell hard and the two does scattered. The second buck then ran into view on my left, cut in front of my stand, turned sharply to my right, circled directly beneath my stand, and bolted away to my left. He had a nice six or eight-point set of antlers, but since my tag had been filled a split second before his appearance, I could only give a regretful glance as he disappeared. However, my first whitetail buck was on the ground, and my mood changed quickly to one of elation and satisfaction. Opening day of any season brings an excitement of its own, but recording your first buck kill before the sun peeks above the horizon takes that experience to a new level!

That first buck was taken across the road from Irling's apple farm. For the 1976 shotgun opener, I chose a location at the top of a ridge only a couple of hundred yards from the scene of my 1973 success. My morning hunt from a permanent tree stand was unsuccessful, without a deer of any sex or size being seen. After a quick lunch at the car, I decided to get back into the woods early with the hope that heavy hunter pressure would keep the deer moving all day instead of their more normal early morning/late afternoon activity. To change my luck, I placed a small folding stool at the base of a large oak tree in the same general area.

At 1:00 p.m., I was settled on my stool, shotgun across my lap, and by 1:15 I was sound asleep, head against the tree! Staying up too late and getting up too early had caught up with me. An hour later I opened my eyes, lost in that disoriented haze of where am I and what time is it! But as my eyes focused, I quickly scanned the woods below, and, to my utter amazement, a forked-horn buck was walking left to right 30 yards below me! (Who says being in the right place at the right time doesn't count in deer hunting!) My shot lifted the small buck clear off the ground, flipped him 360 degrees in the air, and dropped him dead on the spot! The whole sequence of events left me stunned, and hoping it wasn't just a dream. (It wasn't!)

Opening day of the 1977 fall bow season found me back in the same area. During preseason scouting, I found heavily-used converging trails at the base of the ridge where I had taken my shotgun "nap buck". I found an ideal tree and built a permanent stand, allowing plenty of time for the deer to familiarize themselves with the new construction and accept it as a new, nonthreatening member of their environment. The location was approximately 40 yards inside the woods bordering the far end of the open field where we parked. However, the cover was quite thick and afforded terrific protection for deer conducting their normal travel between bedding and feeding areas. In fact, the deer used a long, narrow funnel of trees from my stand area to and across the road leading to the apple orchard. I figured my stand would be most effective in the early morning as deer left the orchard to bed down in the ridgetop thickets during the day. I would then be in an ideal position to ambush them as they passed on the trails below!

Charlie and another hunter friend, Ray Poulke, decided to hunt the orchard side, which I felt would be a boon to me if they missed any opportunities or were scented.

At 7:15 a.m. I saw movement on the trail ahead of me. A single deer was picking its way toward me, confirming its unalarmed state by stopping occasionally to munch some tender leaves or succulent grass. I was downwind, well concealed, and entertained no thought of being detected. As the young deer rounded a bend in the trail 20 yards away and headed straight for my tree, I got the first unobstructed view of its head. Thin eight-inch spikes filled the gap between his ears, but to me, seeking my first bow-killed buck, he represented a worthy trophy. As with many bowhunters, my small buck would serve well as a starting point from which future buck goals would be based and compared. The challenge to get a bigger and better "rack" is a buck hunter's constant motivation.

The buck continued on course and turned to his left 10 yards in front of my stand. He paused briefly, then continued his slow journey, which, within steps, offered me a perfect quartering-away shot at 15 yards. At impact, he exchanged ends and ran wildly back down the same trail.

I knew I had made a good shot and concentrated on watching him until he disappeared from view. That observation enabled me to pick up his trail quickly, resulting in a shorter tracking effort. Approximately 40 yards past the bend in the trail, I jumped him from his bed. (To have bedded that close to where he was hit indicated that the internal hemorrhaging process was taking its toll.) He ran into a dense patch of saplings where I found him piled up moments later. I was thrilled with my first bow kill, and being a buck made it that much better!

Two months later I scored again on the opening day of shotgun season. A light snow had started falling in the early a.m. of that Monday in early December, and by the time I reached my stand on the backside of my productive ridge, two inches were on the ground with no sign of a letup. That white background opened up the woods and eliminated any chance for deer to go undetected in any direction for up to several hundred yards. Any time a hunter can see a deer before it sees him greatly increases his chance for success, assuming wind and concealment are favorable.

With no noticeable wind, conditions were perfect as I waited in the pre-dawn darkness for the official 7 a.m. "opening bell". I was tingling with the anticipation that something good was about to happen. My previous successes in the area added to my excitement, and I had the feeling I was following a carefully prepared script with the actors about to play out their roles. I soon discovered that a rewrite wouldn't be necessary.

Shortly after daybreak, I heard the distinct cracking of fallen branches and the sound of hooves meeting dry leaves and rocks coming from below the ridgeline 30 yards to my right. Due to the steepness of the drop-off, the sound of the approaching deer reached me before I could see them. From the commotion, I knew several deer were moving swiftly towards the crest. I shifted my sitting position toward the noise, released the safety, and raised my trusty "1100" for what I knew would be a quick shot if a buck came into view. My heart was jumping out of my chest as their approach grew louder. The moment of truth was only seconds away.

When the big-racked buck suddenly cleared the ridge, I reacted as if he had caught me by complete surprise. Instead of immediately taking aim behind his shoulder and firing, I hesitated just long enough for a couple of trees to block my shot. Maybe I thought he was going to stop to wait for the others or perhaps greed interfered with my thinking, hoping that an even bigger buck was following. Unfortunately, the lead buck wasn't stopping for anything, and the "bigger" trailing buck turned out to be a considerably smaller six pointer followed by two does. Luckily, that second buck did hesitate long enough for me to fire a shot, and the Remington Mark IV "00" buckshot kept him down.

Charlie and Ray had taken stands on the other side of the ridge, and within seconds of my shot, Charlie's 12 gauge responded with two quick shots of its own. The big buck that eluded me, an old Roman-nosed nine pointer, had run right to Charlie's tree, and, before it could correct its mistake, my partner dispatched it. When I dragged my buck to where Charlie and Ray were dressing out the larger deer, Charlie told me that he must have missed the buck cleanly with his first shot at less than 20 yards, since it didn't flinch or run. Then, he almost lost his footing on the ice-covered stand before quickly regrouping to make the killing shot on his fine trophy!

Charlie's and my opening day shotgun double on two good bucks tops the list of memorable hunts at Irling's farm in Hunterdon County.

My last Hunterdon County buck was taken in 1984, another opening day shotgun success. A local hunting club had leased the Irling farm for its exclusive deer hunting use, and with "club" signs nailed to every other tree, I was resigned to not being able to hunt my favorite Irling haunts and having to find a new hot spot. Charlie and Ray went one step further: They stopped hunting in Hunterdon altogether!

There was a wide trail that extended from the county road that bisected Irling's farm past the orchard and into Voorhees State Park where public hunting was permitted. During one of my several scouting trips to Voorhees, I found an enormous oak tree along a rock boundary wall and close to a drop-off that led to heavy thickets interspersed with numerous, frequently-used deer trails. That oak offered the perfect vantagepoint for spotting deer moving between their beds in the thickets below and Irling's orchard behind me. A huge branch 15 feet above the ground held my portable seat securely.

Not knowing how many "public" hunters would show up in the park that day and being equally concerned about my own safety, I arrived at my oak tree destination by 5 a.m., even though legal shooting wouldn't begin until 7 a.m. I was never fond of reading about hunters being wounded or killed by overly-eager and careless fellow hunters who specialized in "sound" or "movement" shots without first identifying their targets! My counterplay was to be the **first** hunter in the woods and **first** to get above the ground.

The thin layer of crusty snow and dry, crunchy leaves made a quiet approach to my stand location almost impossible, but the extra time I had allowed enabled me to make as cautious an approach as conditions allowed. I knew once I got set up, I'd be happy that the forest floor **was** noisy, since it would provide an early and loud warning system for any deer approaching from considerable distances away.

I had plenty of firepower with me that day in the form of my recently purchased Ithaca "Mag-10" full-choke semi-automatic with a 36-inch barrel. That 10-gauge "cannon" requires

3½-inch shells, and I was packing "000" buckshot magnum loads, which can cut down small trees let alone a thin-skinned deer. Obviously, I don't believe in prolonged suffering!

Once I had climbed to my lofty perch, attached my seat, fastened my safety belt, and loaded my gun, the only chore left before the legal shooting hour arrived was to ward off other hunters arriving late and looking for promising ambush sites, either on or above the ground. If they slowed down in my immediate area, I signaled them with my flashlight to keep them moving, counting on the fact that most hunters will respect another's territory once he's set up. Fortunately, all the hunters save one were considerate and passed through to safe havens beyond, thereby saving the need to give verbal reminders. That one rude hunter, however, meandered into my area at 6:45 a.m. and plunked himself down on the rock wall 75 yards to my right. The flashing of my light didn't deter him, and it was too close to legal shooting time to get down from my tree to "remind" him of good etiquette. That would have made matters worse, so I stayed put and did a slow burn instead! What's wrong with some people, anyway?

While waiting, I also thought about an article I had read the week before in one of the major hunting magazines. The author insisted that through intense concentration, a hunter could literally "will" deer to his location. I had never heard of such mental telepathy tactics being applied to deer hunting and wondered if it applied only to a wilderness setting or if an advanced course could bring them running to your home! Normally, my power of concentration lasts about as long as a golf shot, but I figured I'd give it my best effort. I focused my attention and psychic energy on a trail only 10 yards from my tree and leading to the thickets below.

Shortly after 7 a.m., the shooting began. Series of one, two, or three shots, some at close intervals, others spaced 10 minutes or more apart, could be heard at varying distances. None were close enough for me to get on the edge of my seat and start looking for blurs of brown and white hide. I tried to visualize what those shots represented. Based on my experience, a single shot meant either a clean kill or a desperate shot at a vanishing tail; two shots with a slight pause in between indicated a knockdown shot followed by a finishing shot; and three quick shots in succession usually meant a tag was still unfilled! Occasionally a long series of many shots could be heard, and I would imagine a lone buck running the entire length of a narrow stretch of woods while a party of hunters at 100-yard intervals unloaded three desperate shots each! (File this under "idle thoughts while passing long hours in a tree stand"!)

After half an hour of intense concentration, I was ready to abandon my mental deer calling technique. It seemed obvious the deers' brain waves were on a different frequency than mine - or so I thought! I had just finished my silent self-criticism for even entertaining such a folly when I heard the crunching of leaves from the drop-off below, with the noise rapidly approaching on the trail that had been the object of my attention and source of my concentration since daybreak. Suddenly, a nervous doe came into view, walking rapidly and looking from side to side at her new surroundings on the ridgetop. When she stopped and looked behind her I got very excited, since a doe's backward glance is often the telltale sign of a trailing buck. Sure enough, a handsome eight-point buck topped the hill and came to a halt alongside his female companion! He was on the near side of her and offered a perfect 15-yard shot into his right shoulder and lung area. The Mag-10 had been in position from the first rustle of leaves, and when I squeezed the trigger, the sound alone could have scared him to death. He hit the ground so fast that I thought for a split second I had shot a cottontail instead of a whitetail! He didn't flinch, and after I got down to inspect him, I counted **ten** "000" buckshot holes in his chest area. He hadn't suffered, and I didn't have to worry about some other hunter finishing him off had he been able to run off. As I stood over him, I couldn't help but think that maybe, just maybe, the mental telepathy technique had brought him my way!

Not only did my hunt end on a triumphant note, but a humorous one as well. As I prepared to field dress the buck, lingering a few moments to admire his handsome rack, my late-arriving "neighbor" walked over to offer his congratulations and also to tell me what a fright I had given him. He did appear a bit ashen and his hands were trembling. As soon as he told his story, I realized why. It seems he had taken out a white handkerchief to blow his nose at the instant I fired at my buck. Thinking someone had mistaken his hanky for a buck's white "tail" and had fired at **him**, he dove to the ground to escape a follow-up barrage!

He was unhurt, but badly shaken. I couldn't help chuckling out loud, but inwardly, I hoped the experience taught him a double lesson: (1) don't hunt too close to others, and (2) don't wave white hankies in deer woods during the season! He was a nice fellow but not too smart, so I really couldn't get mad at him. Besides, he offered to help drag out my buck, which, of course, I accepted with heartfelt thanks! That exertion alone should have taught him not to venture too close!

In between my Hunterdon County and Stonehill Farm (see Chapter 12) adventures were some exciting bowhunting moments on several other Colts Neck, New Jersey farms. Colts Neck is located west of the Garden State Parkway in Monmouth County. It was also only a 20-minute drive from my Rumson home, which made Saturday a.m. and p.m. hunts possible, with time in between to do the normal weekend chores! Many large horse and crop farms bordered Route 537 West, and I was able to secure bowhunting permission at three of them: Colonial Farm, Tom Orgo's farm, and Steve Colando's farm. Colando's and Colonial were adjoining, with Orgo's just one farm removed.

They all offered good crops and sufficient cover to support large and healthy deer herds. Only two things remained to insure consistent success: plenty of preseason scouting and shooting practice. The deer, including many big bucks, were there for the taking, and I was determined to get my share!

Colonial Farm was the scene of my 1980 Presidential election day encounter with a monster buck, one that taught me a valuable lesson about his self-preservation and survival instincts. That early November dawn meeting renewed my respect for mature whitetail bucks, in general, a respect I carry with me each time I venture inside their habitat.

I had hunted Colonial several times before that election day and found enough buck sign to keep me going back. Particularly encouraging was a section of woods bordering the corner of a large, cut alfalfa field. Defined deer trails just inside the tree line extended the entire length of both adjoining woodlots and converged at the corner. A huge hardwood with several thick branches 12 to 15 feet above ground added the final touch to a perfect setting for ambushing a buck entering or exiting that preferred feeding spot. The woods deepened away from the field on its south end and contained several overgrown bedding areas deep within its interior.

I arrived at the big hardwood well before the first presidential vote was cast and climbed to the first big limb, which was high enough, wide enough, and strong enough to hold me without the need for a tree stand. A nail wrapped with black electrical tape served as my bow hanger. I had practiced diligently with my Bear Whitetail Hunter compound including the previous evening at my backyard range, so I was confident my sight pins and release would not let me down. The first traces of dawn were appearing when I heard heavy, measured steps approaching from the heavy cover behind me. At first, I thought it was another hunter, since the dry leaves magnified the sound. However, occasional pauses and the lack of any human noises, such as clothing rubbing against brush, quickly convinced me that a big deer was headed my way! I was caught a bit off guard, since I figured any deer I'd see would be walking *from* the alfalfa field to the woods, and not vice versa. My back was resting against the wide trunk, so I had to shift sideways on the wide limb to adjust to the deer's new route.

Within a minute, a large-bodied deer emerged from the thick laurel 10 yards behind my tree. It was still too dark to get a clear view of its head, but the body size told me it had to be a buck. It paused briefly to test the wind and peer out towards the field, then resumed its slow walk right to the base of my tree! I remember smiling to myself as I contemplated a straight downward shot of less than five yards into its spine or, at worst, into its chest cavity on either side of the spine. However, those plans were put on permanent hold when the deer suddenly raised its antlered head and stared directly at me. Our eyes met ever so briefly before he made a powerful sideways leap and quickly disappeared into the surrounding brush!

In the instant he turned his head upward, I was able to capture the awesome dimensions of his rack. Extending well beyond his ears, the heavy ivory-colored beams carried at least four long, thick tines per side, plus generous brow tines that looked more like long candlesticks. He was a magnificent specimen, and had I remembered to apply cover scent to my boots while walking to my hardwood perch, I would have gotten a shot. However, once his nose hit my scent line, his alarm system was triggered and some built-in instinct told him to look above for the danger source. There I was, and away he went! I had counted my chickens too early and ended up eating crow! I quietly praised his extraordinary survival instincts and vowed never again to take anything for granted when pursuing those wise, mature bucks. They don't get big by being dumb, and I learned a valuable lesson about the need to counter their superior senses, especially their sense of smell. I left those woods at Colonial Farm a disappointed but wiser hunter. One win for Ronald Reagan, one loss for Kimber Shoop!

Fonder Colonial Farm memories resulted from the times I took Kimber III there to watch deer feeding in one of the back fields during late afternoons. We sat in a permanent tree stand built just inside the bordering tree line and observed them cautiously enter the clover field from the far corner and feed their way towards us; first the does, then the bucks just before dark. I can still picture the look of amazement and wonderment on his eight-year-old face! Those were special, quality times, and, at the very least, he learned to respect and appreciate wildlife in their natural habitat. Unfortunately, too few children get to observe such wonders of nature.

Tom Orga's farm yielded one good six pointer to my bow on November 9, 1984. I nicknamed him the "cut finger" buck for reasons I will now explain.

I had just returned from a successful woodland caribou hunt in Newfoundland (see Chapter 8) and was eager to get back to New Jersey's bow season. The prerut was in full swing with only a couple of weeks before the full rut reached its peak. I had returned from my Canadian trip on Friday, November 1st, and in the predawn hours of November 2nd, I climbed into my tree stand at Orgo's. My wait was a short one as a young six-point buck ambled toward me on a well-defined trail nearby. He stopped 20 yards away and appeared to be alarmed. He was quartering towards me and didn't offer the greatest shot into his chest area, but I also felt from his body language that he wasn't going to hang around long enough to give me a better opportunity. The result: my hurried shot flew above his back, and he headed immediately for the thicket at the far end of that woodlot. I was disappointed, but I also knew the best of the rut was still ahead.

On the following Saturday afternoon, I eagerly returned to the same patch of woods and set up in a tree at the far end where my missed buck of the previous week had made his exit. Heavy thickets bordered that section, and I was optimistic about seeing deer as they left their beds there to journey to the cornfields bordering the opposite end. Rutting activity was on the upswing, and I figured that factor would encourage more activity. I was "on stand" by 3:30 p.m., and at 4:00 a lone buck walked out of the thicket and stopped 10 yards from my stand! When he held his head high to sniff the air, I got a good look at his rack and realized he was the object of my unsuccessful effort the previous week! It was time to mend the errors of my way! He cooperated fully and stood in the same spot until I slowly rose from my elevated seat, drew, aligned behind his shoulder, and released. A perfect shot resulted and passed completely through my surprised target. I watched him as he sped down the trail below me, turned to his left, and disappeared into the thicket. Then I heard him stop, fall to the ground, and thrash briefly before succumbing.

I found blood immediately, and a splattered trail led to a quick recovery 60 yards beyond. I was pleased that I had gotten a second chance and succeeded. He was a nice trophy with small compact antlers carrying three points per side. My admiration time was brief, and then it was time to get to work dressing and dragging! I reached for my knife, but felt nothing but belt. I then remembered that in my haste to put on my camo suit, apply my camo makeup, and make the mile walk to my stand, I had forgotten my razor-sharp Buck knife! Decision time: Should I return to my Bronco II to get it, or improvise by using a broadhead to perform the "gutting" chore? Since darkness was approaching, and I didn't fancy field dressing the buck in the dark, I chose the latter. It was not a smart decision.

Although I successfully opened his chest cavity, I was not as fortunate when I reached inside to sever his lungs. My right hand slipped on the bloody shaft followed immediately by the unmistakable sting of a razor cut as a broadhead blade penetrated deeply into my index finger! I knew immediately it was a serious wound, which was quickly confirmed when I extracted my hand and removed my wool glove liner. The blade had penetrated to the bone and blood was spurting!

Decision time again: Should I leave the deer and return immediately to my vehicle to drive for medical help, or remove my undershirt to make a tourniquet, stop the bleeding, and then drag out the deer with my bow in one trip? Guess which option I chose? Only after returning home with my trophy did I drive to the local hospital to have my finger stitched up. Just another day in the woods!

Prior to Stonehill Farm, my most satisfying and productive New Jersey bowhunting was experienced at Steve Colando's farm. Steve raised horses on his large spread, and once I convinced him that I was responsible and knew the difference between a deer and a horse, he gave me permission to hunt.

A long dirt lane ran from the farmhouse and stables to the first woodlot a quarter mile away. Those woods bordered the Colonial Farm acreage on the west, which was the scene of my 1980 Election Day monster buck encounter and disappointment. I usually parked at the corner of those woods and walked to my favorite spot in the second woodlot 100 yards to the east. Those trees narrowed to a 30-yard width at one stretch with cornfields on the north side and a road paralleling more woods on the south side. That narrow patch was a hub of deer activity, since it served as both a natural funnel for those traveling between woodlots east and west and a crossing area for those bedding and feeding between the woods on the south and cornfield on the north, respectively. There was a cyclone border fence that also ran east to west alongside the corn, and a three-foot opening in that structure served as the deers' entrance and exit point. I positioned my tree stand 15 yards from that opening, so it wasn't surprising that my sightings were frequent, both in the morning and evening!

As evidence of how "prime" my stand location was, in the two-week period between November 10 and 24, 1985, I saw six different bucks within shooting range. Of that group, I missed a nice eight pointer that appeared earlier than expected one afternoon and caught me with my glasses off and binoculars up glassing the opposite end of the field from which he approached. He came out of a thicket 40 yards to my left front, and by the time I caught his movement, he had closed the distance to 20 yards. I knew I needed my glasses to get a clear sight picture and had to chance making the extra movement to exchange my pocket size Minoltas for single-lens bifocals! It worked. Then, as if on signal, the majestic, wide-racked eight pointer with rut-swelled neck did a "button hook" pattern from his path at the edge of the corn to a point 10 yards to my left near the opening in the fence. He stopped to contemplate his next move and offered a perfect broadside shot save for one **small** problem in the form of a narrow-trunked, multi-limbed sapling about 15 feet high that blocked the path of my "slam dunk" shot. It was the only obstruction in front of my stand, and I quietly cursed the fact I hadn't thinned out the branches or cut it down altogether! It's uncanny how a buck will use cover, however sparse, to his advantage. My unsuspecting trophy was no exception.

Although there was no perceptible wind, I was fearful that the longer I waited, the more likely he'd be of detecting my odor - which normally spreads downward and outward from tree stand locations under calm conditions. Another moment of truth was upon me! I knew he wouldn't stand there forever, so I raised and drew my Hoyt-Easton 60-pound compound in one slow, deliberate motion and settled the 15-yard pin behind his shoulder. I needed a perfect shot to pass between two closely-spaced branches, but my shot ticked the upper limb just enough to cause my arrow to veer to the left two inches in front of his neck. He immediately reversed direction, took two bounds to the edge of the corn, and stopped. I quickly nocked another shaft and shifted my feet in preparation for a second shot, this time at a prepaced 25-yard distance. I'm confident that shot would have found its mark as well had it not been for a branch that caught the top limb of my bow and forced me to make an uncomfortable and unpracticed backward lean in order to come to full draw. That move disrupted my concentration and the unorthodox release resulted in a flight lacking its usual "zip", even though the arrow appeared to be on target. The buck didn't wait around for a third attempt, as he quickly covered the 200-yard distance to the far end of the cornfield and disappeared over a hedgerow. He displayed no signs of being hit, and my subsequent search and tracking effort failed to reveal even one speck of blood. It also did not result in the recovery of my second arrow. Darkness ended my search, and I returned home disappointed about the outcome and perplexed about the "disappearance" of that second shaft. A follow-up search had the same results; neither a trace of the arrow nor any indication of a hit - superficial or otherwise. I was satisfied that my "button hook" buck had survived my attempt and lived to challenge me another day!

During that same two-week period, I rattled in another eight-point buck from across the road to within 20 yards of my stand. He was headed for the opening in the fence, and I decided to let him get closer before attempting a shot. Unfortunately, a light breeze carried my scent to his sensitive nose, and he took off through the narrow funnel of woods before I could raise my bow.

A few days later I passed on another buck, this time a tall "spike" walking along the edge of the same cornfield. Not wanting to waste a good opportunity to experiment, I waited for the "two pointer" to pass 20 yards to my right and then made a series of improvised grunts "au natural". I was curious to see if the sound from my own voice could be as effective as one from a manufactured grunt tube. To my surprise, the young buck stopped, turned around, then retraced the 20-yard distance to his previous location in front of my stand. I got a big kick out of his reaction and knew going forward I could rely on that newest weapon in my arsenal.

The following Saturday, I returned to my spot near the hole-in-the fence and quietly set up in my favorite tree. After my two-shot miss on the big eight pointer, I trimmed all interfering branches and felt confident there would be no repeat of that earlier event. As usual, I was ready for the day's events well before the first streaks of gray emerged from the darkness of night. The peak of the rut had passed, but the recent buck activity told me to be on stand earlier than later. The portion of the cornfield directly in front of me had not been harvested, and the standing stalks were so close and dry that no deer could walk through without being heard, especially on the windless morning of that particular November day.

49

It was in that quiet predawn darkness that I heard the first unmistakable sound of deer approaching through the corn! Muted at first, the noise from brushed stalks grew louder and pinpointed the location of two deer walking steadily on a diagonal path that would eventually bring them to a spot directly in front of my stand at no more than 30 yards. The corn in that area was not as dense and would offer a shot, assuming good light conditions. As hoped, the deer emerged from the heavy canopy of stalks where anticipated, but it was still too dark to even determine their sex let alone loose an arrow. What happened next caught me by complete surprise, but did provide the answer to the deers' identity question. A clash of antlers broke the predawn silence!

For five full minutes the two bucks banged their racks together, twisting and pushing, then disengaging briefly before resuming their contact. It was the first time I had witnessed such a display in person, but based on videos I had seen, the intense scene that unfolded below me seemed more than a mere "sparring" session.

The fighting stopped as quickly as it started, and the bucks, like the players in "Field of Dreams", disappeared into the corn. An hour later, as first light illuminated the "set", I observed the two bucks clashing again at the far end of the cornfield to my left. I watched them through my binoculars until Act II was completed and the combatants exited for good. That was one of my most fascinating bowhunting experiences, and I hadn't even shot an arrow!

My patience and misses were finally rewarded during that busy November when buck number six ventured too close to my favorite hole-in-the fence stand location. The fat six pointer took a double-lung hit on the exact spot where the big eight pointer "ate" my second arrow two weeks earlier. I guess you could call my eventual success a deserved reward, but those two hot weeks at Colando's would still rank high on my hunting memories' list even if I hadn't filled a tag!

To attest to the quality of New Jersey's deer herd, during Thanksgiving 1995, I visited a taxidermy studio in the Garden Sate and saw the enormous typical 12-point rack of a bow-killed New Jersey whitetail buck that green scored **202** Pope and Young points, **well** above the minimum 125 needed for entry into the record book. The rack's symmetry was near-perfect, and I suspect few, if any, points were deducted once the final scoring was completed. Saskatchewan move over!

Other Deer Hunting Adventures in New Jersey - Bow and Shotgun

HARVEST RECORD

1971	Doe	Hunterdon County, Clinton, NJ - Voorhees State Park	Shotgun
1973	Buck (3 pt)	Hunterdon County - Irling's farm	Shotgun
1976	Buck (4 pt)	Hunterdon County - Irling's farm	Shotgun
1977	Buck (3 pt)	Hunterdon County - Irling's farm	Bow
1977	Buck (6 pt)	Hunterdon County - Irling's farm	Shotgun
1978	Doe	Hunterdon County - Irling's farm	Bow
1981	Doe	Monmouth County - Steve Colando's farm	Bow
1982	Buck (4 pt)	Monmouth County - Steve Colando's farm	Bow
1983	Buck (button)	Sussex County	Shotgun
1984	Buck (6 pt)	Monmouth County - Tom Orgo's farm	Bow
1984	Buck (8 pt)	Hunterdon County, Clinton, NJ - Voorhees State Park	Shotgun
1985	Buck (3 pt)	Monmouth County - Steve Colando's farm	Bow
1985	Buck (6 pt)	Monmouth County - Steve Colando's farm	Bow
1986	Buck (6 pt)	Monmouth County - Steve Colando's farm	Bow
1991	Buck (9 pt)	Monmouth County - Stonehill Farm	Bow
1991	Buck (7 pt)	Monmouth County - Stonehill Farm	Bow

December 10, 1973: Kim's first buck, taken on opening day of New Jersey firearm season with Remington 1100 12-gauge and Mark IV "double 0" buckshot. The three pointer was downed near Clinton in Hunterdon County

October 8, 1977: My first bow kill! The three pointer was taken on opening day in Clinton, NJ with Whitetail Hunter bow and Satellite broadheads

December 3, 1984: New Jersey firearm season opening day eight-point "mental telepathy" buck taken with Ithaca "Mag-10" shotgun and "triple 0" buckshot

"Pop" Irling's Clinton, NJ apple orchard in Hunterdon county, New Jersey's best deer-producing county

September 1984: practice makes perfect!

November 1982: four-point buck taken with bow
on Steve Colando's farm in Colts Neck, NJ

(Above) December 1985: six-point whitetail buck taken on Steve Colando's farm (Below) October 1984: "cut finger" six-point buck taken on Tom Orgo's farm, both with Bear Whitetail Hunter bow and Razorbak-4 broadheads

Chapter 6: New York Bow and Rifle Deer Hunts at "Just-a-Farm" (1976-1986)

The best thing about joining the investment firm of A.G. Becker, Inc. in 1976 was meeting J. Wesley Blackwell. I joined Wes as a member of the company's institutional fixed income sales desk. More importantly, we both enjoyed deer hunting, and when Wes extended an invitation for me to join him for the opener of New York's Southern Zone rifle season, I jumped at the chance.

A few years prior, Wes had purchased a 200-plus acre farm in Delaware County's dairy country. He named it appropriately enough, "Just-a-Farm", but its beautiful location in one of the county's vast, winding valleys would certainly rate more than "just-a-setting"! Wes was an absentee owner during much of the fall, winter, and spring months, except for holidays, and, of course, deer season. His family, wife Karen, and children Tommy and Julie, spent their summers at the farm where horses and a man-made pond stocked with bass and pan fish provided riding, swimming, boating, and fishing enjoyment. Wes joined them for long weekends, about a 1½-hour drive from their primary residence in Rye, New York.

Just-a-Farm's huge red barn housed over 50 dairy cattle, which were tended to in Wes' absence by his neighbor, Herb Hait. The two-story farmhouse had four bedrooms on the second floor, ample room for visiting hunters. The main level was highlighted by a large high-ceilinged den, where comfortable, deep-cushioned couches and chairs surrounded a large stone fireplace and contributed to its relaxing, rustic decor. (Many a sniffer of brandy and countless hunting stories were "consumed" while sitting in front of toasty fires during the eleven seasons I visited Just-a-Farm between 1976 and 1986.) Wes kept a winter's supply of cut firewood stacked on the screened-in front porch and in a large storage shed at the end of his driveway. The shed also protected his tractor and other farm machinery from the severe winter weather. Heavy snowfalls and strong winds that whipped through the valley were the rule rather than the exception, and, invariably, the flakes started flying for keeps during the opening week of deer season in mid November.

For that first hunt, I arrived on Saturday, November 20, in order to zero-in my rifle, do some extensive scouting, and select a good stand site for Monday's opener. It was my first deer hunt with a rifle, and, since my personal arsenal consisted of shotguns only, I had to borrow my dad's Remington .30-.06 model 742 Woodsmaster semi-automatic for the occasion. It was plenty of gun for the game I'd be hunting. I just had to be able to shoot it where I aimed! On Wes' advice, I adjusted my 4X Bushnell fixed-power scope until my groupings were consistently three inches high at 100 yards for the 150-grain cartridges I'd be using. That taken care of, Wes gave me a general lay of the land and the benefit of his knowledge of deer movements and sightings.

Wes' acreage extended from the top of a hill 400 or so yards behind his house and barn to the top of the mountain which rose a considerable distance from the county road that fronted the farm. On Sunday we spent several hours walking the property looking for any sign - trails, fresh rubs and scrapes, **and** deer - that would help us determine our ambush sites for the next morning. The land behind the house was a mixture of pastures, cornfields, open woodlands with sparse cover, and, near the top, a series of rock walls which served as boundary markers. Heavier cover and thicker woods grew above Wes' property line, but its owner and his friends would be hunting there. Wes had some past success sitting at the intersection of two boundary walls waiting for hunters above to push deer down to him. That strategy had put a couple of fat does in his freezer while filling his landowner permits during previous seasons. Not being one to break up anyone's opening day ritual, I encouraged Wes to man his usual spot while I turned my attention to the greater expanse of fields, thickets, and woods across the road.

A cut cornfield ran from the edge of the road in front of the farmhouse for 120 yards where it sloped sharply downward to a knee-high stream that paralleled the road. Across that 10-foot wide, fast-flowing body of water, the grade steepened, and the sparse cover of open fields turned quickly into heavier cover marked by small pines and numerous groups of saplings. Established deer trails dominated that second tier of growth, which extended for another 50 to 75 yards before the main body of woods started. That unbroken expanse of trees and dense ground cover extended all the way to the mountain's crest approximately 1,500 feet above. Once inside the woods, a series of rock boundary walls crisscrossed the mountain and served as welcome landmarks when climbing to favorite stand locations in the predawn darkness. After a few years of hunting the farm, I had found several good stand locations at different elevations on the mountain. I could find each one easily in near total darkness - with the aid of only a tiny flashlight - by counting paces from certain walls or trees near the walls. With the number of paces to each location committed to memory, my nighttime navigational system worked to perfection. One such stand was behind a rock outcropping 60 paces above a dead tree located in the middle of the "second" wall. Another was a huge oak tree overlooking a swampy area at the base of the mountain, located exactly 88 paces from a certain tree along the "first" wall! Unfortunately, I didn't have the benefit of such measurements during that initial hunt.

During my Sunday scouting, I located the lower "first" rock wall which intersected with another at its extreme left end as I faced the mountain. Just inside the corner where they joined, a tall, sturdy, heavily-limbed hardwood grew. I could reach its lower branches when I stood on the wall and then climb as high as I wished to attain the best field of view. During a "dry run", I found two solid limbs to stand on 15 feet above ground, and the trunk supported my back. Since I hadn't yet purchased a portable stand and didn't have time to build a platform and seat, the term "tree stand" took on a new and literal meaning! But at least I felt confident I could locate the walls and tree in the next morning's darkness!

The opening day alarm sounded at 4 a.m., and after dressing and grabbing a quick cup of coffee, Wes and I wished each other well and headed off in opposite directions. Wes' neighbor, Nick, and some of his buddies also planned to hunt above the house, so Wes was hopeful they would push something his way. I headed across the cut cornfield towards the stream; the first leg of a half-mile trek to my new "stand." Three inches of snow had fallen overnight, and that added to my excitement about the day's prospects.

I wore hip boots to cross the stream, then changed to my insulated L.L. Bean Maine Hunting boots on the other side. I stashed the hip boots under a tree for my return crossing and, after squirting some cover scent on my rubber- bottomed "Beaners", resumed my uphill journey in search of the three-foot high stone walls. My only chance for error was if I veered too far left and missed both the horizontal wall and the one that intersected it and ran vertically up the mountain. I therefore picked my way through the heavy brush on a diagonal path to the right.

Five minutes later the beam from my flashlight caught the targeted structure, and I breathed a sigh of relief! The walls' intersecting point and my preselected tree were only 20 yards away.

The temperature was in the 20's and a gusty wind was blowing, so I decided to huddle in the "corner" and wait for the first hint of light before climbing my tree and bearing the brunt of the wind chill factor. Increased exposure to the weather, especially on cold, raw days, is the price one pays for getting into the woods earlier than later, but higher success rates dictate that it's worth the effort and discomfort.

As dawn broke, I pulled myself up into the tree and secured my footing on the support branches. I chambered a 150-grain shell and inserted the four-round clip, being careful to muffle the metal sounds with my insulated gloves. I was happy to have the snow cover, since it enabled me to pick up movement a lot quicker and minimized the need to use the Jason 7X 15X35 binoculars that hung from my neck. I had already cleaned and put on my glasses while on the ground, waiting for the body heat rising from my shirt collar to dissipate first to prevent fogging. Overheating resulting from long walks to chosen stand sites in heavy clothing is also why some hunters elect to carry their outer garments and dress on arrival. There's no bigger "red flag" to downwind deer than human perspiration odor. A deer's sense of smell is its number one defense mechanism and is supposedly 25 times more acute than that of man. Preventative measures, including the use of cover scent, are therefore essential to prevent detection.

At daybreak, the wind had lessened somewhat and the sky was clear. Although partially obstructed by clusters of hardwood saplings in the foreground, I could see the Blackwell barn and light gray house with red shudders in the distance. I hadn't seen so much as a stockpiling squirrel during my first watchful hour, but then I caught movement to my left. When I turned my head for a better look, I saw the prettiest sight any deer hunter could hope for. Slowly working his way on a diagonal path toward me from a swampy area below was a beautiful, wide-racked buck with rut-swelled neck and blackened tarsal glands! Due to my short scouting time and low expectation level, I was definitely caught by surprise, as my increased heartbeat confirmed!

When I first saw him he was about 80 yards away, but, due to the thickness of the brush and trees between us, I had no choice but to wait until he entered lighter cover. I looked ahead and picked an unobstructed open area 20 yards to my right. If the buck continued on course, it would give me a clear 30 to 35 yard shot! All I had to do was wait, with just enough time for the nervous tension to build to a fever's pitch.

My best and only buck killed to that point was the small three pointer taken with a bow on "Pop" Irling's Clinton, New Jersey farm – quite a difference from the one then approaching me on Just-a-Farm! Even with the wind blowing and much movement of branches, I kept perfectly still for fear of attracting his attention; although, thinking back, I was probably more conspicuous by my *lack* of movement! At any rate, as soon as he neared my predetermined interception point, I prepared for the shot. I needed to turn to the right and adjust my feet on the support branches, and I looked down to be sure I didn't slip or make any rubbing noise. It was at that moment that my binoculars swung outward and hit my riflescope - metal against metal! Even with the noise from the wind and rubbing branches, the foreign metal *clink* sound caused the buck to stop dead in his tracks and look back in my direction! He didn't bolt and apparently couldn't decipher the source of the strange noise, but I knew I had a very narrow window of shooting opportunity. A deer of his maturity usually runs first and tries to figure the situation out later. With that in mind, I slowly shouldered my rifle, released the safety, aimed behind his right foreleg, and fired. He immediately turned and ran uphill to my right, showing no sign of a hit. I was half in shock and half in a state of panic to get off another shot, and quickly! He was gaining speed with every bound, and my opportunity was fading fast. I couldn't even think about bullet deflection as I swung on the moving blur of brown hide and touched off my second round. He went down hard and stayed there. I kept the crosshairs on his heaving right side, but soon all movement ceased. The trophy was mine! Ironically, as I lifted my cheek from the stock, I saw that my barrel was resting snugly against the tree trunk. I couldn't have swung an eighth of an inch farther! (talk about being **lucky**!)

It was only 7:15 a.m., yet my hunt was over. I'd be happy to have every hunt end as quickly if it resulted in the kind of trophy I took that morning. He was my first "racked" buck, and I never enjoyed field dressing a deer so much in my life. It probably took me longer than usual, too, since I kept stopping to recount his eight typical points and admire his 17-inch outside spread. I had removed my down-filled *10X* hunting coat and required orange vest when I started the "gutting" process, but quickly rethought the wisdom of that move and replaced the vest. If another hunter had been attracted by my shot, I didn't care to end up in his sight picture. Besides, there aren't too many deer around with orange hides!

The snow made my downhill "drag" to the stream an easy one, and, after changing boots, I managed to pull the buck through the stream. However, the resistance offered by the water's flow made me glad it wasn't any wider, and, once on the other side, the upslope made the going tougher and restricted my progress to 20-foot intervals. By resting and switching hands to avoid cramping, I finally reached the farmhouse. I took my time, since I had no reason to hurry and was way ahead of schedule!

When I finally got back to the house, I celebrated my "victory" with a hearty ham and fried-egg breakfast, then called Dad at work to tell him the good news. He was excited and proud and wanted to know the full details. I was more than happy to oblige.

Wes came back from his uneventful morning hunt just before noon and was as pleased about my success as if he had taken the buck himself. It's nice to have friends who can share your joys without any trace of envy or jealousy. Wes is such a person, and it was easy for me to reciprocate a few years later when Wes nailed a big eight pointer of his own from his usual post on the hill behind the farmhouse.

Wes planned to go back out after lunch and stay on stand until dark. I decided to get an early start on the 3½-hour drive home, so after an extended photo session, I expressed my heartfelt thanks and appreciation to my host and began my triumphant journey back to New Jersey. Wes' parting comment was for me to circle the calendar for opening day 1977. I enthusiastically accepted his invitation and immediately started the 365-day countdown!

By the time the following fall arrived, I had a very handsome eight-point whitetail shoulder mount hanging on my wall. It was a constant reminder of my terrific first hunt at Just-a-Farm, and I eagerly anticipated my return.

The preopening day weekend finally arrived, and when I headed north on Saturday, November 19th, I had added some lumber, a saw, a hammer and nails to my usual hunting gear. There would be no standing on branches this time! I planned to do my usual scouting for fresh sign, but unless some dramatic event altered my plans, I had every intention of being in that same lucky tree where I had enjoyed my previous year's success. Only this time I would be higher and more comfortable in a permanent stand and seat!

If anything, my Saturday afternoon and Sunday morning scouting sessions further confirmed that my tree at the juncture of the two stone walls was in an ideal spot. I found numerous fresh rubs along a well-worn trail only 20 yards away. That trail continued to the thick, swampy area below and to the left. Another new trail paralleled the vertical stone wall that ended at my tree. With that encouragement, I built my new platform and seat 20 feet above ground in the upper branches of my favorite hardwood. The additional elevation gave me a much wider field of view in all directions and put me above the many obstructive branches that could deflect an otherwise well-aimed shot. After placing two nails in convenient spots from which to hang my slinged rifle and fanny pack, I was satisfied that all was ready for the next morning's opening bell.

Wes, Nick, and Nick's buddies planned to hunt above Wes' place once again, so, as far as I knew, I would be the only one hunting across the road and stream. The good and bad of that was that fewer hunters would mean less noise and odor to spook game, but more hunter activity would keep the game moving for longer periods during the day. Given the choice, I'd choose fewer hunters than more anytime. Good scouting and stand location can make up for the lack of hunter presence and keep deer following their normal routines.

The rest of Sunday was spent zeroing-in our rifles, treating my host to an early dinner at a local restaurant, and visiting with Nick and friends to swap stories of past and anticipated deer hunting successes in front of a crackling fire. A few adult beverages helped embellish the tales. Then, after many "good luck tomorrow" exchanges, we returned to Wes' to lay out our clothes and gear. The 4:00 a.m. wakeup was only five hours away! Although there was no snow cover or forecast for same, opening morning called for cold, clear weather. With my new stand waiting to be occupied, I felt well prepared and confident. Knowing my location was a "proven" area made me feel that much better.

When the alarm rang, I wasted little time getting ready for the day's adventure. I wanted to get to my stand as early and quietly as possible, climb to my new perch carefully and silently, and get settled and "ready" well before daybreak. I had waited a whole year for that special day and didn't want to make any foolish or avoidable mistakes. By 5:30 a.m., I was prepared for whatever the day brought. My safety belt was secure, my rifle was loaded with safety on, and my glasses were clean and held firmly in place with an elastic strap. I had applied coverup scent to my boots for the walk in, and I squirted additional amounts when I reached my tree. I hadn't as much as brushed against a tree let alone snapped a twig. The table was set!

At first light I was tingling with anticipation, and all my senses were on maximum alert. At any moment I expected the twin of the previous year's eight pointer to make an appearance, following the same diagonal path from the swamp. I guess he hadn't received a copy of the script, since no buck made an appearance; not at 6 a.m., 7 a.m., 8 a.m., 9 a.m., 10 a.m., or 11 a.m.! At 12:00 noon, I decided to climb down and return to the house for lunch. After so much buildup and hopeful anticipation, that morning's hunt was a disappointment. I had seen only three does at a considerable distance, so I wasn't very encouraged by the prospects. I generally get more psyched for morning hunts than for afternoon hunts due to the mystery and suspense of entering the woods in the dark, leaving time for the mind to play games while waiting for the day's events to unfold. However, post-rut and opening day hunter activity promised to keep deer on the move, so I looked forward to the p.m. vigil.

I met Wes at the house. He had seen only does as well. There had been some shooting on his side, and although he kept a sharp lookout, nothing with antlers appeared. I told him about my buckless morning, but promised to return to give it my best shot after a quick sandwich. I encouraged Wes to hunt the "stream" side with me, and by 1:30 p.m. I was back in my tree, comfortable and hopeful. Wes decided to walk towards the swamp and then climb up the mountain for several hundred yards.

At 2:00 p.m., a lone doe appeared on the trail to my right and walked swiftly out of sight toward the swamp. I heard her before I saw her, and the anticipation of the deer being a buck got my adrenaline flowing. At least it kept me awake and alert. However, by 4:00 p.m. my mood had once again turned dour. The two o'clock doe was the last animal of any kind I had seen, and less than one hour of legal shooting time remained. Fifteen minutes later I removed my safety belt, buckled on my fanny pack, and prepared to make my descent. I had removed my rifle from its nail holder and was preparing to shoulder it for my climb down, when I took one last look around.

To this day, I don't know how he got there. The air was still, and the leaves were dry and plentiful; yet, I hadn't heard a single footstep. Nor had I caught the slightest movement. But the truth was that directly below my stand, a mere five feet beyond the horizontal stone wall, stood a six-point whitetail buck! It was as if he had been lowered to that spot by a silent helicopter or giant stork! I was dumbfounded, but my initial shock turned quickly into action. I was actually sitting on the stand's platform about to lower myself to the closest branch when I spotted him. If I had made any noise, it obviously wasn't enough to scare him into flight. However, his ears were "working" nervously, and I knew his suspicion and uneasiness were growing.

He held his position facing to my right as I carefully released the safety and shouldered the .30-.06. At such a close distance and with a clear shot, I decided to aim for his heart, located low in his chest cavity behind his foreleg. As soon as my crosshairs found their mark, I squeezed the trigger. The buck leaped into the air, then ran forward in an uneven pattern for over 100 yards. I knew the jumping behavior was the normal reaction to a heart shot, but I was mystified by the distance he was able to cover, assuming the hit was accurate.

His initial burst was fast and strong, and, as one is supposed to do, I concentrated on watching him as far as I could. Suddenly he slowed and seemed to lose his footing. A few steps farther he swayed, then wobbled, and finally fell on his left side. When I reached him he was stone dead, and his left antler was buried in the ground as a result of the hard fall. When I lifted his head he sported a fine set of antlers with three points per side sans brow tines.

Wes had already started his walk down the mountain when he heard my shot and was soon by my side offering his congratulations. Since it was getting dark, he decided to continue on to the farm and return with his tractor. In the meantime, I finished field dressing the buck and started dragging it downhill to save time. Wes met me before I reached the stream and helped me load my newest trophy for the quick and dry ride back to the farm.

I think I was still in a daze as I recounted my afternoon hunt and surprise encounter. As usual, Wes was his laid-back, matter-of-fact self as he praised my good fortune. His happiness for me was sincere, and, once again, he extended an invitation for the next deer season; a kindness he repeated each year until I moved to Colorado.

I enjoyed other successes during my 11 years of hunting at Wes' farm, including a bow-killed doe, a fat spike buck as he followed a doe out of the swampy area near the stream, and a nice forked-horn buck taken from a rock outcropping high on the mountain. On another opening day, I counted a total of 28 deer, but none carried the required "headgear". Each of those hunts holds special memories, but my fondest remembrances are of the a.m. eight pointer taken in 1976 and the p.m. six pointer shot in 1977, both from that same "lucky" tree. Their mounts are nicknamed "A.M." and "P.M.", respectively!

As a small token of my appreciation, I surprised Wes with a new mailbox before my last hunt with him in 1986. On its sides are pictures of whitetails and the inscription, "J. Wesley Blackwell, Just-a-Farm".

I hope to see that mailbox again some day.

Wes Blackwell's "Just-a-Farm" near Hobert, NY in Delaware County

November 22, 1976: New York Southern Zone rifle season opening day eight-point buck taken on mountain in background at Wes' farm

J. Wesley Blackwell with my November 1976 opening day eight pointer

"A.M." eight pointer (left) and "P.M." six pointer taken on opening days of New York Southern Zone rifle season in 1976 and 1977, respectively, on Wes Blackwell's "Just-a-Farm"

"spike" buck taken on opening day of New York 1979 Southern Zone rifle season at Wes' farm

Chapter 7: Colorado Mulies - My First Guided Hunt (1983)

> **COLORADO**
> Quality elk and deer tent camp hunts using
> horses; archery, rifle, muzzleloader.
> 30 yrs. Experience.
> (Approved NAHC) License #145
> Dick Pennington Gde. Svc., Ltd
> 2371 "H" Rd., Grand Junction, CO 81505
> Tel.# 970-242-6318

When I saw the above ad in the January/February, 1996 edition of *North American Hunter* magazine, I silently questioned how 12 years could have passed so quickly since my first guided hunt. It evoked memories of my November 1983 mule deer hunt with Dick Pennington and his son, Alan. Back then, I remember Dick mentioning being 50 years old, so it was encouraging to know he was still going strong at 62! When you love the outdoors and keep in shape like Dick, there's no telling how long you can go on. It's just another reason why hunters should get out there "while the gettin's good" and the legs are still strong!

Dick operates his outfit out of Grand Junction, Colorado, guiding archery, rifle, and muzzleloader hunters for elk, mule deer, black bear, and cougar in the fall and winter. During the summer, Dick and his family conduct fishing and horse pack trips.

Kimber III and his mom surprised me on my 40th birthday with a trophy mule deer hunt with Dick for November 10 - 15, 1983. I had always dreamed of going on a western guided hunt ever since my dad did so in the 1950's, and now it was to become a reality. I was delighted with their special gift. They had done their homework and couldn't have chosen a more experienced, hardworking, or caring person than Dick. That hunt marked the beginning of what would be a series of wonderful guided adventures over the ensuing years.

In anticipation of my first guided hunt, I had many questions to ask, and I'm sure the cost of my hunt would have been double if Dick had charged me for his phone time! But I wanted to be sure I arrived well prepared from a conditioning and equipment standpoint in order to eliminate as many excuses and alibis as possible and give myself the best chance for success. He was extremely helpful and patient, and his list of personal gear required for rifle hunts provided most of the answers. Dick also recommended sighting-in two inches high at 100 yards and using 150-grain cartridges.

I inquired about getting an elk license as well, since Colorado hosts the largest elk population in the U.S., and good bulls would be in our area. Dick explained that his quota was filled on elk tags, but said if there were any cancellations he would put me at the top of his list. He told me there would be 10 hunters in camp, with a fairly equal mix of those hunting either elk, deer, or both. I remarked that **that** many hunters seemed a bit excessive, but Dick said his territory, equipment, horses, and the number of available guides comfortably supported that number. I felt better.

Dick's ranch was only three miles from the airport in Grand Junction, and he arranged for me to stay at the Holiday Inn, which was only a half mile from the airport. Alan Pennington met my flight and took me to the hotel for my overnight stay before picking me up for our drive into camp. Two weathered 4 WD pickups provided the transportation.

Dick's camp was northeast of Grand Junction, and the backroads' drive to our wall-tent campsite took about 1½ hours. The terrain around our camp was more hilly than mountainous, but we still had to extricate both trucks from a deep muddy ravine via winches within a few hundred yards of our destination.

Dick owned his own packhorses, and they were already corralled in camp. He had asked each hunter for his weight and riding experience in order to match us with the right steed, and he firmly believed that owning versus leasing stock enabled him to learn the temperament and disposition of each animal. That would assure maximum comfort and safety to each hunter, regardless of his horsemanship or physical condition.

The Dick Pennington Guide Service was in reality the Dick Pennington *Family* Guild Service. Dick was a slightly built, wiry man whose stubbled face left the impression he was either taking a temporary hiatus from shaving or was in the preliminary stages of growing a *real* beard. A red checkered shirt, worn jeans, cowboy boots, and sweat-stained cowboy hat with curled brim identified him as a man of the outdoors! Dick had been guiding for over 30 years and was savvy in all aspects of outfitting and guiding, from wrangling to setting up camp, but especially for finding, stalking, and tracking game. He had passed along those skills to his son Alan, and I genuinely appreciated their thorough knowledge of game habits and movements, and their overall effort during my four days of hunting. (As is the norm, a "hunt" includes a day on both ends for travel to and from camp). Both Dick and Alan were quiet individuals, but very pleasant and ever attuned to the needs and desires of their clients. Dick's petite blond wife, Norma, helped with bookings and camp duties, most notably her impressive culinary skills in the mess tent. When it comes to outfitter families, the Penningtons are certainly among the best.

Being my first guided big-game hunting experience, I was eager to learn as much as possible from the experts. I was all eyes, ears, and questions as I observed and picked the brains of not only Dick and Alan, but of the other hunters, too. Collectively, they had been on over 30 guided hunts!

I became more cognizant of wind direction and learned the importance of staying downwind in order to spot more game and be able to work in closer for a decent shot. Being seen will not hinder success as severely as being scented, although it is best to avoid both. From my observation, mule deer possess a certain curiosity which, even if a hunter is detected, will cause them to pause after their initial flight to try to identify their pursuer. Knowing this, a hunter can sometimes get a second chance for a shot and should stay ready in a good shooting position. Elk, on the other hand, never look back. Once they sense danger or are spooked, they stay on the move until they reach heavy cover.

During the second day of our hunt, Dick and another guide, Todd, took four of us hunters on horseback to an area five miles from camp where we observed a herd of over 30 elk on a distant hillside. We dismounted, tied the horses, and started glassing for bulls. Since I was licensed for mule deer only, I didn't feel the adrenaline rush that the others were experiencing, but I was glad to help scan the group for a "shootable" bull. We observed one "spike" and a "four point", but since others were obscured by pines and aspens, we believed a larger herd bull could be present. We stalked to get a closer look and decided, based on a left to right crosswind, to make a wide circular approach through a ravine to our right to a point above the herd. A few minutes into our march, snow started to fly and very quickly became so thick that it obscured our vision and caused us to lose sight of our intended target. Dick made a quick decision to crawl under a large pine tree to wait out the storm. He felt the storm's intensity would subside shortly, and that we'd then be able to regain our bearings. Otherwise, we would be wandering aimlessly with barely 10 feet of visibility.

Once under the tree, Dick cut some low-hanging boughs for all of us to sit on to keep our butts from getting wet. That was just one of many lessons in woodsmanship I was to learn from Dick. For anyone who has been caught in a downpour without his rain gear or has gotten a boot full of water, keeping dry in the field takes on new significance.

Eventually the snow let up, and we were able to resume our stalk. Unfortunately, during the storm the elk had moved deeper into the timber, and, by the time we reached the targeted area, they were long gone. At least I had gained some stalking and weather-avoiding experience.

On another day, Alan Pennington was assigned to take me to an area that offered a good lookout point from a rock outcropping overlooking the valley below. To get there he had to drive one of the trucks along a steep mountain road that was no wider than a horse trail, and which had been partially washed out by recent rains. Sitting on a hay bale in the open bed, I'd be lying if I told you I was anywhere close to comfortable during our predawn drive. I kept leaning toward the uphill side of the truck in order to make a quick exit over the side in the event the ground collapsed and the truck rolled over! Alan, on the other hand, seemed completely unconcerned and in control as he successfully maneuvered through the rocks and bushes at an acute angle to reach our parking spot. From there we walked farther uphill to the rock outcropping aptly named *Windy Point* - a location where the wind blew so hard from left to right that I had to cock my head to avoid getting pelted by the accompanying sleet. We then crawled out to the edge and maintained a prone position to stay concealed from any game below. It was just as well, since standing would have resulted in being blown off our feet!

The area below us was thick with pine, spruce, and aspen. Luckily, early snows provided a good background for observing any game movement within the trees. During our two-hour watch, we spotted a medium-sized 3x3 mulie walking through some pines approximately 200 yards away. Even though he was a decent buck, I had my sights set on a wider 4x4 trophy, and it was still early enough in the hunt not to be tempted to lower my standards. Ironically, the next day Alan guided another hunter to that same spot, and he connected on a nice 24-inch 4x4, the one that was supposed to have walked in front of **my** sights! Those mulie bucks sure do have trouble following schedules – especially showing up a day late!

When darkness fell, everyone returned to camp to enjoy a delicious meal prepared by Norma and to share stories about the day's activities and past hunts. With 10 hunters and the 4 guides (Dick, Alan, Todd, and Tim), there was certainly no shortage of lively conversations, jokes, and hunting yarns swollen beyond their normal exaggeration over the years.

The other hunters represented four states: Tim O'Mara and Tom Wolf from Massachusetts; Fred Hoffman, an insurance company manager from Wisconsin; Bob Williams, owner of an electrical supply company, Melvin Goulds, president of a general contracting business, and another fellow named Jim were from Tennessee; Jim and Harry were aqua farmers from Mississippi, and they brought two coolers of farm-raised catfish to share with everyone. Delicious! Two lifelong hunting buddies, Billy George and Jimmy Oliver ("J.O.") rounded out the Mississippi contingent and kept everyone in stitches with their rich southern humor and friendly digs at each other. Apparently, "J.O." got "scope eye" on every hunt due to never allowing enough eye relief between his eye and the rear scope aperture. Every time he fired, the "kick" would imprint a circular (and often **bloody**!) cut around his right eye. Billy George kept asking him how many scars he intended to collect before mounting his scope farther away!

Billy George happened to be celebrating his 40th birthday with us, and Norma made a special cake to mark the occasion. Upon blowing out the candles, he looked over at me and commented in his slow Mississippi drawl, "Keem, the problem with me is I've got a 20-year-old mind trapped in this 40-year-old body!" That summed up his feeling on reaching 40 in a humorous way. I'll never forget that comment. All the guys were fun to be with and offered an interesting array of backgrounds and careers. The one thing we all shared during those six days together was our love for the outdoors and big-game hunting. There's something to be said for male bonding and the need to get back to nature, if only for a brief period each year. Putting one's family and business responsibilities on hold for awhile also plays a part in that escape syndrome, and I don't recall seeing one guilty face among that whole group!

I had one more good chance to get my buck on the last day in camp. Shortly after daybreak, four of us hunters plus guides Tim and Todd were on foot a short distance from camp when we spotted deer inside a woodline 100 yards away. We all dropped quickly into prone positions, and, since I was the only one in the group with a deer-only license, I was chosen to take the first shot. One of the hunters at the front of our single file spotted a good racked buck, but from my position I couldn't find him in my scope due to scrub pines obstructing my field of

71

view. The frustration grew as I wasted valuable seconds trying to locate him, while the hunter farther ahead had a clear shot, yet wasn't the designated shooter! Good shooting opportunities at trophy game are fleeting, and by the time I gave up my priority spot in the shooting rotation, the deer's growing nervousness had turned into a quick exit. No one took a shot, and the opportunity was lost. It goes to show that luck does play a part in hunting success; for example, if I had been at the front of the column instead of last, if my view hadn't been obstructed by trees, if…if…if… However, that's why they call it hunting, not killing.

Both Billy George and Jimmy "Scope Eye" took small bucks on the last day, with Billy's resulting from an especially long shot across a wide canyon. Billy said he saw the buck standing among some pines on the opposite hillside at an estimated 550 yards, took a high aim over its back, and systematically worked down shot-by-shot until he connected. I hope he gave "J.O." some of the venison to hold over his wounded eye! Bob Williams had hung a nice 3x4 mulie earlier in the week, so the total harvest was four mule deer bucks, but no elk. A reasonable number of elk had been spotted, but only one shot was taken at a decent branch-antlered bull. That lone opportunity came at dusk by Bob Williams on a return trip to camp. The elk "shutout" helped temper my disappointment at not having a license in case that golden opportunity had presented itself. I think if any hunter is asked, he would rather spend the extra money to have all possible licenses than to limit the cost of his hunt and possibly lose out on that once-in-a-lifetime trophy opportunity.

Dick had another camp - located above 10,000 feet - which he normally used for spring bear and early fall hunts. Snow had already closed that camp by the time our party reached his lower site at 8,000 feet. Dick told us that one year while hunting out of his "high" camp, a freak early snowstorm dumped nearly five **feet** of snow over two days, with drifts reaching the top of the tent sides. Realizing the severity of the situation, Dick opted to go for help on horseback and felt very fortunate that he made it. The hunters were rescued, but his horses perished. Weather; another big-game hunting threat and danger!

Dick had scheduled a new group of hunters the following week, so we packed our gear and bid ado to "Camp Pennington". Left behind were the two 10 by 20-foot canvas wall tents that had served as home to our group of outfitters, guides, and hunters, and a similar-sized mess tent with its crude but efficient stove and long table and benches that had served as our meal and entertainment center. Before we broke camp, the horses were fed and watered. They seemed content, but in need of a well-deserved rest until the next crew arrived. I gave one last pat to sure-footed Diablo, my assigned packhorse for the week, took one final look at the panorama, then joined the others for the ride back to the real world. Although I didn't bring home a trophy, I brought back memories of a great experience that made me hungry for more!

November 1983: Dick Pennington, outfitter/guide
<u>Dick Pennington Guide Service, Ltd.</u>

(L to R) Alan, Dick, and Norma Pennington

(L to R) "J.O.", Melvin, Billy George, Fred,
Jimmy, Tim, Bob, Harry, and Tom

Kim, "Mule Deer Hunter", November 1983

Winching our way out of camp

Pennington's "lower" camp

Chapter 8: Newfoundland - The Land of Woodland Caribou, Canadian Moose, and Black Bear (1984)

With a name like Angus Wentzel, he's gotta be good! That name jumped out at me as I was perusing the list of outfitters in the back pages of the July, 1984 edition of *Sports Afield*.

Angus is the owner/outfitter of <u>Deer Pond Camps, Ltd.</u> out of Corner Brook, Newfoundland, Canada. His advertisement for fly-in hunting indicated success rates of 97% on moose and 100% on caribou in 1983, and that was good enough for me. I called him to book a hunt for September 30 - October 7, 1984. The combination hunt included Canadian moose, woodland caribou, and for an extra $50 license fee, black bear. Angus suggested arriving on Saturday, the 29th, with plans to fly into camp early on Sunday.

The hunt got off to a shaky start on two fronts. First, when I arrived at the Stephenville, Newfoundland airport on the afternoon of the 29th, only my cased rifle arrived on the connecting Air Canada flight out of Montreal! My two duffel bags containing all my hunting clothes, ammo, and other gear had not been transferred to the second flight! But at least my early arrival gave me another day to work out the problem before flying into camp on Sunday, the *official* starting day of my hunt. Angus had instructed me to take a taxi from Stephenville to Corner Brook, where he lived and kept his single-engine Beechcraft equipped with pontoons. The 50-mile trip was a blur, since I was preoccupied with making plans to locate my luggage and to receive it in time for my flight to camp. Angus said he would call me at the Holiday Inn in Corner Brook and provide me with details for the next day. I arrived at the motel at approximately 3:00 p.m. and immediately got on the phone to Air Canada's baggage department in Montreal. If my bags could not be located, I would have had to rush out to replace all missing items before the stores closed *that* day. Corner Brook's stores were not open on Sundays! Luckily, I spoke with a handler, Mr. Gousa, who was very apologetic and empathetic and made it his personal project to find my bags. Yes! He assured me they would not only be on Sunday's flight to Stephenville, but would be delivered to my hotel. That conversation alone was quite a relief, and, sure enough, at 3:00 p.m. on Sunday my bags arrived as promised. Thank you, Mr. Gousa! Nothing can mess up a hunting trip more than lost baggage and firearms.

My second concern was that I hadn't heard from Angus. I waited in my room until 8:00 p.m. on Saturday and then decided to call his home. His wife, Madeline, answered and sounded quite upset. As the story unfolded, Angus was flying the previous week's group of hunters from camp on Friday, the 28th, when a strong wind sheer flipped his plane on takeoff, landing it upside down in the lake fronting the camp! Angus and two of the hunters managed to crawl out and swim to shore, but a third hunter wasn't as fortunate and drowned in the frigid water. He was unable to release his seat belt. I learned later that the victim was in his 30's, married, with two young children. He had taken a nice moose on his first guided hunt and was heading home when the tragedy struck. Angus was involved with Canada's equivalent of the FAA investigation of the accident plus arranging for a new pilot and plane for me, since he was temporarily grounded until the investigation was completed! Madeline assured me that Angus would contact me on Sunday and that my hunt would proceed as planned. I was understandably shocked and unnerved by the news. Remote, fly-in hunts always carry an element of danger, but you never expect it to hit so close to home.

When Angus called he seemed surprisingly composed in the face of what had transpired. Part of that had to do with the calm, stoic nature of the Newfoundland people in general, and it showed as he recounted the events of the previous two days without a trace of emotion. He was lucky to be alive, and, as we spoke, it occurred to me that I could have been attending his funeral instead. I think the other part of his reaction was that he had been totally numbed by the experience!

After Angus picked me up at 3:30 p.m., we headed to the pier with my newly-arrived baggage to get loaded into the substitute plane. Angus assured me that the pilot, Dan, was highly qualified and dependable, which I gratefully accepted. However, midway through the 40-minute flight to Newfoundland Game Management Area #37, my concern grew with each of Dan's yawns as he explained how he had been flying charters for 12 straight hours and was tired. Half joking and half serious, I replied that I hoped he wasn't planning to take a nap until we landed! Whew, all of a sudden, airplanes were not my favorite subject, and I was greatly relieved when we arrived at our northern destination in the district of Burgeo and started our descent towards the Cochran Pond Camp, or should I say the Cochran *Death* Pond Camp!

My first water landing was smooth, and we glided to the narrow pier which extended about 20 feet from the shore. My gear was quickly unloaded, and Dan's condition was no longer of utmost concern to me. I assume he made it back safely.

My personal guide, Bryant Payne, was there to greet me. He was a bald, thin-faced man of medium height and build, with a quiet demeanor. A native "Newfy", Bryant made his living by guiding moose and caribou hunts in the fall and winter and by fishing for cod in the spring and summer near St. Pauls, Newfoundland.

Two other hunters, Tom and Joe LeBlanc, Jr. from Linden, Michigan extended their greetings as well, and all helped carry my gear to the wooden trailerlike dwelling that would serve as "home" for the next week. Joe Sr. had business to attend to but would join us the following day.

Our 45-foot long by 12-foot wide shelter was divided into three equal areas: the middle section where we entered was the kitchen and dining area with Eric, the hired cook and camp orderly, in charge; the section to the left was the guides' quarters, and the remaining area on the right contained beds and clothes hooks for four hunters. There was ample storage space under the wood-framed, mattressed beds to keep extra clothes, rifle cases, and other personal gear out of the way. The area was a bit tight, but efficient and comfortable. A wood-burning stove in the kitchen area radiated sufficient heat to warm the extreme sections as well. The wooden dwelling was painted white so it could be seen from a distance, and, since our daily treks for game took us from 10 to 15 miles away from camp, any visual aid to relocate our shelter at the end of a long day afield was welcomed! A separate supply tent and outhouse completed our "community".

Successful hunting was accomplished by walking, glassing, and stalking. The terrain near our campsite was strewn with large boulders, which we used as oversized stepping stones to traverse approximately 100 yards before reaching the typical ground cover, called "the bog" by the natives. That shin-high, sagelike growth was soft when dry, and provided a comfortable cushion when walking. Like sage, you had to pick up your feet or suffer the annoying tugs and pulls if you tried to shuffle along. After a rain, the bog's dirt base softened quickly and slowed our travel considerably! The bog, interspersed with small bushes and saplings, covered the bulk of the rolling landscape, broken only by the occasional three to five acre stands of hardwoods which served as harbors for game during severe weather and heavy snows. I experienced all bog conditions during that week; dry, rain-drenched, and snow-covered. Unfortunately, none compared favorably to a leisurely walk in the park!

On Monday, October 1st, we awoke at 5:30 a.m., dressed, ate a hearty breakfast of ham and eggs, fried potatoes, toast, and coffee and were ready to hunt by 7:00 a.m. Since it had to be light enough to spot game at long distances, there was no advantage to making an earlier departure.

Once outside our abode, Bryant took his only compass reading of the day, and then the boulder hopping and walking began. The early comfortable pace soon slowed due to the distances covered, the rising temperature, and overdressing - the main culprit being my three-quarter length, goose-down filled *10-X* hunting parka. By noon, we had spotted only four cow moose and several cow caribou for our seven mile effort. After a quick sandwich and canned orange drink, the sun beckoned us to take a midday snooze as the temperature reached the mid-80's!

We resumed our hunt at 1:30 p.m. and soon spotted a bull and cow caribou at a distance of over one thousand yards. The sun's reflection off his antlers identified the bull, but he was much too far away to determine his rack's symmetry and size. They were feeding and walking on a left-to-right diagonal route from where we stood and were completely unaware of our presence. The quartering wind was favorable for a stalk as we circled to our left and headed towards a small ravine, which we felt would bring us within 100 to 150 yards of our quarry, assuming they maintained their course.

As the distance closed to about 300 yards, Bryant and I took a more critical look at the bull's headgear. Antler mass even on an average bull caribou is impressive, and the inclination is to shoot the first one you see. The sight through my binoculars was impressive; good height and spread with good "bezes". More impressively, he had the desired double "shovels" extending out to his nose tip. I felt his overall symmetry was worthy of a place on my wall, but since he was the first bull I had ever seen in the wild, I asked for Bryant's assessment. I decided to abide by his "go" or "no go" decision.

Bryant concurred that he was an excellent trophy and emphasized the rare double shovels as a real consideration versus more mass! That observation, combined with the earlier voiced concern about the scarce number of caribou sightings overall, made me rethink the option of holding out for a better trophy. With my mind made up, I wanted to get closer for a good clean shot.

Our good fortune continued as the caribou went into the ravine and casually sauntered their way up the embankment on the far side. With their path leading them away from me, I made my final stalk into the near side of the ravine where I settled behind a small pine tree and chose a branch which afforded a steady rest for my shot. Suddenly, the bull turned and gave me a perfect, unobstructed shot at 125 yards. My .30-.06 Remington model 742 Woodsmaster barked and the 180- grain Winchester Silvertip was on its way to a perfect double-lung hit. I watched through my Leupold Vari-X-III 3.5x10 scope as he lurched forward, ran 20 yards, then circled back before collapsing in the short brush. My woodland caribou trophy was history.

The next thing I knew, Bryant was slapping me on the back and praising my fine shot and quick kill. We hurried to the downed bull, admired his fine 30-point rack, took some photos, then got down to the work at hand. Bryant did all the gutting, quartering, and caping to my complete delight. He kept repeating what a good bull he was, although I suspect, like most guides, he would have been just as complimentary if I had taken a cow!

Although a man of few words, Bryant proved his worth as a guide, and his knowledge of the terrain and game paid off handsomely with my first-day trophy "Bou". I could then concentrate on taking a good bull moose and black bear in the days remaining!

We returned to camp at 4:00 p.m. with the cape, antlers, and two hindquarters. Bryant made an immediate return trip with two other guides, Ken and Joe, to retrieve the rest of the meat. I made a token, rather unenthusiastic offer to accompany them, but they said the three of them could handle it. Happily, I took a nap.

Joe LeBlanc, Sr. had arrived, and, after the three meat packers returned, we all sat down to a terrific meal and discussed the day's events. My caribou was the main topic of conversation, and both Bryant and I were more than happy to recount every detail, from sighting to caping!

Tuesday, October 2nd, belonged to Joe Jr., who scored on a nice 10-point bull moose with a long offhand shot. He and his guide, Ken, had spotted it about five miles from camp while that largest member of the deer family fed in a shallow lake, one of many which dotted

81

the territory. After a careful stalk that brought him within 150 yards, Joe made his shot count. What made his accomplishment more memorable was having his dad and brother along to share the moment!

My Tuesday afield started at 7:15 a.m. and ended at 5:00 p.m. with some incredible sightings, but no "triumphs". During our long 10-mile stroll through the bog, we saw a cow moose, two sage grouse, two mallard ducks, a woodcock, and seven Canada geese. We didn't see a single caribou, which made my previous day's decision seem even wiser. The weather again turned sunny and warm after a frosty morning, but a cool, steady breeze was a refreshing accompaniment during the entire day.

Wednesday, October 3rd was ***nobody's*** day, since all of us were confined to our quarters by a torrential downpour. Even without the rain, strong winds and fog would have made hunting very difficult. We hunters consoled ourselves by playing cards, reading hunting magazines, and eating, while the four guides spent the day retrieving Joe's moose. On a day like that, they certainly earned their pay!

Thursday, October 4th offered little improvement in the weather. Even though the heavy, steady rain had changed to a drizzle, the fog endured, and a chilly wind made the hunting outlook dismal at best. If it hadn't been for Wednesday's confinement, it would have been easy to dismiss any thought of pulling on the boots. However, 24 hours with nine guys cramped inside our small quarters caused a minor case of claustrophobia and created a real need to "break out", regardless of the weather. Bryant decided to try for moose in a new area several miles away, which could be reached faster via water. Since we were getting a late start, using the camp's outboard-powered 12-foot aluminum skiff was the most expedient way to reach our destination via the rough expanse of interconnected waterways.

Unfortunately for us, the weather worsened, and after two futile hours of poor visibility and no sightings, Bryant and I agreed that the game was holding in heavy cover and would probably remain there until conditions improved. Resigned to our fate via the elements, we retraced our path and arrived back at the "cabin" by 2:00 p.m. The break at least preserved our sanity, whereas all others in the party had elected to stay put and watch the walls move that much closer together!

The sky cleared on Friday, and prospects for a good hunting day were in place. Joe Sr. had decided to leave early due to the combination of bad weather and poor physical conditioning. In addition, since Joe Jr. had filled his only tag, I was left in the enviable position of having both their guides available to help Bryant in quest of my moose. In fact, after lying around for two straight days, they *insisted* on going along!

No sooner had we finished the initial boulder-hopping part of our journey (with 50-year-old Joe leading the way like a crazed bull frog leaping from lily pad to lily pad), than we spotted two cow caribou with a magnificent bull standing at the crest of the first hill, silhouetted against the bright blue sky. Our collective mouths dropped open as the surefire Boone and Crockett candidate nonchalantly eyed our approach, as if knowing I had filled my tag and posed no threat. As pleased as I was with my trophy, the bull we saw *that* morning would be difficult to top by anyone, anywhere! Generally, caribou have poor eyesight, and our fuzzy images apparently peaked that bull's curiosity enough for him to walk toward us for a closer look. His approach brought him within 40 paces of our group, and I was able to make a thorough inspection of his rack through my scope, which was cranked up to its maximum 10 power. Long, well-defined points covered his heavy, wide main beams highlighted by 20-inch long bezes with six points on each and massive double shovels at least 12 inches deep in front. Those protective eye guards extended **beyond** the tip of his nose. The guides kept saying how my bull was just as good, but I knew they were only trying to console me. Mine was a good bull. The other was a *dream* bull. I regretted not having my camera to capture a lasting image of that superb specimen, but, then again, it may have served only to prolong my period of "what ifs". As it turned out, that larger bull was only the second mature trophy I saw on my trip; the **other** one came home with me! Greed and regrets should have no place in hunting, anyway. There's too much to enjoy besides the taking of game.

At any rate, "King Bou" got our hearts started and gave us a good adrenaline rush for that day's moose hunt.

We followed a route that Ken felt would produce sightings, and, hopefully, a second trophy for me. I'm not sure how many miles we covered, and I was afraid to ask, realizing it would be an equal number on the return trip! *Knowing* the distance may have proven too tiring mentally, let alone physically. Eventually, Ken and Joe pushed a cow and good bull with maybe

10 points per side from a small woodlot they were driving. Unfortunately, Bryant and I didn't have sufficient time to properly position ourselves before the moose decided to escape. I couldn't respond in time for a decent shot.

As we regrouped to plan our pursuit strategy, we spotted another smaller bull feeding approximately 400 yards away. Ken motioned for me to follow him, and after a 200-yard run through the bog with my tongue hanging out, we peeked over the top of a hill only to see the smaller forked-antler bull standing broadside at 150 yards. If he had been the larger bull, I wouldn't have hesitated to shoot, but the younger male didn't meet the minimum trophy requirement I had set for myself. I passed. That was my last chance that day, and the guides blamed an approaching snowstorm for the lack of further game movement. Sure enough, on our return hike to camp, the flakes started to fall!

When we awoke the next morning, there were five inches of snow on the ground. It provided a terrific backdrop for spotting game, and I was very eager to hit "the bog"! My three-guide triumvirate was in place again as we headed in the same general direction as the previous day. About five miles from camp we picked up the fresh tracks of three moose, one set of which we determined to be a bull. As we followed the tracks, my heart started racing as we picked up our pace, stopping at each rise to glass thoroughly with the hope of catching any dark patches of movement against the snow cover. The tracks led into a patch of timber, and as we slowly inched our way inside, eight eyes strained to catch any horizontal lines in the vertical growth or any movement that would give us the upper hand. Ken suddenly held up his hand and pointed ahead. As my eyes became acclimated to the thick undergrowth, I spotted the long snout of a moose, but with absolutely no accompanying movement. Like "follow the dots", I kept expanding my vision until the entire body was outlined - a cow. At 20 paces she looked like a train, and, when the wind shifted, she *moved* like a train too! The bull and another cow were ahead of her, but the thickness of the cover didn't afford clear identification let alone a shot. By the time we got to the woodlot's edge where they had broken out, 300 yards separated us, and the distance was widening rapidly. Moose may have an awkward gait, but they sure do know how to get the most speed out of it. They don't have the innate curiosity of a mule deer to eventually stop to look back at their pursuers, so once they get on their way, they stay on their way! The bull was only a "spike" anyway, so it didn't bother me that I didn't get a shot.

The sun was causing the snow to melt rapidly, especially with the bog acting as a gigantic sponge. Our background advantage soon disappeared, and more frequent glassing became the order of the day. We did spot two other bulls with two cows crossing a creek a considerable distance away, and their quick pace indicated they had winded us. One of the bulls sported a respectable palmated rack, but with the distance widening between us, we didn't stand a chance to get within range. Besides, it was getting late, and we had 10 miles of soggy bog to traverse before we reached the welcome warmth of our "white house". The ***thought*** alone of carrying more than 100 pounds of moose meat, antlers, or cape over that distance made me weary. As it turned out, I needed every ounce of energy just to make the long trek back without an extra load! My sea-anchor parka didn't make it any easier; however, halfway through our journey, one of the guides volunteered to carry the perspiration-weighted garment for me. Hearty guys, those Newfys!

On our return trip, Joe spotted a small black bear running along a creek bottom, but it disappeared into heavy brush by the time I reached the spot. It would have been fun to have at least seen it, but, like moose, black bears don't stop to count heads.

There were four very tired and hungry people at the dinner table that night, but as I thought back on the day's events, it was a "good" tired with many satisfying memories locked away. Once again, Eric took care of the hunger pangs.

My Newfoundland caribou and moose hunt was drawing to a close, but I had my wonderful woodland bull as a lasting memory. Not a day goes by that I don't admire its shoulder mount on my living room wall and relive parts of my Cochran Pond adventure.

I met good, hard-working people who gave their all to ensure an enjoyable hunt. The self-proclaimed "Goofy Newfys", with their clipped, French/English accents, were very difficult to understand when they spoke quickly amongst themselves; however, they were careful and considerate with their speech when in "mixed" company and slowed down the cadence considerably.

Bryant was as proud to have guided my successful harvest as I was to have scored, and when I gave him an extra tip to show my appreciation, you would have thought I had presented him with a lifetime annuity of codfish! Very humble, very thankful.

Dennis Hynes was the fourth guide in camp, and, even though I didn't have an opportunity to work with him, he invited me to come back the next year to hunt with him and his brother, Wayne, near Rick's Lake. I thanked him for his invitation, knowing I would be moving on to new areas and game in future years. There are just so many interesting places to hunt for the 38 different species of North American big game, that I'm reluctant to rebook with any outfitter, regardless of whether I've taken a good trophy or not.

Another bush pilot "pontooned" in on Sunday, October 7th to take me, my gear, "bou" rack, cape, and meat back to Corner Brook. Angus met me at the ramp at 1:00 p.m., and we drove immediately to the local butchers to prepare the delicious, fat free, sweet-tasting caribou steaks and roasts for my 4:30 p.m. flight from Stephenville. During our ride, Angus told me he had been exonerated from any pilot error concerning the plane crash. I could tell a tremendous weight of uncertainty had been lifted from his shoulders. Losing his pilot's license would have had a crippling effect on his business.

I thanked him for a fine hunt and gave well-deserved praise for all non-weather related aspects; accommodations, food, guide experience and effort, and quality game sightings. These people are gracious, not "goofy", but, then again, gracious doesn't rhyme with "Newfy"!

My flight home went smoothly, and, naturally, all my gear and gun arrived with me at LaGuardia. Lost equipment always seems to occur when flying *to* hunts. I was one happy hunter, but already my mind was thinking ahead to the fall of 1985.

Angus Wentzel, owner/outfitter
<u>Deer Pond Camps, Ltd.</u>

Storage hut and the "white house"
on Cochran's Pond

The LaBlancs (L to R) Joe Jr., Tom, and Joe Sr.

(Front) guide Gordon with (L to R)
Eric, the cook, and guides, Ken and Joe

Joe Jr., Kim, and Tom

Bidding farewell to Bryant Payne

(Above) Kim with his 30-point woodland caribou bull where he fell (Below) his beautiful shoulder mount

Chapter 9: Hunting "The Bob"- Montana's Bob Marshall Wilderness - for Elk and Mule Deer (1985)

After my 1984 woodland caribou success in Newfoundland, I decided to return to the lower 48 to hunt Rocky Mountain elk and mule deer in "Big Sky Country". An ad for Cabin Creek Outfitters out of Missoula, Montana caught my eye, and I was soon making arrangements for a fall 1985 hunt with Pat Ackerman, who, along with Duane "Duke" Dugre, owned and operated Cabin Creek Outfitters. I immediately took a liking to Pat for his friendly nature and willingness to answer all my prehunt questions.

Pat and his wife, Shirley, lived in Stayton, Oregon where Pat ran the family pharmacy. Once hunting season rolled around, however, he crossed the border to join his partner in Missoula. Shirley went along as well to join Duke's wife, Lois, as camp cooks and general organizers.

During my discussion with Pat, I learned that elk and deer rifle hunting in the Bob Marshall Wilderness started earlier than the state's regular season, which afforded the opportunity to hunt undisturbed bulls during the rut! That information certainly peaked my interest, and, shortly after my usual outfitter background check via the North American Hunting Club's *Hunt Reports* and client reference lists, I booked for Cabin Creek's first hunt from September 13th through the 23rd. A day on each end of that period would be devoted to packing in and out of camp, respectively, leaving 8½ days of actual hunting. I arranged for my nonresident license through Cabin Creek and bought tags for elk, deer (either mule or whitetail), and black bear.

As summer drew to a close and with a new hunting season "in the air", I began serious preparation for my Montana trip. I remember visiting the shooting range in Englishtown, New Jersey to zero-in my rifle and not being able to get a tight pattern three inches high at 100 yards. Only after returning home did I realize that my scope mount screws had loosened, which caused the earlier scattered pattern! Since my schedule didn't allow for another visit to the range prior to my departure, I had to count on sighting-in when I arrived. In the meantime, I manually realigned the scope tube, tightened the mount screws, and placed the .30-.06 in my hardcover travel case. Ironically, when I arrived at Duke Dugre's ranch and used his bench rest to sight-in, my first shot hit the 100-yard yard target exactly three inches above center. Perfect! I was relieved and ready.

The direct midday flight from Newark International to Missoula was on time and all baggage arrived safely. Duke met my flight and drove me to his ranch in nearby Greenbough, where Pat and their staff were busy packing food and equipment, plus rounding up the horses to take to the trailhead. The trailhead was at the base of the foothills leading into the Bob Marshall Wilderness and marked the starting point for the following day's 26-mile horsepack trip into the main camp.

The other four hunters had arrived earlier that day, and they had already transferred their personal gear into two-foot by four-foot wooden boxes which would be carried into camp via mule train. Each mule carried two boxes, matched by weight to ensure balance and comfort for those stubborn, yet dependable porters.

The hunters were all friendly and, once again, represented various ages, backgrounds, jobs, and residences. Mark Wheeler was a balding, heavyset member of Sharon, Pennsylvania's first-aid squad. His physical appearance belied his early 30's age. Ben Hogevoll was in his 30's as well, but was noticeably in better shape than Mark and ran an international fishing operation based in Newport, Oregon. Ben had an engaging personality, and his quick wit made him a fun guy to be with. Bill Oetken and "Champ" Husted, both in their late 50's to early 60's, were close friends from West Linn and Milwaukee, Oregon, respectively, who had shared a number of hunting experiences over the years. Champ was the father of Bill Husted, a popular and successful professional bowler at the time. It was to be the first guided elk hunt for all of us, and for Ben and Mark, the first guided big-game hunt of any kind.

Activity was lively at the trailhead early the following morning . The pack horses, which had been trailered from Duke's ranch, had to be saddled and bridled, and the eight mules had to be loaded with the boxes of personal gear plus food and other supplies for camp. After two hours of cinching, hoisting, and tying, we were ready to "mount up" and start our journey. Camp was at an altitude of 9,500 feet, so the ride was a steady uphill climb on narrow trails through pine forests and across crystal-clear streams. The streambeds consisted of green, red, and yellow pebbles, and their colors shone brightly from the sun penetrating the shallow water.

It was a beautiful sight. Several times the trail came precipitously close to the edge of the mountain, with sheer drop-offs of over 800 feet! (Pat told of a forest ranger who lost his life the previous spring when his motorcycle plunged over the edge while he was clearing the trail.) At such points, I quickly leaned toward the mountain and shifted my foot position in the stirrups to a mere toehold. I wanted to be ready just in case my horse slipped or decided to take the short way home - straight down! At least I'd have a chance to bail out versus hanging on for a death ride. At the time, I hoped and prayed that "horse sense" was real **and** that my steed's every thought was on sticking to the trail. As far as I know, there are no documented cases of horse suicides via jumping off mountains! The only incident occurred when Bill's horse started to buck due to discomfort from a cinch pulled too tightly. The situation was quickly remedied, and Bill managed to hang on even though his eyes opened about 10 times wider than normal! The six-hour ride into camp was at a leisurely pace, with the temperature in the 60's, and several stops were made along the way to rest, take pictures, and water the horses at stream crossings. Everyone was relaxed and full of high expectations when we finally arrived at camp in the late afternoon.

Duke and Pat had built their camp in a pristine wilderness setting at the edge of Cabin Creek surrounded by endless acres of new-growth lodgepole pine forests. The lodgepoles served them well as the framework for the four canvas wall tents and several bedframes they built. The stream served as our water source and also provided an additional recreational outlet: trout fishing! All week long, each of us hunters used whatever time not pursuing elk, deer, or bear trying our luck at the sizeable rainbows, browns, and brookies waiting nearby.

The mess tent was the center of Lois' and Shirley's activity, and the meals they produced from that structure were a sight to behold; for example, a full course turkey dinner, complete with dressing, mashed potatoes, creamed onions, and pumpkin pie topped with whipped cream for dessert! At one point I was so amazed by the quantity and quality of food that I looked behind the tent, expecting to find a huge food locker or walk-in freezer. But no, everything had come in with us on the mules!

Besides the mess tent, there were three other sleeping tents: one for the outfitters and their wives, one for the guides and wrangler, and the other for us hunters. In addition, a corral had been built for the mules with an adjacent enclosure for the tack. The horses were allowed to roam freely during the night to feed on the rich grasses surrounding us, its abundance assuring that the wrangler wouldn't have far to travel each morning to find them. A large cowbell was attached to the lead mare's halter to aid the search, knowing that once located, the others would be close by. It sounded a bit risky to me, but it worked!

The last piece of architecture was a raised platform built between two pines with a rope and pulley to hoist camp and game meat, capes, and other consumables to their perch 15 feet above the ground, thus providing ample protection from hungry bears. Both blacks and grizzlies inhabited the area, and, even though grizzly hunting in Montana was on a limited quota basis to help preserve their dwindling numbers, the overall bear population was sizeable enough to warrant preventative measures for protecting food sources. Therefore, the higher the better!

Hunting plans and strategies were outlined at dinner that first night. I would be hunting for elk with my guide, Tim Hoag, in an area approximately 10 miles from camp. Most of the distance would be covered on horseback, but it still required a predawn start. Similar assignments were meted out to the other guide and hunter pairings, and no one was concerned about crowding out or overlapping another's territory due to the vastness of the wilderness involved. There was plenty of room and game for everyone. Tim and I talked at length and got to know each other better. I was as interested to find out how much guiding experience and savvy Tim had as he was to learn about my hunting knowledge, experience, skill, and conditioning. I believe the more compatible a hunter and guide are, the better their chance for success. Tim told me he had guided for Cabin Creek the previous two seasons with *some* success, but admitted he hadn't yet bugled in a bull. He felt his bugling technique was good enough to do the job - if and when the opportunity came - and voiced confidence about the quantity of elk in the area, our timing vis-`a-vis the rut, and the weather. With that said, I felt reassured about Tim's ability as initially expressed by Pat during our conversation months before.

As is the case on every guided hunt I've been on, breakfast on that first hunting day marks the peak of everyones' hope, anticipation, and confidence. Visions of trophy racks replace sugarplums, and each hunter sees himself as the next Jack O'Connor, Chuck Adams, or more recently, Milo Hanson. Thereafter, as each day passes without success, combinations of uncertainty, doubt, frustration, futility, and even desperation replace those earlier, more positive feelings and attitudes in varying degrees, but with increasing intensity. Everyone wants to be included in that group of roughly 20% who tag an elk in any given year and an even lower percentage who harvest a wall-hanging trophy bull; however, that other 80% exists for a reason, and all hunters are aware of the numerous, if not endless reasons which contribute to unfilled tags! Regardless of the odds, hunters in general and elk hunters in particular approach each season with an optimistic belief that *this* will be the year when all the preseason scouting, shooting, and conditioning will pay off and bring them within range of that once-in-a-lifetime trophy, **and** that they won't be seen, heard, or scented before a successful shot can be launched! So it was on September 15, 1985, when Tim and I rode out of camp.

Cut trails led to a series of ridgetops that we followed to Babcock Ridge, our destination. As soon as the sun made its appearance, we tied the horses and continued on foot. We were then only a couple of hundred yards below the summit of Babcock, and our climb to the top would put us in good position to intercept any elk working their way up from the valleys below. Those valleys contained grassy meadows where the elk fed from late afternoon until early morning, when they retreated to their higher bedding areas. My hope for that first day was merely to locate some elk or even to hear a bugle to confirm they were in the area. Anything beyond that would be a bonus as far as identifying a good bull or getting close enough for a shot via successful bugling and stalking. Other factors such as cover, luck, patience, and weather would also play key roles, so we didn't want to get too far ahead of ourselves. However, we knew we had more than a week to withstand the test and meet the challenge.

We walked along the ridgetop for over a mile that morning, stopping every hundred yards or so to bugle and wait for a response that never came. A light rain the night before had dampened the ground foliage, so by the time we stopped for lunch I was uncomfortably wet, both on the outside from the brush and on the inside from perspiration! After a short rest, we planned to backtrack and resume our bugling-and-listening sequence in hopes of getting a bull to answer. In the meantime, we munched our sandwiches, washed them down with water from our canteens, and observed a treeless path a hundred yards wide caused by an avalanche from some time past. The swath covered thousands of vertical feet from its starting point where we stood to its termination point in the valley beneath us. Large pines, snapped like matchsticks and piled up far below, served as real evidence of the awesome and devastating power of such snowslides.

Feeling rested after our lunch break, we headed back along the ridgetop. Following our morning pattern, we stopped a short distance away to bugle, and Tim released a long, multi-pitched call that would have made any herd bull proud! The only difference from his earlier attempts was that a bull *did* respond! Our initial reaction was one of shock and disbelief. The bull was in the bottom of the valley several hundred yards forward of our location, an area we had passed only hours before without success. That fact, coupled with the time of day and not really expecting any action then, caught us both off guard. However, within seconds we swung into action, moving briskly to a point ahead that we felt would place us directly above where we heard the bull's first response. Tim's second call was met with an immediate and louder reply, which confirmed that the bull was indeed parallel to us, moving upward, and quickly closing the gap between us.

Tim signaled for me to follow him down the steep side of the ridge, where we quickly set up on a narrow level area beside a large hardwood. Tim's third bugle was answered by a series of grunts and chortles less than a hundred yards away and moving closer! My heart was in my throat as I chambered a shell and strained my eyes to spot any movement below us. Tim scraped a broken branch against the hardwood just as a bull would do to demonstrate his prefight rage by thrashing his antlers against any and all available saplings and trees! Then I saw Tim point and whisper, "There he is!" At first I didn't see the bull moving directly toward me through the waist-high brush interspersed with assorted sizes of pines and hardwoods. But then he turned broadside 60 yards below and started shredding a sapling with vigorous side-to-side movements of his head and impressive, wide rack. With Tim urging, "Shoot. Shoot.", I placed the crosshairs behind the right shoulder, flipped off the safety, and squeezed the trigger. I lost the sight picture due to the recoil, and when Tim yelled to shoot him *again*, I frantically tried to find the bull in my scope for another shot. All sorts of things flashed through my mind at that instant; did I make a clean miss by shooting over its back due to the steep slope, or did I hit him in a non-fatal area - a wound that would require extensive tracking? I heard myself saying, "I can't find him, where is he?" I then lowered the rifle and looked toward the spot where the bull had stood only seconds before. I saw some movement in the bushes there and told Tim, "I think he's down!" Ten yards into our steep descent I saw part of the bull's rack among the ground cover. Sure enough, I had dropped him in his tracks with one shot that broke his back and then ricocheted through both lungs. By the time we reached him, he was stone dead. He was a beautiful 6x6 trophy with a 40-inch inside spread and identical beam length. I had hoped to bag at least a 5x5 for my efforts, so I was elated to have surpassed my goal. Not only would his shoulder mount help keep the hunt *alive*, but the memories of that classic bugling sequence and setup to intercept the charging bull would live in my mind forever!

Since we were on foot and a considerable distance from the horses, Tim felt there was only enough time to field dress the bull, then return early the next morning with Bryon Wieder, the wrangler, and two mules to pack out all the meat, head, and cape. Quartering and butchering the 800-pound animal was too much for one man in the few hours of light remaining, and we still had to find the horses and ride back to camp. Before leaving the kill site, Tim and I took several precautionary measures to protect the head and carcass from damage in the event a grizzly paid a visit during our absence: first, I removed my orange vest and used it to tie the antlers to a nearby sapling. Tim reasoned that the vest would help anchor the elk and prevent it from sliding down the steep slope, and that my scent on it would deter any bear, especially a grizzly, from eating the carcass or dragging it away; next, Tim hung his elk call on the antlers as an additional human scent deterrent; and, finally, since bears usually give first consumption priority to the entrails, I helped Tim move the "gut pile" 20 yards away and cover it with pine boughs to mask our scent. Satisfied with our thinking and work, we walked to our horses and returned to camp.

Everyone was excited about my success, and Tim and I recounted our adventure in great detail. Pat Ackerman was especially delighted, since "getting the monkey off their backs" early in a hunt relieved a lot of pressure on the outfitters to "produce" and built confidence and enthusiasm for the other hunters in camp. Maybe I should have asked for a discount!

With our retrieval plans OK'd, at least three of us in camp that night knew what the next day would bring, or at least we *thought* we did! No one else had even seen an elk let alone taken a shot that first day, so everyone turned in early in anticipation of better things to come.

Shortly after daybreak, Tim, Bryon, and I rode out of camp with two mules in tow. Each mule was equipped with a pack harness from which large canvas meat bags hung. I was instructed to bring my rifle in case of a bear encounter, either along the way or at the kill site! Horses get skittish at the sight or scent of bears, and if a hunter is thrown, being armed could save his life if his steed heads for the next county!

Along the way, we encountered a bog formed by a runoff intersecting a low point in the trail. Tim's horse just made it through, but mine wasn't so lucky. He sank to his withers as I hung on, not sure whether to jump off and get mired as well, or stay aboard hoping he could extricate himself without losing his balance and falling on me! After a couple of unsuccessful lunges, the stallion harnessed all his remaining energy into a final upward thrust and found solid ground. I could feel his power erupt beneath me, and I was amazed at his effort and strength. Shortly thereafter, we reached Babcock Ridge and proceeded to the point where Tim and I had made our descent the day before. If all went well, my bull would be waiting 60 yards below the ridgetop where we tied our horses. Tension was in the air as we eased down the slope on foot, watching and listening for any movement that might indicate danger. Bryon and Tim were unarmed, but went first. I followed with a firm grip on my .30-.06 with shell chambered, knowing I was solely responsible for all three of us in the event a grizzly was lying in wait!

When we got within 20 yards of our targeted area, it became quite evident that Tim and I hadn't been the last visitors! The ground was torn up and bushes were trampled in a 15-yard radius from the location of the elk carcass, which was completely buried! Only the antlers were visible! The pine boughs we had placed over the entrails were scattered haphazardly, with no trace of what they had covered. My vest was gone, never to be found, and Tim's elk bugle had been ripped into small pieces! On the incline above my buried elk were wide, deep claw marks that all agreed had to be made by a grizzly! After devouring the entrails, he apparently had decided to bury his find and return later to finish his meal. However, later was **then**, and my heart was pounding as I imagined the grizzly watching us from a nearby vantage point, planning a charge intended to put Bryon, Tim, and me on his menu as well. The three of us simultaneously scanned the surrounding brush, and, feeling secure that the bear was not in the immediate area, Bryon and Tim proceeded to butcher the bull, hoping to load up the meat, head, and cape and get out of the area ASAP! My job was to keep guard and maintain a careful vigil in the event the grizzly returned sooner than later!

With axes and knives flying, Tim and Bryon set a new *Guinness* butchering record, and everything seemed on schedule to escape the area unharmed until the mules decided not to cooperate. They had appeared nervous and wild-eyed as we loaded and secured their cargo with heavy rope, and just as Bryon was about to lead them to where our horses were tied, one of the mules spun wildly, bucking and kicking until the harness worked loose and deposited its full load on the ground! The second mule followed suit and was soon stomping on the bull's head and antlers in an attempt to reduce its 12 points to a "raghorn"! Luckily, I avoided its kicks and managed to rescue my trophy before any major damage occurred. A second attempt to repack everything met with the same result, and it was obvious that neither mule was overly thrilled with the pungent grizzly odor that filled their nostrils! Perseverance finally paid off as the mules settled down and allowed the elk meat to be loaded and tied. However, to prevent any further incident, Bryon cradled the elk's antlered head and cape in his lap during the long and uncomfortable ride back to camp! One thing was for sure, we were all glad to get out of Mr. Grizzly's kitchen!

While the others went back into the field the following day, I slept in and then helped Tim "fine tune" the elk cape. I had decided to keep the entire hide to tan and use to make a vest, so I took care to remove all strands of meat that remained from the hasty field skinning. Once the cape and hide were stripped, salted, and rolled up, we grabbed some fishing rods and headed for the stream to challenge some native trout and discuss the following day's mule deer hunt. Tim had a good area in mind, but he was concerned about his injured knee not holding up. He had twisted it while loading my elk, and by dinner that evening the swelling had increased. Tim was forced to pass his guiding baton to Owen Talkington, who had worked for Cabin Creek for a number of years and knew his way around their territory. It took only a few moments' conversation with Owen to feel comfortable with the assignment. His animated talk and enthusiasm complimented the twinkle in his eyes that peered out from behind a fully-bearded face. I was still the only hunter to have scored, so everyone was eager to greet the new dawn.

Owen and I headed out on foot since his designated target area was only a couple of ridges and miles away. He set a fast pace with the hope of reaching the second ridgetop by sunup. We'd then be in a position to glass below and spot any mulies working their way up from their nighttime feeding areas to the elevated safety and security of their daytime bedding areas. Our arrival was delayed by heavy undergrowth and steep slopes with shale slides, which created balance problems. By the time we arrived at Owen's preferred glassing area, the sun was up and no deer were spotted. Either they were already where they wanted to be or weren't in the area at all. We did some still-hunting to no avail, then returned to camp at midday to strategize and plan the following day's hunt. We decided on a new area requiring a horseback ride part of the way, with the balance covered on foot to a high lookout point.

We left camp in the predawn darkness with a light snow falling. I was excited, since the snow cover provided a wonderful background for picking up movement and identifying bucks over greater distances. After riding several miles from camp, we started our ascent up Gordon's Mountain and immediately spotted fresh deer tracks. One set was considerably larger than the others, and we surmised it probably had been made by a buck! I was excited and felt lucky, two feelings that had proven meaningless too often in the past, but at least lent early optimism to the task at hand. Snow was falling, the tracks were new, and, with my elk already tagged, I was relaxed, hopeful, and ready! I had not yet killed a mulie, so adding a nice buck to my bull would certainly be a wonderful bonus to an already fantastic hunt.

The tracks veered to our left on a path that headed around and below the crest of the ridge, but Owen and I decided to head straight to the top, hoping to intercept the deer as they continued their upward journey. After tying the horses and walking 300 yards, we reached a good vantagepoint with a blowdown to sit on. If our calculation proved correct, the deer would appear 40 yards below us as they emerged from a thick grove of small pines.

We hadn't been sitting for more than ten minutes when I caught movement below and to my left that materialized into a set of beautiful, dark, bifurcated antlers bobbing their way through the pines! My quick glance at Owen brought his attention to the emerging buck, and after a quick check of his rack, he whispered, "Take him." I had already flipped up the spring-action scope covers and shouldered my .30-.06. The buck must have caught my movement as he came to an abrupt halt and looked our way! Whether he recognized danger and was planning to escape, I'll never know. My crosshairs had already found their mark, and my shot quickly changed whatever plans he may have had! Owen was watching through his binoculars as my shot ripped through the buck's rib cage just behind his shoulder and penetrated both lungs. The deer leaped forward and then turned sharply downhill. I fired a second shot as he ran away, but

100

fortunately the miss didn't affect the final result as he piled up against a log only 40 yards below the point of impact.

When we reached where the buck had been standing, blood was everywhere, indicating immediate flows from both the entry and exit wounds. One look and I knew it was a fatal shot, and a wide red-on-white trail led to the downed deer! He was a handsome trophy with five points on his right side and six on his left, and the heavy body and rut neck added to his magnificent appearance. After field dressing the buck and carefully marking his location, Owen and I returned to camp to get Bryon to help us pack it out. Since the deer's live weight was an estimated 250 pounds, only one horse was needed to bring the head, cape, and all useable meat back to camp. It was certainly a relief to know those mules didn't have to be used again!

My return trip brought mixed emotions; the obvious elation of retrieving a trophy big-game animal amidst the beauty and splendor of the surroundings, offset by thoughts of my Dad and how he would have loved being there. He had been my hunting teacher, and his death the previous March left a void in my life. We had often talked about going on a big-game hunt together, but once he got sick I knew that dream would never be realized. Those thoughts and reflections brought tears to my eyes as we rode along and injected some sadness into what should have been a totally exciting and enjoyable experience. That one was for you, Dad.

Poor luck and other, more controllable factors continued to plague my hunting partners. By week's end, my two trophies were all we had to show for our collective efforts. A sudden wind shift caused one approaching bull to make a hasty retreat just as it was about to become the backdrop for Ben's crosshairs. On another occasion, he found the fresh tracks of a bull Duane had bugled to within 20 paces, but which had circled behind them and caught their scent in its downwind approach. The bull crashed away before Ben could even shoulder his rifle. Bill, Champ, and Mark were handicapped by poor physical conditioning at the outset, and discouragement added to their woes as the week wore on.

Elk hunting is hard work, especially in the great expanse of a wilderness such as "The Bob". I can't help but feel that seeing so many pictures of hunters posing with their trophies in hunting magazines glosses over the amount of work involved and creates the false impression that *everyone* is successful. The tendency for too many hunters is to think that paying for a guided hunt and merely showing up will produce the desired results. Many factors, including physical conditioning, familiarization with and properly sighting one's weapon, choosing the best area and time of year vis-`a-vis rutting activity, favorable weather, a positive mental attitude, and, yes, "luck" contribute to a hunt's **potential** success. However, there are still no guarantees! Few trophies are harvested by those who choose to hunt close to camp, or worse yet, don't even leave camp due to being tired or hungover from the previous night's imbibing around the campfire. Consistently successful big-game hunting requires know-how and energy to turn that ***luck*** factor in your favor! After eight guided big-game hunts, I've seen enough successes and failures to be able to document those factors and reasons which a hunter ***does*** have control over. Any hunter who does his homework and perseveres can turn excuses and alibis into memorable photos and trips to the taxidermist! Based on the cost of guided hunts alone, I never want to have regrets due to a lack of preparation, either mental or physical!

The night before we broke camp, five inches of snow fell. Unfortunately, it came too late to help the others find their potential trophies. The hunt was over, but at least the winter wonderland effect of the snowfall provided a peaceful setting and some solace to those returning with tags unfilled. It had been another exciting and successful experience for me, and even though I didn't fill my bear tag, it's probably best that I didn't – you know, that "adding insult to injury" thing!

Shirley and Pat Ackerman

Prehunt gathering at "Duke" Dugre's ranch –
Ben and girlfriend, Mark, "Champ", and Bill

Heading into "The Bob"

Ben Hogevoll on "Wheatie"

(L to R) "Duke", Bill, "Champ", Pat, Lois,
Shirley, Bryon, Mark, Ben, and Tim

Shirley Ackerman and Lois Dugre:
Cooks Supreme!

Kim with his 6x6 Rocky Mountain bull elk

Tim Hoag, guide, with my elk and last known
picture of his elk bugle in one piece!

Kim with his 5x6 Rocky Mountain mule deer buck

(L to R) Bryon and Owen packing out my mule deer

The nice 6x6 antlers from my Bob Marshall Wilderness elk

Leaving camp with my elk and mule deer "racks"

Final resting place of my two Bob Marshall Wilderness trophies:
5x6 Rocky Mountain mule deer buck and 6x6 bull elk

Chapter 10: Alaska - The Ultimate Big-Game Hunting Experience (1986)

Ever since my first big-game hunt in Colorado, I vowed that if I were ever successful enough to justify the expense, I would head for Alaska. The stories and pictures of that vast wilderness, covering 586,000 square miles or one-fifth the size of the entire lower 48 states, had built such an indelible image in my mind that what began as a remote dream actually turned into an obsession by the time I started making plans in early 1986.

I had seen George Palmer's Alaska Trophy Hunts advertisements many times in the top hunting magazines and had written to him for information as early as 1984. He was kind enough to send a handwritten reply with his brochure, including hunt choices with respective costs, and a reference list of former clients to contact. George also enclosed his annual Christmas letter, which not only highlighted the just-concluded season's successes, but also contained an update of Alaska's game laws and pending legislation that might affect big-game hunting there, especially for nonresidents. George made a personal appeal for hunters to lend their support to pro-hunting bills, encouraging them to write to legislators in the 50th state to voice their pros and cons depending on the particular law in question. I admire his concern and activist involvement in preserving his state's wildlife treasures and in supporting sporthunting for maintaining healthy herds. George's Christmas message also included information about his family. His oldest son, Marty, was a registered guide and pilot who served as his dad's right-hand man in the family's extensive hunting, fishing, and summer wilderness vacation operation. Any outfitter's work is multi-faceted, difficult, and endless: becoming registered and licensed with their state's outfitter/guide association and state game department/division; advertising and booking clients; determining costs and pricing the various hunts to be competitive, yet profitable; buying or leasing land; building camps; investing in equipment, including airplanes, trucks, horses, saddles, bridles, feed, fuel, tents, beds, and stoves; helping with license applications; printing brochures with price and reference lists, and more. Not only must an outfitter love what he does, but it's almost mandatory to have family members share the workload. That's why it's so typical to have an outfitter's wife handle bookings, mailings, and

111

other correspondence, besides being present in camp to cook, cut wood, and, in general, serve as head "camp meister" when the hunters are in the field.

The Palmer's operation had an interesting beginning. Soon after marrying, George and Jackie decided to settle in Alaska and start their outfitting business, although they weren't exactly sure *where* in Alaska that would be. Trusting their instincts and intuition, they packed their worldly belongings and drove north. Their arrival at a small community approximately 50 miles north of Anchorage ended their journey - **Palmer**, Alaska. It seemed like a good omen.

Fortunately for me, the bond market was continuing its strength based on the lower interest rate trend, and that translated into the kind of income I needed to at least rationalize, if not justify, an Alaskan hunting trip. With my final psychological and financial hurdles cleared, it was time to make serious plans with Mr. Palmer!

I wrote to George in January 1986, expressing interest in a 10-day hunt for the following fall. I mentioned that I was particularly interested in taking a Dall ram and Alaska-Yukon bull moose and asked if that was a realistic expectation for the length of hunt mentioned, and if he could accommodate me sometime in September. I decided to hold all my other questions concerning licenses, tags, clothes, caliber of rifle, and grain of cartridge until I first learned if he had an opening for me. I already had a general idea of George's outfitter fees for various length hunts, which ranged up to $12,200 for a 21-day combination hunt (caribou, grizzly, moose, and sheep). Licenses, tags, airfare, nonhunting accommodations, meals, and taxidermy costs were in addition to that basic charge. So you see, hunting not only gets into your blood, but also into your wallet! My wait for a reply was short, and George called to say he would be pleased to book me on a 10-day combination hunt for September 6–15. I was really excited and gave my verbal acceptance. I quickly went through my checklist of questions, which George patiently and thoroughly answered even though he told me he would provide a complete list of what he'd provide versus what I should bring. He sent his standard outfitter/client contract to read, sign, and return with a one-third deposit. He assured me that by the time September rolled around, I'd have every question answered and would be fully prepared for my adventure. I liked George's friendly manner and attention to detail, both of which lent confidence and reassurance to my choice of outfitters. He had earned his master guide status with over 15 years of experience, piloted his own plane, and had *exclusive* hunting rights to two separate regions covering 1,200-

square **miles** and 2,000-square **miles**, respectively. My hunt encompassed a 600-square mile area within game management units #16 and #19 in the Alaska Range near Farewell, Alaska, 160 air miles northwest of Anchorage.

Years before, George had purchased his crown jewel, Mystic Lake Lodge, located on Mystic Lake, 50 miles due west of Mt. McKinley, and which offered a wonderful view of that majestic 20,300-foot peak beyond the lake. The lodge's pine log construction, with its dining room, kitchen, large living room, comfortable couches, and huge stone fireplace, complimented that rustic setting perfectly and served as the base of operation for all family fishing and wilderness trips. In addition, hunters who scored early or were being flown to other camps would often stop at Mystic Lake for a hot shower, day of fishing, and comfortable overnight stay. The reflection of a full moon on the lake's surface and the cry of loons did nothing to taint the setting!

In addition to the lodge, George had built four hunting "out camps"; The Beanery, Big Salmon, Smokey Creek, and Dry Creek within our expansive hunting territory. Each was situated to take advantage of abundant quantities of all species of huntable game. Depending on game movement and weather conditions, multiple camps provided ample mobility and opportunity for hunters to maximize their chance for success. In that context, it's important to note that Alaska has a law in effect that prohibits hunting on the day one flies. This prevents "spotting" game from the air, landing quickly, and making a short stalk and kill. That law supports the notion of "fair chase", which keeps the advantage on the animals' side of the ledger and forces the hunter to overcome a game animal's familiarization with its habitat and overall superior senses of sight, hearing, and smell to achieve his harvest. This is the way it should be. It's my opinion that modern big-game rifles with their superior optics or even high tech bowhunting equipment offer enough of an offset to the animals' advantage that it shouldn't be compromised any further. There should be no guarantees in hunting. Otherwise, the sport would be called "killing", deplete of the challenges, adventures, and disappointments associated with fair chase *hunting*.

The seven-month wait for my hunt to start was agonizingly slow, but it did afford ample time to ask questions, call references, and match the recommended equipment list against what I already had versus what I'd need to purchase. I planned to use the same .30-.06 semi-automatic that had brought me successes in New York, Newfoundland, and Montana. George stated in his April 8th letter that he wasn't a .30-.06 fan, but added that he wasn't saying it wouldn't do the job: "If that is what you're used to and you are comfortable with the .30-.06, then that is what you should bring. It is adequate for the animals you'll be hunting." George stated his personal preference for 7mm or .300 caliber rifles and 180-grain Spitzer cartridges. His years of experience resulted in his recommending Federal Premium 180-grain partition ammo and "sighting-in" at 2 to 2½ inches high at 100 yards. He closed his letter with the reminder to use a good quality hardcover gun case that would give my rifle "positive protection from the airlines' *destructors*, sometimes called baggage handlers"!

I had already signed and returned the outfitter/client contract with my deposit. It outlined the basic responsibilities and provisions of both parties, including: inclusive hunt dates, which for my 10-day hunt allowed a day on each end for travel to and from camp leaving eight actual *hunting* days in the field (this is typical, but a question worth asking for anyone planning a hunt); basic outfitter fee; deposit requirements and cancellation policy; who furnishes what as far as transportation, food, lodging, care and shipment of meat, hides, horns and antlers; guns and ammunition; licenses and tags; and, number of hunters per guide (usually 2:1 unless otherwise negotiated for 1:1 at a higher fee, which I always choose!) One hunter per guide eliminates another body's movement and odor, and the nerve-wracking coin toss when a trophy animal is sighted! Lastly, a paragraph in the contract reminded clients about the inherent risks associated with such a venture, and that there would be limited liability in the event of injury, loss of property, or death. In other words, responsibility for such risk normally rests with the client except for overt acts of negligence on the outfitters' or guides' part.

Most outfitters can't afford the cost of full liability insurance. If required, there would be fewer of them around, and the resulting supply/demand imbalance would create prohibitive fee structures for most hunters. So, it's better to assume the risk and take your chances in order to keep guided hunts reasonably affordable.

George told me that on a 10-day hunt I could expect to take two trophy animals, but that some clients had taken three or four. Weather and luck played a part, but he seemed confident about my taking a moose and sheep since his hunter success rate was 95% on both in his 15 years as an outfitter/guide. He also cited a 50% success rate on grizzly bear and, for all his combination hunts over the years, 95% of hunters had taken one trophy, 85% had taken two, 60% had taken three, and 35% of his clients had taken four or more. The percentages sounded good, almost too good, and I decided to call a few hunters from George's reference list to get some first-hand feedback. Both Fred Cline from Clearfield, Pennsylvania, and Frank Surovich from Albion, Pennsylvania were in their 50's, very friendly, and helpful in providing their positive comments about their Alaska Trophy Hunts experiences. They each gave high marks for the skill and effort of their guides, quality and quantity of game seen, care and handling of meat, hides, horns and antlers, the condition of the camps and equipment, and meals. Fred commented that the terrain was not too difficult to walk or climb, with enough canyons and crevices to work close for decent shots. He recommended boots with vibram soles and a good rain suit. He had scored on a nice Dall ram using a 7mm with 150- grain cartridges. Frank gave "excellent" marks based on three separate hunts with George during which he scored on a 40-inch Dall ram, 67-inch moose, and 350- pound black bear. He used a .300 Weatherby and 180-grain cartridges, but felt my .30-.06 would do just fine. He added praises for Marty Palmer's guiding ability and closed with the assurance that I'd have a great hunt. Repeat visits speak volumes!

With time on my hands and my hunt still months away, I took advantage of my charter membership in the North American Hunting Club to request hunting reports on Alaska Trophy Hunts prepared and filed by other members who had used George Palmer's operation. All comments were "excellent" (based on a rating of either excellent, good, fair, or poor) for the six main categories of quantity of game, experience of guides, other personnel, camp equipment, food, and accommodations. I felt I had done my homework in a thorough and efficient manner and was pleased with the results. Come on September!

I decided to add a $350 grizzly tag to my $400 sheep and $300 moose tags. George encouraged me to get the bear tag since, as George put it, "You don't hunt them. They hunt you! You never know when you'll see one, but they make a great trophy!" Sounded reasonable to me! George said I could purchase the tags when I arrived as well as my $60 nonresident license. All such assistance and helpful time-savers are greatly appreciated by any hunter arranging such a trip, and George Palmer was quick to volunteer his time and made the effort to help. George explained that my moose tag could also be used to take a barren ground caribou, but that I'd need two tags if I harvested both. One tag was interchangeable for either, but not both. George recommended not buying an extra tag, since few caribou had been sighted since their August hunts and felt that my limited number of hunting days might not allow enough time anyway. That also sounded reasonable to me, and as much as a person hopes everything works out better than expected, a quick reality check told me to be very happy with George's prediction of two trophies: moose and sheep! If realized, that would be fantastic. Why get greedy!

Immediately after returning my signed contract and deposit, I booked my flights; Newark International to Anchorage with one changeover in Chicago. I decided to depart on Thursday, September 4th, to give myself an extra day to get into camp. I wanted to be sure I'd start **hunting** on Saturday the 6th as scheduled. George planned to bring out other hunters on the 4th and then, if the weather cooperated, fly me into Smokey Creek on Friday the 5th, with food, extra fuel, and other supplies to keep me company! My last piece of business before departing was to purchase a new Bushnell Trophy 36 power spotting scope, which was recommended to me for the extreme distances I'd encounter. That taken care of, I began the long countdown to September 4th. At long last, it was time to pack my gear, rifle, ammo, and sleeping bag, and head for the airport!

I quickly learned the meaning of the old saying "the best laid plans can go awry" when I learned my flight had been cancelled, forcing me to do some quick rescheduling. It changed my Chicago connection and necessitated another changeover in Seattle! Visions of lost gear and guns filled my mind as I was faced with six baggage loadings and unloadings by the time I reached my final destination. Flashbacks from my Newfoundland trip consumed me. But my only choice was to climb aboard, cross my fingers, and hope for the best. As it turned out, the "gods of baggage handling" were watching over me as my last flight touched down at 9:15 p.m. in Anchorage with everything on board. What a relief to see both duffels, sleeping bag, and rifle case hit that carrousel! Like I said, never a worry, never a doubt! Whew!

I'm convinced that for traveling hunters, losing one's gear and guns via the airlines ranks just behind getting mauled by a grizzly bear on the "fear and worry" list!

Jackie Palmer met my flight, and I was soon introduced to the other three hunters, all of whom had booked 21-day hunts with George: Lyle Sigg, a retired school administrator, was from Ney, Ohio; and Tom Kenyon and Ron Oehlkers, good friends from Longmont, Colorado, were conservation officers with the Colorado Division of Wildlife. With all gear loaded in the Chevy Suburban, we were driven to our prehunt lodging at the Fairview Motel in Palmer, one hour west of Anchorage. After an 18-hour travel day, that bed at the Fairview felt like the best New York's Plaza Hotel could have offered. It was 4:30 a.m. back East!

Strong winds prevented George from flying back from Mystic Lake on Thursday, and that situation held through Friday. George had learned not to challenge the weather, and it wasn't until Saturday morning that he got the green light to attempt the 160-mile flight to Palmer. In the meantime, Jackie had picked up our four-man hunting party at the motel and drove us to their home, which was only three miles from the local airport. Being closer would save time when George arrived to reload new supplies and hunting gear for the return flight to camp. Since Saturday was supposed to have been my first day in the field, I was chomping at the bit to get going! I was also aware of Alaska's law prohibiting hunting on days one travels by plane, and I certainly didn't want any more delays. Watching a college football game on TV wasn't what I had come to Alaska for!

George finally arrived and decided to take me, Lyle, and the supplies into camp immediately while the weather permitted. I got the first nod due to my shorter hunt, and it made me feel good that he took that into consideration. I was assigned to his Smokey Creek camp and guide, Chip Barker, who was already in camp scouting for game in anticipation of my arrival. We'd be ready to start hunting on Sunday, which is allowed in Alaska. George then planned to fly back to Palmer on Sunday to pick up Tom and Ron and take them to his Big Salmon camp.

We were airborne by 2:00 p.m., and I felt a great sense of relief getting that "teaser" phase of the trip behind me and to finally be heading into the wilderness. It already seemed like a *week* since my Thursday arrival.

The one hour and ten minute flight was smooth and exhilarating, especially when we hit the jagged mountains of the Alaska Range. Mile after mile of snow-capped peaks and green valleys passed below us before George started our descent to Smokey Creek. His single-engine Maule M-5 had oversized tires which were underinflated on purpose to facilitate safe landings on the shale-covered dry creek beds. It amazed me how quickly George brought the plane to a complete stop after touch down - and only 150 yards from the campsite!

Chip was there to greet us, and I liked him immediately! His quick, warm smile gave a glimpse of the pleasant, positive, soft-spoken person behind it. After exchanging greetings and handshakes, the work of unloading the supplies and my gear began. Normally, the task was made easier by the use of an old Air Force jeep that was kept at Smokey Creek; however, Chip had been working on its broken carburetor, so it was temporarily out of service. George explained how he had driven the jeep to camp over a three-year period, having to blaze trails as he went. When snow prevented further travel, he'd cover the jeep with a tarp for the winter and resume the journey after the spring thaw! Talk about determination! I guess the only alternative was to fly it in piece-by-piece and assemble it at camp, but it wouldn't have made as dramatic a story!

Smokey Creek camp was nestled in a large grove of majestic 50-foot tall pine trees which grew alongside a half-mile wide, dry creek bed; dry, that is, during late summer, fall, and winter. However, during the spring runoff and early summer, it transformed into the raging Dillinger River!

Majestic mountain ranges rose on both sides of the camp and extended like parallel ribbons as far as the eye could see. Alders and pines covered approximately one half of their 6,000-foot elevation, with shale boulders and rock outcroppings continuing upward to their snow-capped peaks. The changing colors of fall added to the beauty of the area, and, in total, I was completely awed by the magnitude of my surroundings.

George and his dad had built the camp many years prior. A large 16 by 20-foot wooden storage shed had been constructed at one end with a set of weatherworn moose antlers nailed above its double front doors. To the right of this jeep "garage", et al, was a 14 by 20-foot canvas mess tent, and beyond the mess tent were three 10 by12-foot two-man tents for guides and hunters. With the help of Mike Boissoneault, who was serving his apprenticeship as a "meat packer" until he qualified for his guiding license, we soon had all gear and supplies squared away. Chip then suggested I zero-in my rifle at the 100-yard camp range, complete with bench rest, to be sure all the travel and handling hadn't jarred my scope. I was pleased that my shot group was still at the desired 2 to 3 inches high at 100 yards, which for my caliber and grain bullet would be dead-on at 200 yards, about six inches low at 275-300 yards, and 18 inches low at 350 yards. As long as Chip gave good range estimates, I felt secure in my ability to adjust to the drop in trajectory and to place my shots where I wanted. As we headed to the mess tent for dinner, I felt confident and ready!

At dinner I learned that Chip was originally from Maryland's Eastern Shore, but moved to Alaska during the "pipeline" construction era. He married a schoolteacher and settled in Healy, a small town between Anchorage and Fairbanks. He was a carpenter by trade, but having a working wife and no children allowed him to guide during each fall and be in the great Alaska outdoors, which he enjoyed so much. Ironically, he has relatives in Morrison, Colorado, which is only 11 miles from my present home in Evergreen! Even in Alaska, it can be a small world!

Chip told me he'd seen some good bull moose and Dall rams near the Dry Creek camp, which was an eight-mile hike from Smokey Creek. Since both of my targeted trophies were in that area, George instructed Chip and me to pack one duffel each, including enough food for a week, and head out on foot for Dry Creek early Sunday morning. Now, eight miles doesn't sound that far, but I'd be carrying an 80-pound duffel bag on a backpack frame plus wearing heavy clothing and carrying a rifle. Under those conditions, that distance can become very far very fast, especially when heading uphill. Also, my prehunt conditioning program seemed inadequate. It's one thing to jog three miles on a level surface in shorts and quite another to carry 100 pounds uphill on a bumpy trail for eight miles!

My excitement index was at an all-time high when dawn broke on Sunday. It was hunting time! Marty flew in shortly after breakfast to take Lyle to Big Salmon, but first he and Chip worked on the jeep's carburetor and had it purring like a Rolls Royce in no time. It goes to show you how versatile and multi-talented hunting guides have to be! At 10:00 a.m. Chip and I began our trek to Dry Creek. The first three miles heading south from camp along the creek bed wasn't too difficult. Chip set a steady pace and stopped to rest—more for me than him—at comfortable intervals. However, once we hit the trailhead and turned east heading uphill, the going got tough. The weight of the duffel felt no less than a load of cement blocks, and my legs were starting to buckle when our "spike" camp, a 10 by 14-foot canvas wall tent, finally came into view. I soon learned where the term "feeling like the weight of the world has been lifted from your shoulders" came from as I eased the pack frame to the ground. Chip had the advantage of knowing *where* the Dry Creek camp was located and could better prepare himself mentally for the arduous hike, whereas I was locked into a one step at a time *forever* approach. Having to carry just my rifle during the next several days was a welcome thought!

As soon as Chip flipped open the front tent flap, chills went down our spines. Strewn about the dirt "floor" were pieces of the rear canvas wall, slashed by a grizzly as if run through a paper shredder! One mattress pad had multiple eight-inch claw marks in it and was apparently in the bear's path when he made his angry entrance. Chip guessed that the odor of bacon grease from the tent's stove had drawn the bear to the tent, and, unable to find an open entrance, he made his own! We repaired it the best we could, but sleeping with one eye open became the order of the day. I remember lying on that clawed pad each night wondering if a second visit was on that carnivore's schedule!

With repairs done, gear unpacked, and wood cut, Chip suggested we head out to a nearby lookout point to do some glassing. Although moose and sheep had been spotted in the area only a couple of days prior, there was no guarantee they would stay put, especially the Dalls which constantly move among the numerous peaks and bowls. The huge Alaska-Yukon moose are a bit more territorial, but with miles and miles of wilderness at their disposal, "territorial" becomes a relative term; similar to letting your dog out to run around the state instead of your yard! That was the vastness of our environment. In two hours of searching mountainsides, pine thickets, and open meadows, we saw seven Dall ewes, but no moose. We then discussed the possibility of packing a couple days' supply of food plus sleeping bags to hike and glass until we found game! I wasn't overly excited about eating granola bars and sleeping under the stars, but if that's what it would take, I was willing! Chip was the expert, and his years of successful guiding convinced me to follow his lead and not second-guess his plans. We decided to head back to the tent, have our freeze-dried turkey goulash dinner, get a good night's sleep, and *then* discuss whether to stay or move after more glassing on Monday morning. Unfortunately, those plans were literally washed away as severe rains lashed our area and kept us tent-bound all day. Luckily, I had packed a back issue of *Outdoor Life,* which I read cover-to-cover including all ads. With a couple of naps thrown in, I managed to keep my sanity, though barely.

It was still drizzling on Tuesday morning, but after Monday's lock-in, *nothing* was going to prevent us from going afield. We headed to our lookout well rested and with renewed enthusiasm and vigor. That's the great thing about hunting. Each day is a new adventure, with the hope and promise of harvesting that desired trophy. Yesterday's misfortune has no bearing on today's potential triumph!

The steep 300-yard climb to our lookout perch a half mile from the tent put us in a position to view a 360-degree vista encompassing various types of terrain; pine thickets, meadows, ridges, and bowls; all of which was prime moose country. We had decided to hunt for moose first, then look for a good ram.

We hadn't been glassing for more than 15 minutes when Chip excitedly exclaimed, "What a bull!" He had been looking through his spotting scope at a small meadow about a mile away when a huge bull moose emerged from the surrounding trees. Even at that distance his enormous palms were visible with the naked eye and gave him a jack rabbitlike appearance! Chip was almost speechless, and this from a guy who had viewed and evaluated hundreds of moose in the wild. He certainly got my heart pounding when he told me it was the largest rack he'd ever seen and estimated the spread at 80 inches versus the 55 to 65-inch average. It was difficult for me to visualize a rack almost seven feet wide! He felt certain we were looking at a candidate for the top five Boone and Crockett heads, and possibly a new world record!

Since it was only 10:00 a.m., we had plenty of time to make a stalk, even with the rough terrain we had to cover. The bull was meandering around in the meadow, and Chip made a calculated guess that it would likely bed down there for a post-feeding rest. It would be secure there with the surrounding trees only a short distance away in the event of approaching danger. Relying on our "guesstimate" that the huge bull would stay in that area, and with the crosswind in our favor, Chip and I started our stalk. Eager to hit the tree line as quickly as possible, we slid and stumbled down the snow-covered slope.

We began our approach by heading towards a small rise that extended from below the meadow for approximately 300 yards to our right. Once we reached the ravine below our elevated lookout, our view was obscured by a huge pine forest we'd have to cross before reaching the rise. However, a checkpoint and intermediate target was a grove of aspens whose leaves had already turned their famous golden yellow. Once we reached that grove, we knew we were halfway to the hill near the meadow. Later, still-hunting along the base of that slope enabled us to keep downwind until we reached the meadow. All went as planned as we worked

121

into position to scan the meadow and listen for any movement in the surrounding trees. My heart was pounding so hard during that last stage of the stalk that I was sure it could be heard as readily as a fire alarm. Anticipating the appearance of a potential world record moose with each step is a titillating experience to say the least. Even though Chip and I did everything right as far as route direction, approach, keeping downwind, etc., the big bull decided not to cooperate! We neither heard nor saw him. We figured he probably hadn't bedded down after all and had, instead, walked through the meadow and continued on a path parallel to our approach. If our theory was correct, we probably hadn't been closer than 200 yards at any given point. I was disappointed, but it had been an exciting adventure! Just to **see** a potential world record big-game animal in the wild during a hunt is a rarity, and my attempt to enter the record book provided great memories. As Chip and I headed back to camp, my thoughts were already focused on the next day's possibilities.

On Wednesday, after an unappetizing granola and Tang breakfast, we headed back to our lookout point, hoping to spot the monster bull again. Before we even began our climb to the summit, Chip spotted movement across the valley below us, approximately 600 yards away. A look through the binoculars revealed a very respectable bull moose walking among the pines interspersing the distant hillside. He was on the same path we surmised "Mr. Big" had taken the previous day, and I think Chip had fixations about having another go at him when he commented that the new bull was just *average* and felt we could do better. I told him I wanted to get a better look, to get close enough to check out his rack. **Then**, I could decide whether or not to take him. Chip agreed, and we headed down the ravine on a path that would intersect the bull's route. We noted that he was headed along a ridgeline that would take him into a bowl to our left. Once we got on his tracks, it was easy to follow his path, and we were able to spot him standing in the bowl approximately 250 yards away. The wind was in our faces and he hadn't seen us, so I told Chip I'd belly-crawl to a group of small pine trees 50 yards closer to the bull. Once there, I was able to steady my rifle on one of the tree's branches and take a good look at my potential trophy. I liked what I saw! He cooperated very nicely and remained stationary, with an occasional turn of his head that revealed terrific brow tines and wonderful symmetry. I decided to shoot.

I took a comfortable stance, anchored my rifle on the branch, and held it tightly against the trunk via my sling. I then had to wait for him to move slightly to afford a better broadside shot. As if on cue, the bull turned, walked 20 yards closer, and stood broadside against a patch of snow. My target couldn't have been better, and, figuring the distance at 200 to 225 yards, I placed the crosshairs high behind his shoulder and squeezed the trigger. I momentarily lost the sight picture when the .30-.06 kicked, but I quickly found him again in my scope and prepared for a second shot as he started walking forward. However, just before I started applying pressure to the trigger, the bull stopped, shuddered, and fell over! He never moved again.

Chip had watched the whole sequence through his binoculars and was soon at my side. We were both very excited and quickly covered the open ground to the downed trophy. The closer we got, the bigger **he** got! We discovered that the bullet struck just above the spine in his "hump", which serves as the boiler room of his nervous system. Although I had aimed for the lung area behind his shoulder, my shot proved fatal, and with no damage to the meat. A large Alaska-Yukon bull moose can weigh a ton, and my "average" 56-inch spread specimen was in the 1,500-pound range. Where they go down is where they stay, too, and we had to cut away several bushes and saplings to free up some working room. We spent the next six hours gutting, capping, quartering, and removing the antlers via a dull handsaw through the solid bone skull plate. We then hung each 100-pound quarter on pine branches well above the ground to afford some protection from roaming grizzlies until the "packers" could carry the meat back to camp. In Alaska, it's unlawful to leave any meat in the field, so the packers are *not* optional personnel!

By the time Chip and I had carried the 100-pound cape and 60-pound antlers plus other equipment, gear, and guns the two-mile distance from the kill site to our satellite camp, we were two very tired, but happy guys. Chip also carried back our evening meal, the enormous "back strap" which had to be three feet long and six inches in diameter! I can't tell you how delicious that pure tenderloin tasted, cooked to medium-rare perfection on our little stove! If that marauding grizzly had ripped through our tent just for bacon grease, you can imagine what havoc he could have wreaked for a chance at some of that moose steak! Neither Chip nor I had any problems sleeping that night, despite the potential danger from a hungry visitor! All in all, it had been a great day; one bull moose down, one Dall ram to go!

On Thursday morning we decided to head back to Smokey Creek camp for several reasons: our food supply was down to powdered Tang and cheddar cheese; the moose cape had to be salted to preserve the hide for mounting; and, since we hadn't seen any sheep or their tracks since our Sunday arrival, Chip felt there were better ram opportunities elsewhere. So at 9:00 a.m. we packed up and headed back. The return trip was easier since I had worked myself into better shape, and the walk was **downhill**. Chip added the cape to his load, but recommended leaving the antlers at the trailhead where he would pick them up on his return trip to Dry Creek that afternoon.

We reached Smokey Creek at 11:30 a.m. and immediately raided the mess tent for the type of breakfast we'd been craving for four days; eggs, bacon, pancakes, and coffee. Chip salted the cape, then headed back to Dry Creek and didn't return until 6:30 that evening. No one else was in camp, so I decided a siesta was in order and returned to my tent. When I discovered Tom Kenyon's duffel there I surmised he and George were hunting sheep, which was confirmed when they arrived back at dark. They had spotted over 200 sheep in two days, and Tom passed on one full-curl, 35-inch ram since he was looking for an older one with heavier, broomed horns. As it turned out, Tom and Ron had flown in on Sunday just before bad weather hit.

When Chip returned, we all sat down to a delicious moose steak dinner and stayed up until after midnight giving updates and swapping stories. Plans for the next day called for Chip, Mike, and Tom to hike eight miles to Peggy's Creek, a productive sheep area for George over the years, and for George and me to take the jeep along the Dillinger riverbed closer to camp.

Upon awakening on Friday, September 12th, my first thought was that it was my son's 13th birthday. His becoming a teenager made me realize how quickly time flies by, but it also made me reflect on the pride and love I felt for him. I'd already exercised my bragging rights about Kimber III's acting career and starring role in the made-for-TV movie, "The Teddy Kennedy, Jr. Story". I missed him and didn't feel right being away on that special day.

At 7:00 a.m. the weather was clear with the promise of sunny skies. After breakfast, Chip, George, Mike, Tom, and I walked down to the creek bed in front of camp to set up our spotting scopes to look for sheep in the mountains behind us. Sure enough, there were seven sheep in one bowl including five rams, one of which was a respectable broomed trophy in the 35-inch range. When additional sheep entered the bowl, George decided to send Chip and me to get a closer look at what we had just observed. George, Mike, and Tom proceeded to Peggy's Creek as planned.

Chip and I started out at 9:00 a.m. We had to cross a two-foot deep creek before reaching the mountain's base, so I wore my ankle-tight hip boots and carried my leather ones to change into after the crossing.

We charted a route that would take us to a ridgetop on the right side of the bowl we had previously glassed. Once across the creek, we headed up the mountain through pine timber and alder bushes, which grew thicker and taller as we progressed. We glassed at each rest stop, often having to shinny up pine trees to obtain a clear field of view. We soon spotted three sheep moving quickly to our right about 500 yards away followed by a group of nine, including some rams that had emerged from a ravine. The larger group was feeding and moving at a slower pace away from the bowl we were heading for, and we weren't sure if they were the same sheep spotted from camp. However, a couple of the rams deserved a closer look, so we angled to our right to try to get ahead of them and narrow the distance. To get to our intended interception point, Chip and I had to fight our way through 600 yards of heavy alders, often having to backtrack and move sideways to find openings. We eventually located a game trail that made the going a bit easier, and, finally, we reached the upper edge of that maddening jungle.

Simultaneously, we spotted the nine sheep 250 yards above us and still moving to our right. Chip set up his spotting scope and quickly identified two good rams with full curls. He motioned for me to belly-crawl through some low brush to a point at the edge of the brake that would give me an unobstructed view and closer shot if I so decided. I found a good prone rest, checked both rams through my scope, and decided to take the lead one with a beautifully flared tip on his right side. Since he was walking broadside to me, I could see only his right horn and *assumed* his left side was as impressive. That would have been a disappointing assumption on my part had Chip not shouted, "Don't shoot!" From his position he could see that the ram's left horn was heavily broomed and considerably shorter. It also had a strange white ring around the horn about midway between the base and tip, something genetic I guess! I'm glad he stopped me in time and saved me a disappointing lesson of not checking the trophy quality **thoroughly** before pulling the trigger. The significance of that lesson would become evident only a few short hours later! I crawled back to join Chip and, together, plot a new strategy.

125

We decided to work our way towards the bowl on our left and had cautiously approached to within 75 yards of its surrounding peak when a young "sickle horn" ram appeared on the horizon and stared down at us! We froze in our tracks and remained motionless for what seemed like an eternity, realizing that if we moved and spooked him he'd probably run into the bowl and alarm any sheep that might be bedding or feeding there! The wind was in our faces, and, fortunately for us, the young ram's inexperience with man made our 10-minute standoff an exercise of curiosity, rather than fear, on his part. Eventually he turned and walked back over the ridge, and we resumed our ascent to the rim of the bowl. Our scoping quickly revealed a total of 22 rams bedded below us! Our attention was drawn to a group of eight resting in the middle of that 700-yard wide depression. All had impressive heads, but one in particular carried a full curl with slightly flared tips, which put him on my most-wanted list! Our only problem was accessibility. From our position, the group was at least 500 yards away, too far to chance a shot. Also, there was too little foliage between us to attempt a stalk even under ideal conditions, and the existing snow cover *completely* negated that possibility. The only thing we could do was wait and hope they would eventually get up to feed and move towards us. In the meantime, viewing those magnificent creatures of the wild through our scopes was a wonderful way to pass the afternoon. We even had a return visit from the young short-horned ram, which decided to bed down only 20 yards below us! Something told me he had never been shot at!

At 5:30 p.m. the eight rams arose in unison and started walking and feeding in our direction. Our patience was beginning to pay dividends. However, our attention had been so riveted to this group that we failed to keep abreast of a new visitor to the bowl. Having backed away from the scope to rest my eye, I caught movement on the far left rim of the bowl. I quickly repositioned the tripod and focused on the source of that movement. I could hardly believe my eyes! Working his way down into the bowl was the ram of a lifetime, a truly spectacular male carrying heavy, full-curl horns with flared, unbroomed tips. Chip quickly confirmed my excitement with such comments as "He's the one." and "You won't find a better ram in this whole range!" Even at that distance he felt we were looking at a 40-inch curl or more, which I later learned are carried by only 12 of every 1,000 Dalls taken in Alaska in any given year! The pressure was building! Would he come in our direction and, if so, close enough for a good shot?

Our eyes were glued to his every step, and if ***wishing*** plays any part in such matters, then such a mental process was at work. Slowly but steadily he fed his way closer. If he held his line, it would bring him approximately 350 yards below us. That would be a long shot, but one I felt confident about. At that point, Chip suggested an idea he felt would result in a closer shot. He pointed to a rock outcropping 50 yards below us and said we could crawl backwards slowly and carefully from our location to make a low semi-circular approach to those rocks, which would provide good concealment and a solid rest for my shot. I agreed, and 10 minutes later was in position with shell chambered! "My" ram was maintaining his course toward us, as were the eight other rams - which very quickly had become insignificant to us! Fifteen minutes later they joined together, and all nine continued feeding directly below us. The moment of truth had arrived!

Chip wanted to take a last look through his binoculars to confirm the position of my ram. Once we agreed he was the third from the left, I prepared for the shot. I eased forward with my sling looped securely around my left arm. I had already picked out a V-shaped opening between two rocks for my anchor point, and as I nestled in and eased the safety off, I felt solid, steady, and confident. My scope was cranked up to its maximum 10 power, and the crosshairs settled at the base of the ram's neck between his shoulders. The bullet's path would be almost straight down, with little if any trajectory during its 300-yard split-second journey. A perfect shot would break the ram's spine and continue through its lungs and heart. I took a deep breath, exhaled slowly, and squeezed. Instantly, the other eight rams bolted, but I was only concerned about the one that didn't. The big Dall flipped over on its back, kicked twice, then laid motionless!

At that moment I was in my own little world of concentration, but was quickly snapped out of it by Chip's shouts of "You got him!" and "Great shot!" Slaps on the back, hand shakes, and more "congratulations" followed before Chip suddenly took off over the side of the ridge, running and stumbling over the loose shale which covered our side of the bowl. I had enough presence of mind to put my safety "on", remove the clip, and even retrieve the empty shell casing for a souvenir! I was surprised how calm I felt immediately after the shot, but then I followed Chip's hasty, excited descent to my trophy!

My shot missed its mark by one inch, entering at the top of the back on the right side, but effectively penetrating the lungs and heart. We found the spent mushroomed

Winchester180-grain Silvertip – another souvenir – just under the skin behind the sheep's left foreleg. I'm always grateful for a clean, quick kill, and that trip had produced two of them.

My trophy Dall ram was even more spectacular up close, with its pure white coat and yellow eyes, crowned with perfectly symmetrical 40-inch, full-curl and one quarter horns that spanned 28 inches from tip- to-tip. There was no sign of brooming, and Chip estimated its age at 13 years.

I made the shot at approximately 7:00 p.m. and even though there would be decent light until 9:30, we still had a lot of work ahead of us. We both took many pictures from all angles and then caped and quartered the trophy. The average weight of a mature ram is about 225 pounds, of which 40 percent is consumable; so, with approximately 100 pounds of meat stuffed into Chip's backpack and over 50 pounds of head, horns, and cape resting on my shoulders, we started our descent to camp at 9:00. The fact that it was downhill offered little relief to the agony of that trip! Darkness soon enveloped us, and fighting through the alder thickets became a nightmare! It was bad enough during the day, when at least we could *see* what we were stumbling over, but at night, it was impossible. Tripping and falling became the norm, and when not picking ourselves up, there always seemed to be some branch hitting a face, pulling off a hat, or snagging a rifle barrel or sling! Besides the alders, there were shale slides and steep sidehill pitches to negotiate while trying to keep our balance. It felt like trying to fight our way out of a pitch-black, barbed-wire jungle. My hat's off to you, Bre'r Rabbit! My mood changed from complete ecstasy to complete frustration in an hour's time, but finally we reached the base of the mountain. Even though we were battered, bruised, and exhausted, our mission had been a successful one!

When we reached the creek bed, I was too tired to change boots and just waded across without hesitation. We finally reached camp at 10:15 and were greeted with much fanfare and excitement by George, Mike, and Tom. Everyone was impressed with my ram, but it was especially meaningful to hear George's praise - he said my ram was the best taken by any of his hunters that year - since he was the "ultimate judge", having witnessed hundreds of ram kills. Tom had scored as well on a mature ram with heavy-based, broomed horns. We certainly had reason to celebrate, although there was little energy left with which to do it!

After changing clothes, we met back at the mess tent for a late meal. The full impact of what had transpired during that long day finally hit me, and I was overwhelmed with feelings of exhilaration and excitement! Tom and I were both on cloud nine as we rehashed the events that had started 16 hours earlier! Tom had displayed amazing coolness under pressure in taking his ram. Somehow his scope had been knocked loose, and his first shot was three feet off at 400 yards! However, with George and Mike marking his shots, Tom was able to adjust and compensate well enough to make a clean kill on his 35 incher!

When I finally turned in, my adrenaline was still pumping. What a long and exciting day it had been, topped off by the tremendous Dall ram trophy I had been dreaming about for several years. It was a perfect setting for the Old Milwaukee beer slogan, "It doesn't get any better than this." Through all the excitement, my last thought before closing my eyes was that I hoped Kimber's birthday was as happy as my hunting day!

The excitement of Friday's events came flooding back when I awoke on Saturday. Confirmation that the events were real and not imagined came when I saw Chip meticulously "caping out" my sheep near the mess tent. He used a scalpel to separate the hide around the ears, eyes, and nose in one piece, which is essential pretaxidermy preparation. I certainly planned to have shoulder mounts made for each of my trophies, and the first step starts in the field with proper caping and hide preservation via salting. Most outfitters provide such services, but it's always wise to check before booking a hunt so there'll be no negative surprises once in the field. Hides will spoil and the hair or fur will fall out if they aren't removed and salted immediately. At that point there's nothing a taxidermist can do. Trying to find a replacement cape can be an expensive proposition at best, and for more exotic game like moose or sheep, a very remote possibility, if not impossibility, at any price. Therefore, the importance of cape and hide preservation and preparation can't be overemphasized, and most guides have that talent in their bag of skills.

One of George's guides, Tom Shankster, doubled as a taxidermist, and George recommended him highly for his Dall sheep work. I decided to have him do my shoulder mount at his Palmer shop and ship it to me. I couldn't be happier with the results. That magnificent head adorns my den wall and looks as alive as that September 1986 day when he wandered a bit too close!

An interesting event occurred on that same Saturday in camp. Shortly after breakfast I went down to the river bed to observe the scenery and fall colors. As I was absorbing the beauty, a *horse* bolted out of the surrounding pine trees and ran wildly through the camp. It wasn't the fact that it was a horse that shocked me as much as where did it come from and what was it doing **there**?! Neither George nor any of his staff had mentioned owning or using horses in their operation, so you can imaging how startled I was to see one in the remote expanses of the Alaska Range! Soon everyone in camp was alerted to its presence and watched its frolicking in amazement. The steed was a huge chestnut gelding and appeared to be very healthy. George explained that some trappers had brought in four packhorses to Smokey Creek several years prior and had built a corral and shelter to protect them. According to George, the trappers eventually quit the business and abandoned their stock, of which our visitor, "Blaze", was the lone survivor. Miraculously, that horse had already survived several harsh Alaskan winters alone in the wild, having to find his own food sources and avoid predators, including grizzlies. As a result, he had become as wild as his environment, and all attempts by us to befriend him were unsuccessful. He was high-strung, and all his senses were on full alert and geared for escape and avoiding danger. I greatly admired his ability to adapt and survive and quietly wished him well in his awesome struggle against tremendous odds. (In a subsequent correspondence, George informed me of Blaze's death during the winter of 1992 at an estimated age of 22. George found his bleached bones 300 yards above the east end of the landing strip at Smokey Creek.)

With my moose and sheep capes, antlers and horns in good hands, George flew Tom and me to Mystic Lake for a little "R&R" at the lodge before resuming our hunt, which for me would be for grizzly bear! The flight from Smokey Creek took only 15 minutes, but the scenery was awesome, with Mt. Foreaker and Mt. McKinley in full view beyond the lake.

After taking a much-needed shower and tending to equipment cleaning and repair needs, Tom and I went fishing. Actually, only Tom had a fishing license, but I was glad to steer and relax while Tom landed our evening meal, a five-pound lake trout! He also hooked a huge northern pike, which we almost boated before it shook loose. Size and weight can be deceiving when a fish is in the water, but that fish had to be at least 40 inches long with five inches separating those menacing eyes! After dinner, George flew us back to Smokey Creek where I zeroed-in again just to be on the safe side in case a nasty grizzly decided to make an appearance!

On Sunday, Chip, Mike, and Tom headed for Dry Creek to hunt moose and grizzly. The latter seemed an especially promising possibility vis-à-vis the presence of my moose's gut pile from the previous Wednesday. Of course, by then it had to be either very ripe or very gone! George and I took the jeep in the opposite direction along the riverbed towards Peggy's Creek, where George had built several bear observation platforms on the hillside along that stretch. Those log towers afforded a high, safe place to glass for several miles in each direction. As George explained, grizzly bears are not territorial and are constantly on the move looking for food, whether it be berries, roots, or **flesh**. Therefore, "glassing and stalking" is the modus operandi, and the wider the expanse covered, the better. Bagging an interior "Silver Tip" demands a lot of luck and patience. George and I had enough of the latter, but "Lady Luck" was not on our side that day. The only reward for our glassing was to observe a group of eleven Dall ewes working their way down the mountain behind us. Surrounded by that awe-inspiring landscape, I concluded that there are *no* bad days in the Alaska Range!

After we returned to camp, George checked the weather forecast and found that a bad front was expected late Monday. He mentioned that such fronts could last several days. Flying back to Palmer would then be problematical and could result in my missing my return flight. He told me to think about what I wanted to do, but, from his experience, advised not to challenge the weather. Since I had achieved my two primary hunting goals and knew that the odds of killing a bear on my last scheduled hunting day were low at best, I opted to fly back that night. We loaded my gear, including the moose antlers, cape, and meat, then flew some supplies to Mystic Lake where George discussed hunting plans and strategy with Marty for the other hunters. We finally took off for Palmer at 9 p.m. It was a smooth trip, with a full moon and bright stars lighting the way. At last count, all four of us hunters had scored on sheep. Lyle, Ron, and Tom had until the 26th to fill their other tags, and by the time they returned home, all three had bagged bigger moose than mine. Also, both Lyle and Tom added fine barren ground caribou bulls to their lists! George Palmer's Alaska Trophy Hunts final 1986 tally showed his typical 100% success on both moose and sheep!

Unfortunately, my decision to fly back early left me with three rather boring and uneventful days before my scheduled flight home on Wednesday. I was locked into my low super-saver fare which I learned would cost an additional $600 to change to an earlier flight! That option gave me no choice but to wait it out and keep fresh salt on the moose cape in my motel room! I bought an extra duffel bag for transporting the cape and prepared the antlers for the flight by covering all twelve large "points" with sections of split garden hose per airline policy.

George took my sheep cape and horns to Shankster's taxidermy shop on Monday, then flew his last hunter of the season into camp. When George returned on Tuesday, he and Jackie drove me to Anchorage to await my late flight out on Wednesday. That additional wait made me wish I had stayed in the field longer, since George had flown back without a hitch on Tuesday. On the other hand, that time "on hold" served as an unwinding and regearing period for making the transition from the dream world of adventure to the real world of family and work. It had been a wonderful experience, but I looked forward to seeing my son, especially since I had missed his birthday. My extra days of waiting also enabled me to cover my guilt with extra shopping for late birthday gifts. I think we'd both agree I covered myself pretty well!

Before flying out, I spoke with Tom Shankster's wife about proper care of the moose cape until I got it to my taxidermist. She assured me that additional salting would work just fine for drawing out unwanted moisture, and that it should survive the trip in good shape. I had decided to have my moose mounted by my local taxidermist, Larry Obuchowski from Bordentown, New Jersey. Larry is a real artist, and I was very pleased with the previous work he had done for me. Another consideration was that the charge for shipping a moose head from Alaska to New Jersey would have required taking out a second mortgage!

My return flight took off at 8:45 p.m., and as I bid farewell to Alaska, I was thankful for a wonderful experience and grateful for the warmth and hospitality extended by the Palmer family and George's staff. After a transfer in Chicago and six hours of time zone changes, I arrived at Newark International at 8:10 a.m. All baggage, rifle, cape, and antlers were present and accounted for, a fitting ending to a tremendous trip and hunting experience. It has been stated that once a person visits Alaska, he can't wait to return. I couldn't agree more.

The epilogue to my Alaska hunt is that Tom and Larry produced excellent shoulder mounts of my sheep and moose, respectively, and their work serves as a daily reminder of my exciting and memorable visit to "the land of the northern lights and midnight sun".

George Palmer, outfitter and master guide,
<u>Alaska Trophy Hunts</u>, September 1986

Beautiful scenery in front of Smokey Creek camp, looking down
the dry bed of the Dillinger River towards Peggy's Creek

(L to R) Ron, Tom, Kim, and Lyle

Hunting for grizzly bear near Peggy's Creek

Chris in our Dry Creek spike camp tent with repaired canvas
from grizzly bear's "forced entry" in background!

Chris Barker, moose guide, with my trophy

My 56-inch Alaska-Yukon moose

Happy hunter and guide, Chris, at Dry Creek
spike camp with my moose antlers

137

(L to R) George, Mike, Tom, and
Chris scoping for rams

The "jeep" in front of Smokey Creek camp with the "bowl"
in background where I shot my trophy Dall ram

Our fearless "sickle horn" visitor

In the "bowl" above our Smokey Creek campsite
with my full-curl, 40-inch Dall ram

Kim's magnificent full curl and one quarter 40-inch Dall ram, shot from top of shale slide in background

(Above) Returning to camp with Dall ram head and cape; tired, but happy!
(Below) Tom Shankster's wonderful work

141

Tom Kenyon poses with five-pound lake trout he caught
at Mystic Lake Lodge with Mt. McKinley in background

Tom with his beautiful 378 Boone and Crockett points
barren ground caribou bull

Tom with his 62-inch spread, 212 Boone and
Crockett points Alaska-Yukon moose antlers

Ron poses with his 55-inch spread moose rack

Chapter 11: Monster Whitetails - Alberta, Canada (1987)

Having lived most of my life in Delaware and New Jersey, it is understandable why many of my big-game experiences have involved the whitetail deer. Through 1986, I had harvested 15 bucks and 4 does in New Jersey and New York via either bow, rifle, or shotgun, the largest being my Delaware County, New York eight pointer in the 160-pound range. Although stories circulated about some monster bucks in excess of 250 pounds inhabiting the big hardwoods of Maine, most whitetail hunters I know would be *very* content to fill their tags with one of the few *200*-pound mature bucks taken each year. In fact, New Jersey gives special recognition each year to those lucky hunters who qualify for the "200 Pound Buck Club". With that background, you can imagine how my interest was aroused when I read about huge *300*-pound whitetails being taken north of the border, primarily in the Canadian provinces of Alberta and Saskatchewan.

I regard a mature whitetail buck as the smartest and wariest of all the big game animals I've hunted. Their basic nocturnal existence makes them a very elusive target, with a hunter's best opportunity for success coming during the rut when breeding urges cause them to let down their guard, however briefly. In my case, I seemed to be jinxed by small mistakes and oversights when those rare opportunities to bag a **real** trophy did present themselves. Similar frustrations are shared by thousands of other big-game hunters, which is probably why a trophy whitetail buck sporting a high, wide, and heavy eight point or better set of antlers remains their #1 priority. My dream was to someday take a big 10 pointer!

I had read in a hunting magazine long ago that "when you hang up the head of an honest-to-gosh *trophy* whitetail, you have done the most difficult thing in American big-game hunting, something most men hunt all their lives without accomplishing. It takes more than just time, money, and perseverance... It takes a real *hunter*, and that's a title money can't buy".

After my successes on woodland caribou, Rocky Mountain elk and mule deer, Alaska-Yukon moose and Dall sheep from 1984 -1986, I decided 1987 was going to be my year to pursue a trophy whitetail buck in Alberta, Canada. I started my search for a good outfitter and hunting area that February and soon settled on Big White Outfitters in Sterling, Alberta,

145

Canada, owned and operated by Neil Courtice and Al Barvair. I had seen several of their ads during my perusal of the major hunting magazines I subscribe to, and my subsequent phone call to Neil provided the answers and confidence I regard as essential before booking a hunt. I threw out blind faith years ago and developed a long list of appropriate, revealing questions to ask instead. Such "Q & A" sessions serve as the basis for my decision to use any outfitter, and it hasn't failed me yet. It's all a part of doing your homework - only this time you don't have mom or dad to help you!

During my initial conversation with Neil, I voiced one of my main concerns: determining the best time to hunt Alberta whitetails in relation to their rut, an event that could differ from the northeast breeding period I was used to. Based on how far north or south and the changes in daylight, the rut can kick in at different times such as mid November in the northeast versus mid December in the Texas brush country. Contrary to many hunters' thinking and belief, weather plays a lesser, if not negligible role. As such, I wanted to be sure that I booked my hunt with Big White Outfitters at a time that would maximize my chance for success! As part of my normal "checking" process, I spoke with two former clients of Big White, and both gave glowing reports about the size and number of bucks I could expect to see and high marks to the other factors, especially the experience and expertise of Neil and his guides. Satisfied with the information I had gathered, I booked for the week of November 15-22, 1987.

Neil and Al's deer camp was located in a small farming community 170 miles east of Edmonton near the rural town of Provost. Neil met my flight in Edmonton, and, after a brief stop for supplies, we headed for Neil's eastern camp. There was a light snow cover during the early part of the trip, but it soon gave way to the cheerless, drab brown backdrop of the cut grain fields interspersed with pockets of brush, which stretched as far as the eye could see. That was typical of the terrain we would be hunting, and Neil commented that the openness and lack of heavy cover worked to the deers' advantage, since they could spot potential danger - e.g., approaching hunters - from considerable distances. Traditionally, long shots on the run are the order of the day, with many misses resulting. That's one reason so many bucks in the area live long enough to achieve their enormous body size. Additionally, good genetics and rich nutrients contribute to heavy antler growth, with the cumulative result being beautiful, **large** trophy whitetails!

The lack of snow was certainly not a plus, since our game plan was to glass numerous grain fields from Neil's pickup, then stalk when bucks were spotted. Ideally, a white backdrop would have helped, but we rationalized if the deer would be harder to spot without snow, then we would be as well! I had paid extra for a 1x1 hunt, and my early request for Neil to be my guide was granted. He felt confident that buck activity would be on the upswing with the rut fast approaching, and that we'd see our share of good candidates, snow or no snow.

Camp was actually a single cottagelike structure that housed everyone; hunters, guides, and cook. On arrival, I met Neil's partner, Al, whose broad smile and energetic handshake made me feel immediately welcomed. Al had served as the guide for the #1 Pope and Young Dall ram bow kill during the previous fall, so his credentials were well established. I was also introduced to the other three hunters: Jackie Raines, a big, strong, happy-go-lucky resident of North Lake Park, Florida; John "Grafton" Gray, an older hunting enthusiast who owned "Mr. Sportsman, Inc." in Russellville, Alabama; and Jack Hinkle, Jr., a young fellow from New Jersey who was on his first guided big-game hunt. All four of us had hunted whitetails in our native states, but it was the first attempt by each of us to try for one of the so-called "Monarchs of Alberta".

Although known for its huge whitetails, Alberta also offers excellent mule deer hunting, and the area I would be hunting had ample numbers of both. Therefore, I arranged through Neil to purchase an additional mule deer tag just in case one of those bifurcated racks appeared!

Shortly after arriving, I paid the balance of the outfitter's fee, got my non-resident license and tags, sorted out my clothes and equipment, and checked my rifle and scope for any sign of travel wear or damage. The balance of that first day was spent getting acquainted, swapping hunting stories, and enjoying a delicious prehunt steak dinner prepared by Al. Jackie kept us all laughing with his tales about hunting wild boars and whitetails in the Florida swamps, and how he had built a custom-made swamp buggy to negotiate the thick, wet terrain. He was the epitome of a good ol' boy with good ol' stories!

Grafton and I got into a discussion about hunting rifles and how he felt his bolt action .270 Ruger was "the best choice" for hunting deer. I assumed since he carried the Ruger line at his sporting goods store that his thinking was somewhat slanted! Knowing that each person has his own caliber and cartridge favorites, hunters' discussions about same are more informative than persuasive, realizing, like politics and religion, that each is going to continue using what works for him and what he feels comfortable with.

Neil soon took over the conversation as he explained how, where, and with whom Monday's first day of hunting would proceed. It was my first hunt using a pickup truck to locate game, and, as such, we didn't have to rise in the predawn darkness to get to a predetermined ambush site before sunup. Using unquestioned logic, Neil stated that "You can't spot what you can't see." With that as our credo, Neil and I climbed into his truck at 6:30 a.m.

We hadn't gone half a mile when Neil pointed through my window and exclaimed, "Look at that buck!" Unfortunately, the sun was not yet up, and the early dawn's mixture of grays and browns made it difficult to pick out individual forms. My effort to locate that buck was futile. My "deer" eyes were not yet acclimated to the dimly lit surroundings, and, after factoring in the moving truck, I decided to give myself a quick pardon for that oversight! Neil had hunted the area for several years and wanted to check out a few neighboring farms where he had seen several large bucks feeding during his preseason scouting. Neil explained during our drive that the majority of the local farmers were friendly, cooperative, and agreeable to allowing outfitters like himself access to their land. Flexible gates consisting of three strands of barbed wire attached to loose wooden posts could be quickly disengaged from anchored wire loops to allow entry to the fields for cruising and glassing. Signs with such pleasant messages as "please be considerate" were posted as a constant reminder for visitors to reattach the gates after passing through. Based on the appreciation of outfitters and hunters alike for such access privileges, I'm certain those gate-closing requests were rarely, if ever, violated! What a pleasant change from the "posted - no hunting" signs seen with increasing frequency in the United States.

At about 7:30 a.m. Neil spotted two good bucks standing near a woodlot several hundred yards away. He felt one deserved a closer look and brought the truck to a stop to steady his binoculars on the steering wheel. Unfortunately, both deer retreated into the woods, but not before Neil got a good look at his target buck, which he described as "a nice eight pointer with good height and mass". He felt we could make a wide circle on foot to get within a couple hundred yards of them. Assuming the bucks held their position just inside the woodline and the wind continued in our favor, we would then be within reasonable shooting distance. We took our time and used all available cover to make an undetected approach, but when we raised our binoculars, the bucks had vanished. Closer examination revealed two sets of fresh tracks heading for a heavy thicket at an unhurried pace. Convinced we hadn't been detected, Neil motioned for me to circle the thicket and "post" while he crawled through the brush to push them out. Either they had already passed through or held tight during Neil's penetration, but when neither buck appeared, we decided to abandon our pursuit.

We returned to the truck and continued our surveillance of the surrounding fields and woodlots. At 8:45 a.m., Neil again looked through my passenger-side window and pointed to a big buck moving away from us across a cut grain field. It was walking at a leisurely pace and with each step widened the initial 200-yard distance from our stationary vehicle. A mist hung over the field, but it didn't prevent us from gaining a clear image through our binoculars of a large-bodied whitetail with high, heavy antlers extending beyond his outstretched ears. My heart started pounding as Neil announced, "He's a beauty. Let's try to get him!" Without hesitation, we jumped out of the cab and over the barbed-wire fence that paralleled the gravel road!

The buck was out of view as we angled to our right towards a small woodlot 200 yards ahead. Our route kept us at a higher elevation than the path taken by the buck, since the field sloped downward to the left. We figured the woods would help conceal our advance, whereupon we could glass to relocate the buck without being detected. Neil set a quick pace, and I soon started to feel the weight of my heavy Woolrich suit and rifle as I tried to keep up. The traditional red and black checkered wool pants and jacket are welcome companions on a deer stand in sub-freezing weather, but *running* in them, even in mild weather, turns such an outfit into a suit of armor! There was also a 50-pound weight difference between Neil and me which made me a bit less nimble of foot, and by the time we reached the patch of woods, I was soaked in perspiration. Luckily, the pace slowed considerably as we worked our way towards the right edge of the trees, where we gained a clear view of the field once again. My heart sank as our scanning revealed only distant cattle in the field. We were positive the buck hadn't seen or scented us during our stalk, but the question remained: Where did he go? The broad expanse of field was broken only by a narrow, brush-choked ravine, which snaked its way along the plot's right boundary for several hundred yards. Neil and I had no sooner exchanged glances concerning the concealment potential of the ravine, when out he came! The big bruiser had apparently headed straight for that spot to check one of his fresh scrapes. The buck was loping on a right-to-left diagonal path away from us, and Neil's quick assessment of his trophy quality necessitated my making a quick decision and shot before he started putting *serious* distance between us. Attempting an extremely long shot which might only wound him and result in a long tracking effort with no recovery was not on my list of preferred options. So, with my window of opportunity closing quickly, I decided to take action. It was "now or never"!

Since we had moved forward into the open field, there were no trees close enough to provide a good anchor for the 200-yard plus shot I faced. Every second was crucial, and the buck was widening the gap with every stride. I immediately got into a kneeling position, rested my left elbow on my left knee, and, with the sling wrapped around my left arm, steadied myself as well as possible for the shot at hand. The crosshairs were wavering as I tried to calculate the right lead and elevation for my moving target. Neil quickly responded with "about 225" when I asked for his yardage estimate, and, with that, I held at the base of the buck's neck on a line even with the top of his back and squeezed off. My hope was for my bullet to hit the lung area behind his shoulder about 10 inches below and behind my point of aim.

I soon had the answer to my quick calculation as the buck toppled to the ground. As he struggled to his feet, I finished the job with a perfectly placed shot into his "boiler room". He fell heavily and stayed down, but I continued to cover his rib cage with my scope just in case I had only stunned him with a glancing shot off his skull or antlers. I had read enough stories about "dead" bucks miraculously jumping up and running off after such hits, while the hunter stood with mouth agape, his gun propped against a tree with deer tag in one hand and skinning knife in the other! I wanted to be sure my name wouldn't be associated with such a disappointing ending! However, once I was certain he was down for keeps, I let out a ceremonial "whoop" and received Neil's congratulations and accolades for two good shots under hurried conditions. I was proud of my shooting given the circumstances of the distance involved at a moving target, and less-than-ideal anchor position! My face became one large smile as I started to move excitedly toward my prize.

Neil's cry of "Wait!" contained such a tone of alarm and concern that it stopped me in my tracks. I looked back to see him waving for me to follow him in his quick retreat toward the **truck**! I was totally confused, but as I caught up with him he provided answers that caught me completely off guard! It seems the field we were in was one of the few that Neil *hadn't* secured permission to hunt! It wasn't that he couldn't have gotten permission, but rather an omission that he had forgotten to, and, just to play it safe, he wanted to get off the property in case the owner came to investigate the shooting. I didn't know what to say, but I wasn't about to hold a debate with Neil at that point and jeopardize the recovery of my buck! I just assumed he had done all his homework and had gained the necessary permission from **every** landowner whose property we'd hunt. I wasn't prepared for that reversal and possible disappointment. I was also exhausted by the run back to the truck, and that added to my growing frustration at Neil for his "oversight". He sensed my mood and assured me we'd recover my deer, but just wanted to take precautions. He stated that most of the farmers returned home for their noontime meal, and that we'd take advantage of that break to retrieve my buck. It was then only 9:45 a.m., and the next 2¼-hour wait seemed like a week. I had plenty of time to play and replay the worst case scenario in my head about how much I had spent in time and money to harvest the whitetail trophy of a lifetime, only to have it confiscated due to an inadvertent trespassing violation.

Fortunately, that nightmarish ending didn't come to fruition. At noon, we drove to the far side of the field and pulled up to one of the gates previously described. I assumed Neil planned to drive into the field, load my deer, and make a quick exit. Wrong again. For whatever reason, Neil didn't want to take his truck onto the property even though the grain had been cut and the ground was frozen. Driving wouldn't have caused any damage. From our location we could see my dead buck through our "binocs", lying in the same spot where my second shot had dropped him. The only difference was instead of being 225 yards away, he was then over 500 yards away! Neil's second announcement was that he didn't want to take the time to field dress him until **after** we removed him from the field. With that statement, I again suggested the quickest and less taxing solution was to use the truck. As far as I was concerned, the odds of being detected on foot were greater than in the truck due to the longer period of time it would take us to drag the huge carcass to the truck, and mostly in an uphill direction, as well. With my request denied, "General" Courtice led "Private" Shoop on his 500-yard forced march toward our objective! In anticipation of the arduous task ahead, I shed the bulk of my heavy clothing, which, in retrospect, probably saved a premature heart attack! Our approach on the downward-sloping terrain was relatively easy and without pain, but as the distance to my quarry narrowed, I knew the return trip would be a stiff test of my strength and endurance.

My buck was enormous! Lying there, he looked more like a small cow than a whitetail deer, at least the ones I was used to seeing. The left beam of his rack arched upward and carried three high and heavy points in front of a six-inch brow tine. His right antler carried six points including a sticker point and matching brow tine. A 20-inch inside spread added to the beautiful symmetry of his rack that would later green score at over 140 B & C points. I couldn't have been more pleased with my handsome whitetail specimen, whose shoulder mount would occupy a place of honor on my trophy room wall a few months later.

The two-man trophy admiration society quickly adjourned as we prepared to exit as quickly as possible; quickly, that is, as a herd of **snails**! Maybe from a psychological standpoint, Neil should have refrained from announcing his estimate of my buck's weight. Perhaps I could have pretended it was a small doe and convinced myself that an uphill 500-yard drag in a half-stooped position wasn't really that tough. However, when the words "three hundred pounds" hit my ears, all those mind games went out the window in a hurry. Admittedly, the first 50 yards weren't too bad since we were "fresh", and the ground with its thin layer of snow was relatively flat and offered little resistance. After switching sides to prevent cramps in the grip hands, we matched our initial effort. At that point the ground started its upward slope, and the weight of the buck began to take its toll. My grip hand cramped with greater frequency at shorter intervals, my back ached, and my heart pounded in sympathy with my labored breathing. Our 50-yard breaks were soon down to 20, and my thigh and calf muscles were complaining big time. And that was during the *first* 250 yards! Needless to say, by the time we reached the truck, there were two completely exhausted "draggers" who didn't have enough energy to lift the buck into the open bed! One attempt convinced us to rest in the cab until we regained enough strength to complete our 300-pound "clean and jerk"! We then drove to a safer area to take pictures and field dress my "monster".

It had been an up-and-down day that ended on a high note, and one happy hunter made his triumphant return to camp with the well-earned trophy in tow! The one last thought that crossed my mind that night was that if Neil is ever faced with the same situation and decision we had that day, you can bet the ranch he'll drive instead of drag!

I spent the rest of my hunt trying to find an equally impressive mule deer buck, but without success. I passed on two small 3x3 mulies on separate occasions, since I was only interested in taking a buck that bettered my Montana trophy, and meat was not a necessity.

The other hunters had mixed success: Jackie took another "hog" whitetail, whose nine-point rack had good symmetry, but lacked the mass of mine. It also amused me how Jackie could make his deer look normal sized when standing next to it!; Grafton took a nice 3x4 mulie buck on the last day, but never got to prove his Ruger prowess on a big whitetail. Final score: Remington 1, Ruger 0!; Jack Hinkle missed a big mulie buck in fading shooting light on our third day afield and never got another good opportunity during the rest of the hunt on either species. I felt particularly bad for Jack, since I know he had saved for several years to afford the hunt. Although not taking a trophy doesn't mean a bad hunt, in Jack's case it would have been a fitting ending. I couldn't help but think of a second big whitetail buck that Neil drove out of a thicket within 20 yards of my posted position while we were trying to fill my mulie tag. If Jack had been me that day he would have gotten his trophy. But we all know that the "what ifs" and "should haves" are as much a part of hunting as guns and ammo, and, without them, the triumphs and successes wouldn't be as sweet or memorable!

As an interesting sidelight to the trip, one of our frequent visitors during that week was a teenager named Kevin West. Kevin lived with his family on a nearby farm and had gotten the deer-hunting bug from his dad, whose prowess was well known among the locals. In fact, Kevin took me to his home to show me the mount of a mulie buck his father had shot, and I can only say I haven't seen a bigger set of antlers before or since! Kevin was really into bowhunting, but at that point had only frustrations and near misses to show for his effort. I could only encourage him to pay attention to the little details, and that patience would eventually bring success. Years later, I read a magazine article about hunting for whitetails in Alberta, and guess whose picture was shown with the whitetail equivalent of his dad's mulie buck? You guessed it! I'd like to believe my early advice contributed to that success!

Kevin was also a fledgling bull rider, which I always felt required a mental imbalance to get involved with - until I met Kevin. He was a nice, polite, soft-spoken kid who didn't seem to possess the brash, if not cocky, self-assurance required for such a sport. Nevertheless, I started to follow Kevin's career, and I'll be darned if he didn't win the bull riding championship and

153

$50,000 first prize at the premier Calgary Stampede a few years later! He's quite a talented young man, and I wish him well, wherever he is; most likely, sitting in some tree stand in Alberta!

Another enjoyable hunt was over, but memories of my adventures in the field, trophy taken, and new friendships formed were locked in for future review! Each of us defines a successful hunt in different ways, with many factors contributing to the end result. In that regard, each part of my Alberta trip added up to one very educational, rewarding, and satisfying experience!

Neil Courtice's <u>Big White Outfitters</u> hunting camp
near Provost, Alberta, Canada

Typical Alberta whitetail country – heavy pockets
of brush amid wide expanses of cut grain fields

Outfitter and guide Neil Courtice poses with my
monster 300-pound, 10-point whitetail buck

Kim and his Alberta 10-point beauty in the field

Big Jackie Raines poses with his equally "big" nine pointer

(L to R) bullrider Kevin West, Jackie Raines, and Jack Hinkle admire John"Grafton"Gray's Alberta seven-point mule deer with John in the foreground

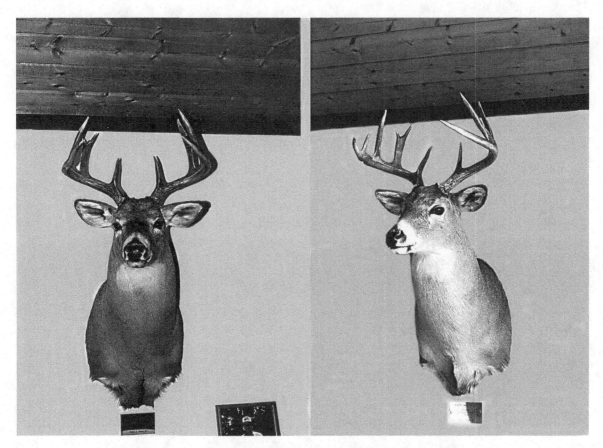

Shoulder mount of my Alberta, Canada 10-point
whitetail buck adorns wall of my Colorado home

Chapter 12: Stonehill Farm - Whitetail Bowhunting
at its Best (1987-1991)

Sometimes the best hunting adventures and memories are those that occur closest to home, and that was never truer than the many enjoyable mornings and afternoons I spent pursuing whitetail bucks on Stonehill Farm in Colts Neck, New Jersey from 1987 through 1991.

It all started one November day in 1987 while goose hunting on land adjacent to Stonehill's 360 acres. I met Tim Arner, Stonehill's manager, who was investigating my shooting to be sure I wasn't trespassing. Satisfied that I wasn't, we struck up a conversation that began a friendship and hunting relationship that exists to this day.

Tim's true love is hunting waterfowl, and he planted corn on the majority of the farm's tillable land to draw in ducks and geese during the fall and winter seasons. I told Tim that my real passion was bowhunting for whitetails, but that it was becoming increasingly difficult to get private landowner permission to hunt. Tim said he did little if any deer hunting, but that the farm was loaded with them, including several large bucks. He did have a problem with trespassers, however, and offered me bowhunting rights in exchange for being his eyes and ears to keep unauthorized persons away. Talk about a great bargain! He even took pains to identify boundaries, locations of thickets and swamps, and the most promising edges where his morning and evening buck sightings usually occurred. The farm had entrances from two different county roads, and Tim showed me both and even where to park near the farmhouse and main barn where Tim maintained his office. He invited me to follow him on a walking tour of the property and showed me where a couple of permanent tree stands were located in case I wanted to use them! To have such a chance meeting turn into a dream come true was the epitome of being in the right place at the right time, and it opened up a four-year door of great bowhunting thrills and memories.

Immediately after Tim's invitation, I obtained aerial photos of Stonehill's acreage from the Federal Land Bank office in Freehold, NJ and ordered a topographical map of the area as well. Besides my extensive and thorough scouting, those additional aides helped pinpoint bedding and feeding areas, holding areas, and escape routes which saved me valuable time in determining the bucks' normal travel patterns and best tree stand locations for intercepting them.

Stonehill's acreage was divided into two almost equal sections by Muhlenbrink Road, with the farmhouse, barns, Tim's house, cornfields, interconnected woodlots, pine groves, swamps, and Stonehill itself located on the western side. More cornfields, woods, and heavy, almost impenetrable thickets and swamps covered the eastern side. That eastern portion of the farm's acreage was also referred to as "the Vortex", resulting from a government aircraft tracking station located within its perimeter. A long gravel road leading to that government installation's lone white-towered facility served as my parking area when hunting that section. There was an abundance of deer trails, rubs, and scrapes throughout the farm's woodlots, and Tim had observed "racked" bucks in all the fields. So where does one start? I decided to hunt the western half first since it had a little bit of everything as far as deer habitat was concerned. There was also an apple orchard behind the farmhouse, and it drew deer like a magnet when the apples started to drop. At the very least, it gave me a starting point for observing and patterning the bucks in that area. I was also drawn to a deep ravine 10 yards wide, which ran for several hundred yards along the southwest boundary. It contained thick cover, which made it a perfect escape route, and numerous trails emerged from the ravine and extended to the edges of several fingers of woods leading to the surrounding cornfields. Those little juts of woods were classic holding areas for bucks waiting for dark before entering the fields to feed.

Stonehill itself is approximately 100 feet high, 80 yards wide at its base, and 300 yards long running east to west. The hill is completely wooded, with the trees extending from the base of the hill on both sides for another 30 yards to adjacent cornfields. Those narrow stretches of open woods and the hilltop itself serve as travel corridors leading to a larger expanse of woods running perpendicular to the extreme western end of the hill. Fresh trails indicated deer activity during my initial scouting trip, and that was confirmed later by sightings of the actual trailmakers themselves!

Stonehill was so named from a large boulder located on top of the western end of the hill. Of historical note are the arrowhead markings chiseled into its surface, pointing towards the east. Speculation has it that local Indians used the "stone" as a trailmarker to indicate direction to the Atlantic Ocean, located approximately 25 miles away.

I approached Stonehill from my parking spot behind the barn on the eastern end of the property and set up on either the northern or southern slope of the hill, depending on the wind and/or thermal currents. On all such approaches, I allowed extra time to keep a slow pace and to position my tree stand with care in the predawn darkness. By doing so, I minimized, if not eliminated, unwanted human noises that could spook any deer in the immediate vicinity of my stand location. Part of a hunter's learning curve has to do with attention to details. Snapping twigs or rustling leaves on the way to a stand because one is late or in a hurry can kill any chance for success before the sun even peeks above the horizon! Any hunter who's heard a doe's "blowing" warning knows that sinking feeling of the hunt being over before it has even started! A hunter who ignores wind direction and the need for stealth in preventing unnatural sounds will be constantly frustrated and consistently unsuccessful.

I had seven different stand locations on Stonehill Farm. Some were used only in the morning or evening depending on their proximity to bedding or feeding areas, and some were effective at either time. However, the critical consideration in making my choice in all cases was wind direction and thermal current movement. In the a.m., I set up downwind from feeding areas so I wouldn't be detected when deer headed for their bedding areas. Conversely, for my p.m. vigils, I placed my stand downwind from their bedding areas so the wind would carry my scent away from the deer as they meandered toward their feeding areas. On days with no apparent wind factor, I was ever mindful of the effect of thermal currents, which generally flow downhill as the evening air cools and uphill when the morning air warms. Thermals explain why a mature buck is often the first to leave a feeding area for an elevated bedding location at or before first light while the cool air currents are still moving **towards** him, warning of any danger ahead. Delaying his exit could prove fatal, since the warming currents would then be at his back, eliminating a whitetail's primary warning device - its nose - and leaving its less acute ears and eyes to detect a hunter's presence. For his p.m. travel to lower feeding areas, a mature buck leaves his bed while the warm thermals are still moving **upward**. Then, once he nears the food plot, a buck will wait and watch from a protected holding area until dark before venturing forth. At that point, he is protected by either low or no shooting light and favorable downward flowing thermals. Because deer have a distinct olfactory advantage over man, a hunter must keep wind and air flows at the top of his priority list and choose his stand location accordingly if he hopes to be successful, especially when pursuing big bucks. For example, when determining a stand location at Stonehill in the a.m., I tested the wind/thermals via a piece of thread tied to the top of my bowstring and chose whichever side, north or south, was downwind from the surrounding cornfields. A wind out of the east or west gave me the option of hunting either side or on top without my scent alerting the feeding deer. I rarely hunted on days with strong or blustery winds, since the deer often stayed holed up in the thickets, unable to rely on their noses to pinpoint potential danger under those conditions. When they can't trust their "sniffers", deer stay put or drastically restrict their daylight travel. Besides, sitting in a swaying tree with little chance of success is no fun!

Due to its proximity to the surrounding cornfields and the cover provided by the woods and thickets for deer traveling to and from their bedding areas, I always found Stonehill to be a better a.m. than p.m. location.

The following four stories highlight the fun and excitement I experienced while bowhunting for whitetails on Stonehill Farm.

I.   Middle of the Rut Madness! - 1988

The peak of the rut in New Jersey and most of the Northeast occurs in mid November, when decreasing daylight triggers a buck's pituitary gland and causes increased testosterone levels, a phenomenon called *photoperiodism*. With these changes, the annual fall breeding period affords the best and possibly only opportunity to harvest a wary, old, dominant trophy whitetail buck, whose activity and movement during the rest of the year is almost entirely nocturnal.

On Saturday, November 12, 1988, my alarm sounded its 4 a.m. call. That was 15 minutes earlier than usual for my Saturday bowhunting ritual, but the rut was in full swing and I wanted to get to my stand without having to rush. Proper preparation required adequate time to attend to such details as applying fresh cover-up scent to my felt boot pads to conceal any odor while walking to my stand, and placing Kodak film canisters filled with doe-in-heat soaked cotton at the base of trees to which I knew the exact yardage from my stand. Since I had only two pins on my bowsight at the time, one set for 10 yards and the other for 20, I could easily adjust for in-between or longer shots by using a higher or lower point-of-aim. However, I always try to take shots at 20 yards or less to prevent misses and needless wounding from deer "jumping the string", or by deflections from unseen twigs and branches. I also allowed extra time to attend to such chores as removing dead leaves and twigs from the stand's surface to prevent unwanted noise, and for attaching or screwing in my climbing steps, portable seat, and bow hanger. Paying attention to details and covering the long list of "little things" often determine success or failure for a bowhunter, and I wanted to be extra careful that day!

On that particular crisp fall morning, a faint breeze was blowing from the north, so I headed for the permanent tree stand Tim had built on the north side of Stonehill. I followed a narrow, leaf-strewn path just inside the woodline for its entire 300-plus yard length to a point parallel to the stand, located 30 paces inside the strip of woods at the base of Stonehill. Weathered "two by four" rungs were nailed into the two hardwoods leading to a narrow plywood platform 10 feet above the ground. I generally prefer a higher perch, but Tim had chosen a good location with numerous intersecting trails nearby. To negate the stand's height problem, I was especially careful to keep any movement to an absolute minimum, and using the permanent structure also saved me the time and energy of putting up my own portable steps, stand, and seat! Setting up earlier than later also provided that extra half hour or so to let the woods quiet down and allowed time for me to attach my safety belt, clean and adjust my glasses, nock my arrow, recheck my windage thread, and take a couple of warm-up draws; in general, to relax and start focusing on the task at hand! I concentrated on the cut cornfield in front of me.

By 5:15 a.m., with all preparatory work completed, I started my quiet listening and watching routine. The emphasis was on listening, since it was still too dark to take a shot even had a buck walked within range. Ten minutes later I heard the distinct, steady *crunch* sound of deer hooves on leaves coming from **behind** me and to the left. The broken cadence told me there were several deer approximately 30 to 40 yards away but coming closer, their progress broken only by occasional pauses to test the air and listen for possible danger. I was not in a position to see them, and the lack of light would not have made that an easy task anyway; however, I knew the closer they came, the greater my risk of being detected from my upwind location. They stopped 20 yards from my stand, and the lead deer started stomping a hoof on the leaves, which usually indicates having seen something out of place, hoping to elicit a movement response to confirm friend or foe. Within seconds, the sound no deer hunter wants to hear—a deer's sudden exhaling or *blowing*—reached my ears, followed instantly by the fast retreat of all members in the direction they came from. They had caught my scent just as I feared. However, I was certain from their numbers and behavior that they were does, and I just prayed that their exit wouldn't frighten away any bucks in the area. I was encouraged by the fact that it was the peak of the rut, and the old adage "to find the bucks, locate the does" came immediately to mind!

Within minutes, my concern about bucks vacating the area proved needless as a ghostly figure sporting an eight-point rack appeared on the same trail I had entered from, having emerged from a thicket farther to my left. He was walking slowly toward the spot where I had buried one of my doe-in-heat canisters in the leaves, and, with the wind in my favor, he didn't have a hint about my presence 40 yards away! If he stayed his course, he'd be within that magical 20-yard shooting distance in less than a minute, and in a perfect broadside position as well! My problem was the shooting light, or lack thereof! A quick glance at my illuminated watch hands showed 5:45 a.m. If only I could stall him for 10 minutes! Maybe he would smell the canisters and hang around, thinking there was a receptive doe in the area. A lot of thoughts were racing through my mind simultaneously, and I knew an important decision had to be made sooner than later! The transition from night to day was just beginning, and even at 20 yards I couldn't see my sight pin clearly enough to be certain my aim would produce a quick kill. I could make out the buck's light-colored antlers and general body outline, but, just as a seasoned duck hunter picks out a single bird and avoids shooting at the whole flock, I wanted to focus with certainty on that eight-inch lung area behind his shoulder instead of the entire form! Even with my glasses on I was unable to get a clear sight picture, and my frustration ***and*** heartbeat increased as decision time fast approached!

As anticipated, the buck stopped to sniff the interesting odor rising from the base of the "canister" tree! I knew that tree was exactly 22 paces from the front of the stand, and the buck appeared to be standing slightly beyond it. He seemed relaxed and unaware of any impending danger. He sniffed the air and looked in several directions in an attempt to locate the doe he felt certain was nearby. Several agonizing minutes passed, but at least the previous darkness had started turning to the first gray tinge of dawn. The buck moved several steps forward to my right. At that point I slowly raised my bow, drew back the Easton "Camo-Hunter" XX75 2315 shaft tipped with a 4-bladed Razorbak broadhead, and settled the bottom 20-yard pin behind and slightly above his shoulder to allow for the extra yardage. The sight picture looked good and the release felt smooth as the string slid across my finger tabs and sent the arrow towards its target. Impact! The buck immediately bolted into the cut cornfield and disappeared beyond a bordering hedgerow. I felt good about the shot and confident of recovery! I was sure it was just a matter of allowing time for his chest cavity to fill with blood, which for a double-lung shot usually occurs within 100 yards.

I had taken my shot at 5:55 a.m. and decided to stay on stand until 6:15. By then it would be light enough to pick up his blood trail and tracks in the rain-softened dirt between the rows of corn stubble. During that waiting period, I replayed both my decision to shoot and the shot itself and decided both were good. I got excited at the thought of standing over my trophy!

When I inspected the spot where my arrow struck, my euphoria turned to concern and doubt. My pace-off ended at 27 yards, not the 22 to 23 yards I had estimated! Instead of finding frothy red blood evidencing a good lung hit, I found **none**. Only white belly hair indicating a paunch hit marked the area. Instantly, my "good" shot had turned into a not-so-good one! It is well known that paunch-hit deer can travel great distances if pushed, so a longer waiting period is required to allow the animal to bed down and weaken as quickly as possible. Chances then increase for a shorter tracking effort and recovery or finishing shot. In hopes of finding blood to confirm the type of hit by its color and/or content, I followed the buck's deep and widely-splayed hoof prints into the adjoining field. Twenty yards into my search I found my arrow and "first blood". They didn't contain the telltale food particles of a stomach hit, and that was encouraging. However, neither did they nor other blood that followed reveal the desired bubbly lung texture or the dark red color of a fatal liver wound. That was discouraging.

While weighing possible options and considering the next move, my attention was drawn to the rustle of leaves and movement near my tree stand, then 50 yards away. To my complete surprise, a huge, high-racked buck was chasing a doe back and forth in front of the stand I had occupied only moments before; and there I was standing in an open field completely exposed!

It was only because the buck's attention was riveted to the estrus-driven business at hand that he didn't see me and run off. I was helpless to do anything but squat down and watch the spectacle to completion. At times like that, second guessing and "what ifs" take over (e.g. what if I had passed up the marginally acceptable shot on the first buck only to be rewarded for my patience with a closer shot at the larger buck!). What were the odds of having a pair of eight-point or better bucks come within shooting range of that stand within such a short time span! During the peak of the rut strange things can happen, and little did I realize as I stood in that field that there was a lot more to come!

Once I recovered from the shock of that rut-crazed chase, I decided to continue tracking my buck. A light rain had begun to fall, and I was concerned about the blood trail being obliterated. His trail took me through the mentioned hedgerow into an adjoining cut cornfield on the north, and drops of blood were evident the entire way as I followed his new path for 200 yards before it turned east towards the barn. A second hedgerow separated me from another field, but the buck chose to parallel the near side of that hedgerow and head south! In effect, he was traveling in a circular route that brought him to the eastern end of Stonehill and the cover and safety of its woods. It was there that I lost both his tracks and blood trail.

After a futile effort to locate new sign, I went to find help. Tim wasn't home, but his good friend and hunting partner, Dennis Donnelly, was at the shop and offered to give me a hand. Dennis is one of the most enthusiastic "up" people I know, and that carries over to his love for hunting! Dennis, like Tim, spent the bulk of his hunting time in duck and goose blinds, although Dennis did participate in New Jersey's shotgun and muzzleloader deer seasons. At that first meeting, he hadn't even shot an arrow at a paper target, let alone a deer! When I related the events of that morning he could hardly contain himself, and we soon found "last blood" and resumed the search. We decided to walk along the top of Stonehill and look down both the north and south slopes for sign or movement, figuring that the buck would be bedded down at or near the crest. About one third of the way along the ridge, I dropped off to the left to probe a heavy thicket. Just then, Dennis shouted "There he goes!", as my buck jumped from his bed and bounded away on the south hillside I occupied. I didn't see him , but a pool of fresh blood in his bed confirmed it was my buck. My hope was renewed as I dropped farther down the slope in case the buck decided to circle back. Dennis continued along the top, peering down into the thickets that pocketed the terrain. Fifty yards farther I heard the *crunch* of leaves coming down the hill. At first I thought it was Dennis, but then a small six-point buck appeared 20 yards in front of me! Simultaneously, we put on our brakes and stared at each other for an instant before he dashed out of the woods and across another field. I hadn't even had a chance to yell to Dennis about that buck when I heard Dennis shout again that **three *more*** bucks were headed my way! I felt like I was in a turnstile as I kept spinning around to pinpoint their location. I never saw them. Dennis told me later that they had stayed near the top and followed the ridgeline in the direction of the barn.

We continued the search for my buck for four more hours without success. We both were satisfied that the wound was a superficial one and that he'd make a full recovery. Not another speck of blood was found after we jumped him on top, an indication that the healing process had already started. We both felt we had exhausted every possibility to find him if he had been mortally wounded and left the woods knowing we had given it our best effort. Maybe I'd get a second opportunity at him later that season or the next year when he'd be bigger. However, you could count on him being wiser and more cautious, as well!

It had been a memorable day on old Stonehill. If I had any doubts before that day about the effect of the rut on buck activity, then I certainly became a believer with my near miss plus five other bucks found in that one small area. Who knows what other buck activity occurred on the farm that day!

My memory of that peak-of-the rut day at Stonehill Farm is quite vivid. It was a day filled with excitement, surprises, hope, and disappointment. However, through all the emotional ups and downs one fact stands out: November 12, 1988 marked the beginning of Dennis Donnelly's bowhunting career, and his whitetail successes since attest to his knowledge, perseverance, and skill.

A valued friendship and hunting relationship was born that day!

II.   "Big Boy" - November, 1989

I kept in touch with Tim and Dennis during the off-season and received immediate feedback of buck sightings from Tim's daily travels about the farm. One such late summer conversation grabbed my attention when Tim reported seeing a group of bachelor bucks, one of which was a "monster" carrying at least 10 points. Though the buck was still in the velvet, Tim could tell from his overall mass that the dominant buck's antlers had the tall, wide, and heavy trophy quality that any hunter would drool over. When I mentioned the buck to Dennis he told me it might have been the same one he missed during shotgun season two years earlier. He had taken a long, low-percentage shot to the top of the ridge from the low stand on Stonehill, but couldn't resist the temptation due to the buck's size. He said if his was the same deer Tim had seen with two additional years of growth, then he must be *really* big! From that day on, we referred to that buck as "Big Boy"!

Tim saw the big whitetail on two other occasions before opening day rolled around. By that time, all my preparation, scouting, and thoughts were geared to one objective—finding and getting an opportunity to harvest "Big Boy"!

For me, opening day of New Jersey's bow season was more symbolic than productive. It represented a change of seasons, a time to put away the golf clubs and crank up the old compound, an opportunity to get *into* the woods after spending the summer "rounds" trying to stay *out* of them. My excitement and anticipation levels were always high at the start of each bow season, but more with respect to the entire season ahead versus opening day per se. I regarded those late September/early October days as an extension of my preseason scouting; continuing to look for fresh sign and trails and watching for deer movement and travel patterns between bedding and feeding areas to determine the best stand locations.

Being a "buck" hunter and especially with a specific challenge and goal set for the fall of 1989, I was realistic enough to know my best and perhaps only chance at "Big Boy" would come during the mid-November rut, when he might let his guard down just long enough to make a mistake in my favor. In the meantime, he'd have no reason to divert from his safe pattern of nocturnal feeding and spending daylight hours bedded in heavy thickets or standing corn.

Until Tim harvested the farm's corn crop in late October, Stonehill's deer had those vast acres of additional cover and protection. Thereafter, their concealment was reduced and limited to the woods, thickets, and darkness of night. Big mature bucks, like the one I was pursuing, take full advantage of the nocturnal factor as their prime survival option and, generally, violate their seclusion routine only when the stronger mating urge takes over during the brief prerut and rut periods each fall. For that reason, my expectation for any premature encounter with "Big Boy" was low.

The weather also contributed to my casual "come what may" early season attitude. Early fall temperatures are usually quite balmy, if not summerlike, and make long hours on stand quite comfortable, but don't provide the mood and atmosphere of those crisp mornings and evenings later on! Warm is to golf as cold is to hunting!

Trees and bushes carrying their full compliment of leaves give the deer another early season advantage regarding good concealment, low detection, and narrower shooting lanes. However, once those leaves fall, the woods open up for the bowhunter, providing advantages not available previously. Dry leaves signal a deer's approach long before it comes into view, allowing valuable time for the archer to shift into shooting position without being seen or heard. Those early season "sight" and "sound" advantages enjoyed by the deer slowly shift to the bowhunter's side of the ledger as changes in cover and rut-induced behavior occur.

October 1989 passed without even a glimpse of my trophy objective. I hunted him hard and often during that month on both sides of Muhlenbrink Road and from many stand locations. After staying on stand until 9:30 or 10:00 a.m., I'd still-hunt for another couple of hours, always looking for tracks, rubs, or any sign that would indicate his presence. All efforts failed.

Early November in the Northeast marks the prerut, a time when scrapes start to appear, mapping the territories of those dominant bucks preparing for the busy breeding period ahead. Increased testosterone levels cause the bucks to flex their muscles by sparring with other males which will soon be their archrivals competing for mating rights among the does. When the rut nears its peak - namely, that 24 to 48-hour window when does reach estrus and are ready to be bred - dominant bucks guard their expanded breeding territory with a vengeance, chase off smaller satellite bucks, and sometimes engage in ferocious fights when other dominant bucks invade their turf. Dominant bucks do the majority of the breeding to ensure that the best genes will be passed along, and it's not uncommon for such animals to lose 20% of their body weight during the rut. Constant checking of scrape lines for receptive does and breeding takes precedence over all else; a 24 hours-per-day activity leaving little or no time for eating. Another indication of prerut activity is the appearance of fresh "rubs" on trees where the bark is removed in shreds by bucks rubbing their antlers against it, an annual fall ritual caused by those chemical changes leading up to the rut. It is believed such rubbing serves the dual purpose of strengthening their neck muscles for defensive purposes and for leaving identifying scent from their preorbital glands located just forward of the antler bases.

The sudden appearance of such prerut sign throughout the woods bordering Stonehill Farm's newly-cut cornfields set the stage for my hunt on Saturday, November 11th.

Conditions were perfect as I drove down the farm lane towards my customary parking spot behind the barn. The forecast, which called for seasonably cool temperatures, clear skies, and no rain, was right on the mark. It was 40 degrees on that moonless night, and the stars shown brightly. A glance at the thread hanging from my Bronco II's aerial indicated no wind. During the 20- minute drive to the farm, I kept thinking back to the six-buck day on Stonehill that Dennis and I had experienced the previous year. With the rut again in full swing, I was hoping that "Big Boy" had added the Stonehill area to his breeding territory. After applying my camo makeup and making a last minute equipment check, I headed for the familiar permanent stand on the north side of Stonehill!

I took extra pains to approach the stand with a minimum of noise, slowly sliding my boots through the leaves toe-and-heel fashion, feeling for twigs and branches as if they were land mines! By 5:15 a.m., I was on stand and ready for whatever happened. Other than a grey squirrel scampering through the leaves, the woods were quiet. Muffled sounds of distant traffic and an occasional dog's bark from a neighboring farm broke the silence at varying intervals as the minutes ticked by. By 6:00 a.m. I hadn't seen even a doe let alone anything with antlers! The sun rose, strings of Canada geese traded back and forth, but still no deer. By 7:00, any hope for a repeat of the previous year's buck frenzy was fading rapidly! At that point, the appearance of a "spike" buck would have been a welcome event!

At 7:30, three does emerged from a distant hedgerow, slowly walked the perimeter of a cut cornfield, then disappeared into the woods at the far corner. Watching them helped pass the time and lifted my spirits slightly in what was thus far a disappointing day. Maybe I was wrong to build up my expectation level, but everything seemed so "right". After six bucks the previous year under similar conditions, I didn't think it was unreasonable to expect *some* buck activity again. However, upon further reflection, I realized that each situation is different, that there are no guarantees in hunting. To assume otherwise, let alone to feel entitled to certain results, is wrong. Faulty or unrealistic expectations can only lead to letdowns and disappointments! Who needs that!

At 8:25, my reflective trance was broken by the rhythmic sound of hooves crunching dry leaves, faintly at first, but increasing in volume with each step. Whatever was causing the noise was near the top of the ridge behind me and to my right (I was facing the cut cornfield with my back to Stonehill). I stood statue-still, afraid that the slightest movement would reveal my location. I could feel the breeze that accompanied the sunrise against the back of my neck, and I was relieved that my scent would not reach the approaching visitor! The sound filling my ears was being made by a single deer, a *large* single deer! There's a telltale difference between the *pitapat* step of a young doe and the heavy, swaggering gait of an old buck. I didn't even have to look to know what was heading my way. My long- awaited confrontation with "Big Boy" was at hand!

My heart was racing as I turned my head ever so slowly to the right, my eyes straining to pick up any movement. Suddenly, I saw him working his way down the side of the hill, more majestic in appearance than I had imagined! He was 60 yards away, and his steady, measured pace and regal air was befitting such a king surveying his domain. His body size was awesome, a conservative 230 pounds on the hoof, and his heavy chest and shoulder muscles rippled with every step. As he closed the distance between us to 40 yards, his huge dark antlers grew even bigger; a beautiful, symmetrical rack with five long tines on both sides including generous brow tines. I also noticed a two-inch long "sticker" point on his back left "G-2" tine, which rose 12 to 14 inches off the main beam. The enormous full curl of those massive main beams came within four inches of touching in front, and the inside spread carried well beyond his outstretched ears.

His calm demeanor displayed no awareness of my presence. I had managed to turn my body sideways in agonizingly short increments and noted that his diagonal path would bring him within 10 yards of my stand if he continued on course. At such close proximity, I couldn't risk the slightest movement until he passed in front of my low perch. Then, once out of his line of vision, I could take a quartering-away shot behind his left shoulder at no more than 15 yards. At least I had a game plan. Now all that "Big Boy" had to do was cooperate!

173

At a distance of 30 paces, he stopped in front of a large hardwood and tested the air. He looked in my direction and worked his ears back and forth. I was downwind and well-concealed behind one of the stand's support trees, so my only risk was movement. He was standing to my right front, and since my bow was hanging on the left side of the tree, any attempt at a shot would have entailed too much shifting and motion. My only option was to hope he resumed his original route. Another 5 or 10 yards would put him within decent range for a shot if I dared, although it would be risky and difficult to raise my bow and draw without being detected. Time stood still as the standoff continued.

I'll never know why or what caused "Big Boy" to stop where he did. Maybe bucks that survive several hunting seasons and grow to be his size develop some uncanny sixth sense when it comes to detecting danger. Whatever the reason, that magnificent trophy turned to his right and walked directly away from me! At about 40 yards he paused again, as if knowing he was safely out of reasonable bow range, and scanned the woods ahead. From my rear view, I marveled at the awesome proportion and spread of his antlers, and in a desperate attempt to get him to change direction, I blew my grunt call. He turned his head to the right, which gave me momentary pause for optimism, but apparently I wasn't convincing enough. He continued his forward movement. I figured my only remaining option was to somehow get to the ground and stalk him, but I dismissed any possibility of that idea succeeding as quickly as it came to mind.

The drama ended abruptly when I inadvertently brushed against the tree that had served as my concealment. The resulting sound was both just loud enough and alien enough to trigger his uphill flight. I can still picture those powerful, almost laborious bounds that carried him to the crest of Stonehill, then a split-second hesitation and backward glance before disappearing over the top. It's as if that last gesture was his way of telling me he was still the "king" of those woods and planned to stay that way! I quietly lauded his survival instincts, and, although I never saw "Big Boy" again, I felt privileged to have had that one memorable encounter.

III.   The "Vortex" - 1991 Opening Day Nine Pointer

I spent the entire 1990 bow season in pursuit of "Big Boy" without ever seeing him. I hadn't heard or read any stories of his demise by either bow, gun, or car, so I was hopeful he would make another appearance. I was concerned that neither Tim nor Dennis had spotted him during that spring or summer, but I wanted to believe he was still alive. To my knowledge, he was never seen again by anyone, but in my mind's eye he will always be just over that next ridge!

As the 1991 archery season approached, I again contacted Tim Arner for the latest information on crop plantings and deer sightings. Included in his update was news about a good buck that one of his workers had seen on several occasions entering a small patch of woods on the "Vortex" part of the farm. I knew the cover he was talking about and decided to scout it out the following weekend, which would be just one week away from the September 28th opener.

Prior to my scouting mission, I studied my aerial map of the area and was interested to see that the oval-shaped, eight-acre woodlot was completely surrounded by cornfields. A narrow, tree-lined ravine extended from those woods to Muhlenbrink Road, a distance of about 250 yards. The ravine served as a perfect funnel for deer traveling from the farm side of Muhlenbrink Road to the Vortex side, and the patch of woods seemed like a natural bedding or holding area for deer using the surrounding cornfields as their main food source! I was excited about the prospects and eager to give the area a thorough inspection!

My scouting mission confirmed my earlier thoughts and revealed much more. Fresh tracks and droppings covered the narrow strip leading to the main body, and multiple, fresh trails led to briar thickets within the woods itself. My aerial photographs made the woodlot appear level with the surrounding cornfields when in fact it was recessed like a basin. As I walked along the wood's perimeter looking for trails leading to and from the corn, I peered down into its interior, looking and listening for deer activity. I eventually found a fresh trail and opening in the tree line, and, just as I started down the slope, a buck jumped from its bed and exited on the opposite side into the sanctuary of the standing corn! That was all the confirmation I needed that I had found a "hot spot"! I immediately aborted my scouting activity in order to leave the area undisturbed until my return on opening day.

Since I had to work prior to the Saturday opener, I didn't have an opportunity to select a good tree, let alone set up my portable stand ahead of time, which I would have preferred to do. I could only make a mental note to allow sufficient time for the extra work I'd be faced with.

Opening day of bow season 1991 was mild and dry with no wind. I planned my setup strategy on the way to my parking spot at the end of the gravel road leading to the Vortex installation and running parallel to my targeted area on the left.

I entered the woods on the near side, having felt my way through the darkness and shrouded rows of corn. I walked slowly, being careful not to bang my tree stand or bow against the stalks. I used my Mini-Maglite flashlight as little as possible to prevent detection and kept its beam as narrow as possible when I did. My progress was slow, often having to back off when heavy patches of briar blocked my path. After penetrating the tree line where the bedded buck had exited during the previous week's scouting trip, I estimated the bottom of the "basin" to be 30 yards wide before sloping upwards to the cornfield on the other side. I wanted to set up in the bottom of that basin area and knew if I hit the upslope, I would have gone too far. Such was my "compass" as I groped along in the dark!

I finally reached the desired location and was immediately faced with the task of selecting an appropriate tree with no obstructing branches to install my wind-in steps and portable stand. In order to minimize noise and save time while completing that arduous task, I waited for more light. I wanted my first choice to be my last! As black turned to gray, I looked directly ahead and quickly identified my tree of choice. Fifteen minutes later I was perched 15 feet above the ground with screw-in portable seat and bow hanger in place. The dawn of a new bow season was fast approaching.

Opening day excitement is difficult to explain to anyone who's never experienced it personally. It would be the same as someone trying to explain the exhilaration of a bungy jump to me. You can only truly know by doing. For me, the **excitement** part of hunting has more to do with the anticipation of events, the mystique and suspense associated with the unknown, the lack of predictability, and the challenge, than with the actual outcome itself, successful or not!

At first light the woods was dead still, and only the *honking* of migrating Canada geese overhead broke the silence. I was relieved that my stand was positioned correctly, facing the cornfield at the top of the 15-foot slope, which put its edge at eye level. A well-defined deer trail passed within feet of my tree and extended from the far end of the woods on my left to a heavy thicket of briars 30 yards to my right. The woods continued beyond the briars for another 25 yards to the adjacent corn. Since I was near that northern end of the woodlot, I had a commanding view of its entire edge in front, to the right, and behind me. The trees were spaced far enough apart to provide good shooting lanes in all directions, and the heavy ground cover of briars and honeysuckle did not hinder a good shot from above. A ground blind would have been completely ineffective from both a sighting and shooting standpoint. Besides providing a wider field of view and unobstructed shots, tree stands placed high above the ground keep a hunter's odor above the game and permit greater freedom of movement without being detected.

I was facing the cornfield, alert for any movement or sound. My bow was hanging within easy reach, arrow nocked. At 7 a.m. a single deer entered the woodlot from the cornfield 30 yards to my left. It stopped momentarily behind a mound to check out its new surroundings, then entered a patch of honeysuckle. I saw only its body, so I still didn't know if it was a buck or doe. I did like the fact that it was traveling alone and was displaying the wariness of a buck. I already had gripped my bow and removed it from its hanger when the deer emerged from the cover heading in my direction. It *was* a buck, and he had a nice, multi-pointed, tight set of antlers. He reached the trail and continued toward me for 10 paces before pausing between two trees. I smiled to myself since I had paced off the distance to the tree on his right just before climbing into my stand. It was exactly 20 paces, which equated to a 20-yard shot!

He seemed nervous, as if he sensed danger, but couldn't determine what it was or where it came from. He held his position and moved his head left and right with both ears cupped and moving in every which direction in an attempt to identify any foreign sounds. That movement afforded me a good look at his antlers, and I quickly counted four points per side on his small, but well-proportioned headgear. He was a worthy trophy by any bowhunter's standards, and the conclusion of my analysis and assessment was to attempt a shot if and/or when the opportunity presented itself. He was already within range, but his body angle and the brush presented problems. He wasn't quite in a head-on position, but his stance would have required a very precise shot into the partially exposed lung area—not a high percentage shot. It was further complicated by the deflection potential of the tangled cover that reached mid-body. I had no reasonable choice but to wait for the buck to move into a better position. I just hoped his growing nervousness wouldn't cause that next movement to be one of flight! Such shoot or wait decisions determine success or failure for most hunters, but the pressure created by those make or break choices is a meaningful part of the total hunting experience.

After a few short minutes, which seemed a *lot* longer, the buck stepped to his left presenting the broadside shot I had hoped for. Without hesitation I drew, placed my 20-yard pin just behind his shoulder, and made a smooth release. The dependable Easton aluminum shaft flew straight and true to its mark, penetrating high in the buck's lung area. He immediately "swapped ends" and ran out of sight down the trail. I felt good about the shot and felt confident he would not go far. After his initial post-impact burst, he quickly slowed to an unsteady walk, which told me the hemorrhaging process was well under way. I waited 20 minutes, then climbed down from my stand and went to where my arrow made contact. I found blood almost immediately and my arrow 10 feet beyond. Its entire length was covered with the bubbly, crimson substance that indicated a lethal, double-lung hit. I found him piled up a mere 30 yards down the trail. Death had come swiftly.

He was a healthy young deer, probably about two years old. A closer inspection of his rack revealed an additional one-inch sticker point protruding from the base of his left antler. I was proud of my accomplishment, gaining special satisfaction from the fact that I had put all the pieces together, from scouting and stand placement to the shot itself, to achieve my success. Of my 10 whitetail bow kills to that point, he was by far my best buck. Little did I realize that he would soon become my second best!

IV.   Return to the Vortex - 1991

With my opening day success, I had the balance of the "regular" **and** "extended" fall bow seasons to hunt for a bigger trophy. (I had been successful in my application for the coveted "extended" season, which covered the important November rut and carried through the first Saturday in December.) In addition, New Jersey provided a three-week winter bow season in January, and **each** of the three seasons entitled a hunter to two deer of either sex! Add to that number a maximum of four more bucks or does during the shotgun and muzzleloader seasons, and New Jersey's total allowable annual harvest per hunter was one of the most generous in the United States at the time!

Just as the answer to the question "how do you eat an elephant" is "one bite at a time", so too my bowhunting success could only be measured by one buck at a time! I returned to the Vortex at my first opportunity.

I had stopped by Dennis Donnelly's house to show him my opening day buck, and he was genuinely excited for me. If there's one true test of who your good hunting buddies are, or should be, they're the ones who show unselfish support for and sincere delight in others' success. Tim Arner and Dennis are two such people, and since Dennis was just getting into bowhunting, I was determined to contribute to **his** first "score". I was convinced other bucks were using that same woodlot where I had taken my nine pointer, so I offered to give Dennis a personal tour and set him up. Being the good sportsman he is, he was reluctant to horn in on "my" territory, but finally bowed to my insistence. I told him there were other Vortex areas I wanted to explore and was happy to relinquish my proven spot.One of the spots I had in mind was a strip of woods that bordered a small unplanted field several hundred yards east of Dennis' newly inherited territory. In fact, that field was adjacent to the cut cornfield where I had been goose hunting the day I met Tim. On that day I made a mental note of the promising habitat for deer and was eager to take a closer look.

My new stand site was on the "long" west side of the rectangular 100 by 200-yard field, with a head-high briar thicket on the north, a mature pine grove on the east, and a narrow hedgerow on the south, with said cornfield on the opposite side. I could almost "feel" the deers' presence. Fresh sign was everywhere, and deer trails crisscrossed the field at close intervals. During my initial visit, I followed one such trail into the woods and found a great tree for my stand at the intersection of another trail only 15 yards inside the woodline.

As far as I was concerned, my primary objective on that afternoon hunt with Dennis was to help him get his deer. I was content to use my stand time for scouting purposes, hoping to see or hear deer to pattern their movements for future hunts and hoped-for success. I was resigned to collecting information, not venison.

After wishing Dennis "Good Luck", I doused my scent pads with cover scent and headed for my new tree, with stand, seat, and bow in hand. It was 3:30 p.m. when I carefully made my way along the edge of the field, surveying the area as I walked. I entered the woods on the trail that led to the base of my preselected tree.

I gently laid my bow on the ground and went to work screwing in my eight metal steps, which took me to a height of 15 feet. There, with one foot on the top step and the other on a branch, I secured my stand and seat. After putting my full weight on both, I felt confident that the combination of sharp metal prongs and support braces dug into the bark and heavy chains wrapped around the trunk would hold both solidly in place throughout my vigil. My final chore was to place the bow hanger at the correct height and angle so I could easily reach and remove my bow from a sitting position. That done, I sat down with my back against the trunk. It was four o'clock.

I was facing the field with the deer trail on my left only five feet from the base of my tree. Other trees grew in clusters, and all still had their leaves, which partially blocked my view of the field. I made a final visual check of my Hoyt-Easton compound, bjorn-nocked arrow, sight pins, arm guard, and finger tabs. I had already cleaned my glasses, and a safety strap held them snugly to my head. Only 10 minutes had passed since I sat down.

Any deer hunter with serious stand time under his belt has watched the stealthy movements of deer in their habitat and experienced their sudden ghostlike appearance in a spot that a blink before was empty. It's uncanny and quite nerve-wracking!

To this day, I can't explain how he got there. I only know that 30 seconds later a seven-point, wide-racked, big-bodied buck was standing on the trail 10 yards below me! He was facing me, which meant he had entered the woods on the same trail I had used only moments before. Hadn't he heard me or seen me setting up? I couldn't believe what I was seeing, assuming it wasn't an illusion.

Once the surprise wore off, I knew I had to take action with no time to waste. He was standing still sniffing the air, with his ears moving constantly to detect any foreign sounds. I remained "frozen" in my seat, fearful that even the slightest twitch on my part would send him on his way. I felt certain he hadn't smelled me or he wouldn't have come that far, but his head-on position at such a close distance would enable him to detect any unnatural movement.

Unless he turned and faced away, my only chance to reach, remove, and draw my bow would be to time his head movements. When he put his nose to the trail, I inched forward on my seat and slid my feet under me. When he raised his head, I froze. When he turned his head to his right, I reached forward with my left hand and grabbed the bow's grip. When his head returned to the forward position or turned to his left, I froze again. The next time he sniffed the trail, I was able to raise the bow off its rest and slowly pull it toward me, and at the same time shift my body to the right to get into a better shooting position. That slow motion start-and- stop process continued for at least five minutes, and the buck seemed to be getting more nervous by the second. He hadn't moved one foot forward since all this started, but then he suddenly turned to his left as if to retrace his steps back to the field. His move took me out of his direct line of vision and gave me a perfect broadside shot. Without hesitation, I stood and drew in one motion, placed my 10- yard pin behind his shoulder, and released. The arrow hit high, but I felt the downward angle would produce the lung penetration I wanted. At impact he completed his turn and raced into and across the field. The trees, which had prevented my seeing his entrance, also prevented me from seeing where he entered the pines on the other side. However, I felt confident the buck was mine, and since it was not yet 4:30, I gave him time to lie down; hopefully, for the last time.

As I followed his deeply-splayed and widely-spaced tracks across the field, I didn't find either one drop of blood or my arrow along the way. That indicated to me that the arrow was still in him, and with only an entrance cut, most, if not all, of the bleeding would be internal. With no blood sign, I had only his hoof prints to rely on for tracking purposes. That sole option was not what I had hoped for, but it seemed like a workable solution, ***until*** I reached the needle-covered floor of the pine forest. The needles not only made tracking more difficult, but the amount of recent deer activity in that area made distinguishing my buck's tracks an impossibility! I felt helpless as I meandered to my left through the pines, sometimes even crawling with the hope of finding upturned needles or one fresh track in an occasional patch of dirt. I reached the northern end of the pines without success and decided to go back to his last known tracks where he entered the pines from the field. Once located, I turned right and continued my search in the direction of the hedgerow. Twenty paces later his white underside caught my eye as he lay dead under some low-hanging pine boughs!

I was relieved and ecstatic as I ran to examine my trophy! My arrow was still in place, having penetrated to one half its length through both lungs. I lifted his head and counted four points on the left and three on the right. His rack was considerably heavier and wider than my previous "best", and I just sat there for a few moments reviewing the quick succession of events that had occurred during that last hour. I savored my accomplishment.

After field dressing the buck and dragging him back to my vehicle, I went back to retrieve my bow and other gear. When Dennis returned to the car after dark, he could tell from my face that my good luck was still intact! Again, he was as excited as I was about my good fortune, and I reviewed every detail with him as we loaded the buck into my Bronco II for the ride to Tim's house.

I enjoyed each and every whitetail hunt at Stonehill Farm and had other successes, misses, encounters, and sightings, including a rare eight-point albino buck. I'll be forever grateful to Tim Arner for opening the farm's gates to me and for the hunting enjoyment that followed. Most important to me are the friendships I developed with Tim and Dennis and their families, and I will value them for the rest of my life!

It should be noted that in 1993 Stonehill Farm was purchased for a reported $6 million by its new "boss", singer Bruce Springsteen, and "No Hunting" signs were posted immediately. It just made me that much more thankful that I had enjoyed my hunting time there while the opportunity existed!

Kim and loyal lab companion, "Freddy", next to the tree used to take the "Vortex" nine pointer

Kim and handsome nine pointer taken in woodlot "basin" near the "Vortex" on Stonehill Farm

My smile reflects the pleasure of having harvested these fine seven and nine-point whitetail bucks with a bow on Stonehill Farm

A happy hunter and his "Vortex" seven pointer taken with a Hoyt-Easton 60-pound compound and Easton aluminum arrows with Razorbak-4 broadheads

Dennis Donnelly: great friend, great hunter!

Chapter 13: Wyoming - "Pronghorn" Country (1992)

At one time there were an estimated 50 million antelope roaming the American plains, but, like the bison, they were practically annihilated by the end of the 1800's. In the 1920's only an estimated 13,000 animals remained, but through successful conservation programs, today's population approaches one million!

Ron Platt of <u>Platt's Guides and Outfitters</u> is one of Wyoming's foremost and most successful antelope icons. I don't recall where I first heard about Ron's expertise in helping his clients consistently harvest some of the best bucks, but I do know my hunting adventure with him did nothing to hurt his reputation.

Ron and his wife, Mayvon, own a large ranch near Encampment, Wyoming about 15 miles northwest of the Wyoming/Colorado state line on Highway 230. Between their summer pack trips and fall hunting trips for elk, mule deer, bighorn sheep, black bear, mountain lion, and trophy antelope, the Platt family operation is busy year round. Through 1991, Ron had been a multiple winner of the Wyoming Outfitters Association competition for best trophies, capturing the #1 award for antelope at least five times along with many #2's and #3's, as well. With over 35 years of experience outfitting in the south central part of Wyoming, I felt confident I'd be in good hands when I placed my call in late January 1992.

Ron instructed me to contact the Wyoming Game and Fish Department in Cheyenne to obtain their 1992 *Nonresident Hunting Information and Applications* and suggested I fill out the "special" antelope permit application. Even though the cost was higher than the regular permit ($250 versus $150), it would almost ensure my success in the July 15 draw. Ron reminded me of the March 15 application deadline and told me to send him the completed application for preferential processing. He had achieved tremendous success on trophy antelope during his private land hunts and recommended my indicating area #108 as my first choice. His hunts there, approximately 85 miles west of Encampment near Rawlins, were conducted on the Bolton Ranch, 17,000 acres of rolling hills, ravines, and sagebrush, otherwise known as prime antelope country! A buck with 15 to 16-inch horns and good mass scoring in the high 70's to 80-plus Boone and Crockett points was a realistic goal in that area.

As Ron had anticipated, I drew my special permit for area #108, but I was still thrilled since it was one of only 200 limited-quota licenses issued for the September 19 through October 14 season! I immediately booked a standard three-day, 2x1 hunt for September 22-24 and sent in my 1/3 deposit towards Ron's $1,175 fee. Since only one other hunter, John Johnson from Lathrop, California, would be in camp with me, Ron said he'd guide for both of us. All three of us could fit comfortably in his pickup's cab, from which we could do our glassing. Once a shootable buck was spotted, we'd flip a coin to determine who would get the first stalk and shot, then alternate thereafter until we both scored.

Ensuing conversations with Ron included the customary discussions about equipment, clothing, rifles, and ammunition. He concurred that my trusty Remington .30-.06 was adequate for most big game, antelope included, and suggested 150-grain cartridges, since the lighter shell would have a flatter trajectory for the long shots normally required. Three inches high at 100 yards would be "right on" at 200 yards, and I could adjust from there. Ron suggested arriving at his ranch around midday on Monday the 21st to zero-in at his range, if need be, before making the two-hour drive to camp. I had planned to fly out early anyway since I had just accepted a job in Denver and wanted to look for a new home, so I arranged my schedule and flight accordingly.

Since temperatures would vary from sub-freezing at night to 60 - 70 degrees during the day, "layering" was the key word with regard to clothing. Other than that, a sleeping bag with ground pad, rain suit, orange vest and hat, and binoculars would take care of my gear requirement. And, oh yes, a good pair of sunglasses to cut the sun's glare and prevent terminal squinting was a recommended inclusion as well! Ron reminded me to obtain the required Wyoming Conservation Stamp, and that I could make the $5 purchase at any sporting goods store upon arrival. With all questions asked and preparations made, I eagerly awaited September's arrival!

I should have known it was going to be a good hunt with Ron, since, upon my early arrival in Colorado, I found my dream home at the top of a mountain in Conifer. Besides offering tremendous views from virtually every window, it had the cathedral ceilings and ample wall space needed for my growing collection of big- game trophies. I immediately put in my bid before heading north to Wyoming and left Ron's phone number with the realtor in case the seller accepted my bid. (He did!)

There was a noticeable change in the topography as I headed north on I-25 past Ft. Collins, Colorado, connecting with Route 287 to Laramie, Wyoming. The Rocky Mountain range gradually faded out of sight to the west and was replaced with great expanses of sagebrush-choked rolling plains and hills interspersed with ravines and small woodlots. The beautiful color mix of Colorado provided by the gray rocks, dark green pine forests, and pockets of aspen - some of which had started turning their mid-October golden yellow - changed to the brown of cut grain fields and pale green of sage. Fewer trees gave an "incomplete" grade to the new landscape. However, it was ideal terrain for antelope, and **they** are what drew me there! I made numerous sightings of sizeable antelope herds during my drive along Route 130 from Laramie to Encampment. I was starting to get excited!

I arrived at Ron's ranch in the early afternoon after stopping to buy my conservation stamp and a quick lunch. His residence is an enormous, modern "lodge" constructed of massive logs, stonework, and other native materials with spacious rooms and large windows affording beautiful views of the distant Medicine Bow National Forest. Ron and Mayvon rebuilt the lodge with their own hands after a fire destroyed the original dwelling, along with many of the big-game trophies belonging to Ron's father. The crown jewel of their rebuilding project was a massive trophy room with numerous specimens of every species of big-game animal available to Ron's clients. Some of the impressive heads and full-bodied mounts were of record book quality taken by both Ron and Mayvon! A family that hunts together stays together!

Since John Johnson hadn't arrived yet, I had time to fire a few rounds from the bed of Ron's Chevy pickup to a 100-yard target set up on an adjacent hillside. I was satisfied with my grouping and felt confident I could hit the small-bodied, but tough "lope" when the opportunity came.

Shortly thereafter John drove up in his diesel truck equipped with an extra fuel tank secured behind the cab. It was not unusual for John to go on multiple hunts each fall, and carrying his own fuel supply saved both time and money as he made his annual loop of several western states. He owned an electrical contracting business in California, but when hunting season rolled around, he put his supervisor in charge and took extended *vacation* time. John was a real character, and his constant chatter included great stories, both hunting and non-hunting. Based on his cowboy hat and boots, suspender-supported jeans, slow drawl, and swagger, I was convinced he was a good old Texas boy until I learned otherwise. But I couldn't have chosen a better companion, and we each were seeking our first antelope buck.

With supplies loaded, John and I formed a caravan behind Ron and headed for the Bolton Ranch. That antelope mecca is located right on the Continental Divide, south of Route 80 and west of Route 71, less than an hour's drive from Encampment. As we neared camp, the rutted dirt roads became very bumpy and dusty. However, during heavy rains those roads became mud holes, which explained Ron's recommendation to have a stable 4WD vehicle in case we encountered bad weather.

Our campsite was in a very picturesque setting. The 10 by 14-foot wall tent used for meals and congregating and two-man sleepers were nestled at the edge of an aspen grove whose leaves had started changing to their golden fall hue. A high ridge collared the grove, and on several occasions curious antelope peered down at our group from the rim. Our view in front was of rolling hills of sagebrush extending for several hundred yards to the base of a flat-topped mountain range. If you can imagine the high-peaked Rockies after a giant machete sliced off the top half then you have an idea of the appearance of those Wyoming cousins! The high point of our location, however, was provided by the nightly star shows. Their dazzling clarity against the pitch-black sky made the constellations appear within one's reach, and most of our evening conversations outside the tents were conducted with heads tilted skyward. Good eye contact aside, it was a marvelous sight!

Ron's game plan was to leave camp at dawn, follow the truck-formed dirt roads until we spotted a herd, then glass to find any good bucks and decide if they were of trophy quality. Ron reminded both of us that patience would pay off with good trophies since the ranch contained many quality bucks, several of which would exceed the Boone and Crockett 82-points minimum. Since neither of us had shot an antelope, he cautioned against wanting to take the first *decent* buck we saw. Ron assured us he could pick out the real "keepers" from the average heads and said to trust his judgement and experience. He further boosted our confidence by adding that the hunt was scheduled for only three days for a reason: antelope could be found in greater numbers in more open areas than other game animals. Our shots would come. ***Choice*** was the big factor.

There's something special about the first day of a hunt, when the feelings of anticipation, confidence, and excitement are at their optimum. Thereafter, as each day passes without success, each or all suffer and decline to some degree. Some hunters give up, at least mentally, and that's usually when "the hunted" widen their advantage and catch their human pursuers well below their maximum levels of alertness and concentration! Quite often one's success or failure in taking a trophy big-game animal depends on a five-second period of decision and action. Those caught napping or flat-footed are the same ones you later hear relating their "coulda, shoulda, woulda" stories around the campfire. As master guide and Colorado outfitter Dick Pennington once told me, ***preparation*** and ***anticipation*** separate the successful hunters from the unsuccessful. The first determinant takes place before the hunt as far as physical conditioning and familiarization with one's firearm and ammunition, and the second factor occurs in the field, being ready at all times for that trophy of a lifetime to appear and taking immediate action to put him in the "win" column!

John and I had matching "readiness" readings of 100% that first day as Ron headed his truck toward the crest of the ridge behind our camp and the rolling prairies that laid beyond. We all had good quality binoculars, plus Ron had his window-mounted spotting scope to gain a "second opinion" once a respectable head was spotted. Antelope can withstand the midday sun and heat better than most game such as deer and elk; therefore, they remain visible for longer periods, which eliminates the need to follow the typical pattern of hunting the dawn and dusk hours when much game is moving to or from their bedding and feeding areas. In addition, antelope have superior eyesight and an ability to run at speeds exceeding 60 miles per hour, enabling them to elude or avoid danger from most predators. Unfortunately for them, the modern rifle cartridge travels faster!

Within an hour after our departure we sighted a small herd of pronghorns 500 yards away. Among the group was one very promising buck that each of us glassed for some time. Its horn length and mass were good, and he had large, curved prongs. Ron thought the horns were in the 15-inch range, which he considered only average and would keep its scoring in the 70's at best. Overall, he felt it was a nice trophy and one that I could be proud of if I decided to take him. I concurred, and since I had won the first shot coin toss at breakfast, I decided to attempt a stalk. Wind is not as important as keeping out of sight when it comes to getting within "comfortable" shooting range, which in my case would be about 300 yards, give or take a few! Therefore, within minutes of leaving John behind in the truck, Ron and I were belly-crawling through the sagebrush with only an occasional "peek" to check the position and mood of our target. We had closed the distance to about 400 yards when Ron suggested I try a shot. There was a possibility of working a bit closer, but the herd was looking our way, which meant they were alerted to and suspicious of our presence. Therefore, my only option seemed to be to try a shot. I was as concerned about the stiff breeze and using the unstable sage as a rest as I was with the distance, but those factors would have been present even if I had shortened the distance by another 25 to 50 yards. I decided to make the best of it. The buck was broadside facing to my right, and when the group convinced themselves they weren't in imminent danger, I made my final preshot movements to get as comfortable and steady as possible. I allowed for a six to eight-inch drop for the 150-grain cartridge over the calculated distance and figured a similar wind drift from left to right. With all numbers crunched, I placed the crosshairs at the top and middle of his back, took a deep breath, exhaled slowly, and pulled the trigger. At the report, dirt kicked up above the buck's back, and all members gave a momentary look our way before bolting in unison. They were in high gear within seconds, and their quick exit prevented a second shot. The miss left me with mixed feelings; initial disappointment at not accomplishing my goal replaced quickly with the promise of other, and possibly better opportunities!

With my miss I also had to pass the baton to John for the next try, and his opportunity came in short order. As we topped a ravine, a herd of 30 antelope were grazing and walking on a right to left diagonal path away from us. Ron looked at the largest of the five bucks in the group, and his excitement was immediate. Ron had glassed tens of thousands of antelope over the years, but he was as excited as a kid on Christmas morning gazing at that particular specimen! When John and I focused on the object of Ron's affection, we knew instantly why he had reacted as he had. The majestic trophy carried high, heavy, and widespread horns with horseshoe-shaped curves and ivory tips. Large, deep prongs added the crowning touch to the wonderful symmetry of that rare buck. Ron felt for sure he would score in the mid 80's or better, with a horn length of over 17 inches! John and Ron made a cautious stalk only to have John "blow" a standing broadside shot at 200 yards. The herd instantly ran into the next county, and, with that, our score was tied at "0". Ron was as disappointed as John about the big one that got away, since there's an ongoing competition among outfitters to have their clients harvest the biggest and the best to secure bragging rights and, more importantly, bookings based on their success. John's potential buck was just such a catalyst! Even with the disappointment, Ron was optimistic about locating the big buck again, since antelope are territorial, choosing home ranges from one half to one mile in size.

Once again I was in the "shooter's" seat, eager to find another big pronghorn. We ate lunch in the truck and continued to drive and glass the vast expanses of the ranch. By mid-afternoon we had scrutinized several bands, but none of the groups held a buck that met Ron's minimum standards. The great thing about hunting is that fortunes can change in a minute, and I was about to experience such a swift turn of events.

As we proceeded along a ridgetop, we spotted a large group of antelope to our left at a distance of 800 to 1000 yards. Our binoculars revealed a mature, long-horned lead buck trying to control his harem of 15 to 20 does with mixed success. As he darted after one straying female to bring her back into the fold, another would break away, and he'd give chase with the same determination. That pattern continued for 10 minutes, and all the while the entire herd was moving uphill to our left. Ron and I agreed that this "herd master" was a good one, with good length and prongs, although lacking the heaviness of that morning's "king". I told Ron I'd like to try for him, and we immediately planned our stalk. With the herd heading up and left on an elevated flat area between two ravines, we decided to hustle down to the left ravine from our high lookout and use its cover to make our approach. If everything worked as planned, we would then walk and crawl up the side of the ravine to an ambush point within 300 yards of the unsuspecting buck. Don't think you can't get winded scrambling downhill. We knew we had no time to waste in order to reach our interception point, and I was right on Ron's heels as he scampered toward the ravine. It should be noted that *scampering* takes on a different meaning when one has Ron's 6'3" wiry 170-pound frame, versus my 6'0" 210-pound bulk!

The buck and his ladies continued moving in the same general direction as we steadily narrowed the distance between us. By the time we reached our target depression, 500 yards separated us. We then scooted another 200 yards, bent over at the waist to keep as low a profile as possible without sacrificing too much speed. We finally reached the point where our 15 foot ascent to the top of the ravine commenced. Within a couple of minutes, we peeked over the edge and spotted my trophy standing broadside on a knoll above us, outlined by the clear blue sky! Ron calculated the range at 375 yards while I chambered a 150-grain Winchester Silvertip and got a comfortable rest for my shot. I figured I needed to hold over its back to allow for the drop at that distance, but my first shot was a clean miss! No dirt kicked up beneath the buck, so the logical conclusion was that I had missed high. He held his position. I quickly lowered my point of aim from six inches over to the top of his back and touched off round number two. Again, I missed high! At that point the buck was staring our way and starting to move forward. I was frustrated but not frazzled, and, with my mind still focused, I put the crosshairs behind his shoulder and launched my third attempt. This time, the confirming **whomp** of a hit was heard, and the trophy bolted downward to his left and disappeared into the other ravine.

After my first two misses I couldn't be sure where the third shot struck, and, from the way he took off, my first thought was that I hadn't hit a vital area. Otherwise, he would have fallen or at least stumbled! My heart sank and my stomach was doing flip-flops before Ron interrupted with encouraging words. He thought I had made a good hit and felt that even if it were a "gut" shot, it wouldn't go far. Instantly, we ran to the spot where my shot connected to check for blood and hair and mark his escape route. There was no "sign" at the impact area, but 25 yards along his trail we found first blood. We followed the blood trail across the plateau, down and through the brush-choked ravine, and up to the next "flat". As we gained our footing and stood up, Ron pointed ahead and said, "There he is!" I couldn't locate the buck at first glance and tried to follow Ron's point on a tighter path to the buck, again to no avail. Then, on my second visual sweep of the area, I spotted him standing in waist-high grass 100 yards ahead looking back at us over his right shoulder. A quick off-hand shot connected, but, once again, he kept his footing and ran off! Although I admired his tenacity, I knew my hunt was about to end on a positive note! He ran only 50 yards after my second hit before stumbling and falling for the last time.

While helping Ron field dress the buck, I expressed disappointment about my poor shooting. When I described my points of aim on the first two shots to allow for bullet drop, Ron quickly corrected the error of my ways and pinpointed the reason I had missed. He explained that on any shot to a higher elevation I should calculate the distance as if the game were on flat ground, which would be a shorter distance than to the elevated point. It was really a refresher course in high school geometry, where the base of my "shooting" triangle (the accurate 200-yard flat ground distance) was considerably shorter than the 375-yard *hypotenuse* distance I had calculated to the antelope's elevated position. My mistake was in calculating the first two shots at 375 and holding over its back instead of the "true" 200-yard distance, which was why my "right on" third shot connected! After the explanation and realizing my ignorance, I felt fortunate and relieved that my trial and error method had succeeded versus the mathematically correct way. It also made me realize that all of my past hunting successes had resulted from shots at or **below** ground level!

While Ron went to get the truck, I had ample time to examine and admire my pronghorn's beautiful coloration and trophy qualities; coarse, tan and white hair, black cheek patches typical of a mature buck, and the sleek, thin-legged body designed for speed! His matching 15 3/8-inch horns seemed to grow out of the top of his eye sockets, and their curved tips gave a heart-shaped appearance when viewed from the front. He had two small "sticker" points on the inside of each horn just above his generous, curved prongs, and they gave him a mark of distinction. His horns flared from a width of six inches at the base to an outside spread of 12 inches where the crowning three-inch curls began. Overall, he was a trophy to be proud of. Later, back at camp, Ron green-scored him at 77 6/8 which put him well above the Safari Club International's 72-points minimum entry score, but below Boone and Crockett's 82-points minimum. Ron estimated my buck's age between six and seven years, which put him past his peak and may have accounted for his horn's extra protuberances.

With my tag filled, I slept in the next day and hung around camp while Ron took John to try to relocate "The King". They were gone all day, but when they returned there was a 85 3/8 Boone and Crockett trophy buck lying in the bed of the pickup! A perfect ending to John's story would have been that his trophy was the same magnificent animal he had missed the previous day. Only it wasn't! As the story unfolded, Ron **did** locate that huge buck again, and he and John did make a careful stalk to within 100 yards, only to have John miss again! If the first miss was a disappointment, then the second was a disaster! I guess the only thing that can be said about John's uncharacteristic double miss was that it wasn't meant to be. However, he quickly regained his composure and shortly thereafter executed a longer, more difficult shot on his equally impressive trophy.

Hunting causes a lot of head scratching and mumbling from apparent easy chances turning into misses and difficult ones becoming clean, one-shot kills! Sometimes there's just no explanation. However, I have the feeling that John's "consolation" buck soothed his earlier pain and disappointment very quickly. At least that's what his broad, toothy smile told me!

With our two-buck goal accomplished, we prepared to break camp. Ron caped out John's buck just as he had mine the day before. He planned to drop off both capes and sets of horns in Cheyenne with his friend and taxidermist, Don Peel, and have the meat processed at another location. However, before all that was accomplished, we had one last night to spend in that beautiful Wyoming country. We celebrated our success with a delicious meal, a lot of unprintable jokes, and many stories of past hunting trips and experiences under that unforgettable star-filled sky. It was a fitting conclusion to another exciting and enjoyable hunting adventure.

Four months later I drove to Cheyenne to pick up my completed shoulder mount. I was very pleased with Don's masterful work, and by day's end my Wyoming trophy was hanging in my downstair's den. It brought to seven the number of different North American big-game species I have harvested. However, since there are **thirty-eight** big-game categories recognized by the Boone and Crockett Club, I'm sure my time and/or money will run out before I can complete the list!

Ron Platt's Encampment, Wyoming home

A few of Ron's outstanding Wyoming trophies

A view behind our Bolton Ranch camp where antelope
could be seen observing us from the ridgetop

Rolling, sagebrush-covered hills in front of our camp
with flat-topped mountains in the background

(Top left) my hunting partner, John Johnson; (Top right) outfitter and guide, Ron Platt; (Bottom) Ron, John, and camp cooks relax after a hearty meal

Kim poses with his antelope buck, which sported 15 3/8-inch horns and green scored 77 6/8 Boone and Crockett points

Chapter 14: Spur-of-the-Moment Elk Hunt – Eagle, Colorado (1993)

When I moved to Colorado from the East Coast in October 1992, my plate was too full with a new home and job to participate in my newly adopted state's big-game hunting seasons that year. Besides, I didn't have time to determine where to hunt or which of the three big-game rifle seasons would be the best choice for the area chosen. I also needed to satisfy the state's six-month residency requirement to apply for the much less costly resident licenses. With all those needs, pressures, and problems, I decided to do my homework and be better prepared for the 1993 hunting season.

By the time fall 1993 arrived, I had acquired not only the necessary residency time and knowledge of where and when to hunt, but a new wife, too! Having just tied the knot in September, I was somewhat reluctant to leave my bride alone in our mountain home for any extended period of time to go hunting. Something told me that saying "see you in five days, I'm going on an elk hunt" was not the best way to start a marriage! However, Lisa was from a Texas hunting family, and she was quick to note my enthusiasm when I picked up a flyer at a local sporting goods store advertising a private ranch hunt by Triple G Outfitters out of Eagle, Colorado. That was on Saturday, October 16, and the first rifle season had started that day! With a "I don't have anything to lose by calling" thought, I took the flyer home with me.

I spoke with Ike McBride, the one-man owner and guide of Triple G. When he told me he had a prime private ranch loaded with elk, but no hunters signed up for that first 10-day season, I became very interested very fast! Ike told me there were leftover private ranch licenses available, and that he charged only $125 per day with no trophy fee! It all seemed too good to be true; so, after a brief discussion with my very understanding partner, I arranged for a maximum three-day hunt beginning Monday, September 18. That gave me time to pack and make the two-hour drive from Conifer to Eagle to meet Ike on Sunday afternoon.

I wasn't sure if I'd have time to zero-in my trusty old .30-.06 semi-automatic, but I felt confident it was still accurately sighted from the previous year's antelope hunt. To maintain consistency, I decided to use the same 150-grain Winchester Silvertip cartridges I had zeroed-in with and used successfully in Wyoming. Given the opportunity, I would have preferred using the heavier 180- grain cartridge for elk, but the trajectory adjustment I'd have to make wasn't worth the risk or effect on my confidence.

Ike told me there was an old cabin available for my use at the ranch and to bring a sleeping bag to unroll on the couch inside. A woodburning stove would supply the heat if needed, but food and beverages were my responsibility (no surprise at only $125/day!). Ike had two reliable packhorses for us to ride to the ranch's mountain summit. From there we could glass and stalk. Ike also mentioned owning a temperamental mule that he would use to pack out my anticipated bull. I liked his optimistic outlook and looked forward to our agreed 3 p.m. Sunday meeting at the Eagle exit off Interstate 70.

Confident that Lisa was safe and comfortable, I loaded my Blazer 4WD and headed west toward Eagle, approximately 130 miles from my home. As usual, I allowed more travel time than necessary and arrived at our rendezvous point an hour early. However, that extra time served me well, since I met a young man at a local restaurant who had heard of Ike McBride and said he was reputed to be an excellent guide who knew how and where to find elk. The fellow assured me I'd have an enjoyable and, very possibly, successful hunt with Ike!

By the time Ike arrived, my confidence was soaring! He even **looked** like a successful guide complete with jeans, cowboy boots, and a black cowboy hat crowning his rugged Native American features. He had a quiet and pleasant demeanor. After exchanging introductory comments, Ike instructed me to follow him for the nine-mile ride along Brush Creek Road and Bruce Creek Road to the 1,700-acre ranch.

After securing my gear in the cabin, which Ike informed me had served years ago as one of the earliest base lodges for skiing in Colorado, I decided to use the remaining hour of daylight to glass the adjacent meadow and mountainside. Results were immediate! I had no sooner set up my Bushnell Trophy spotting scope on the hood of my Blazer than a herd of approximately 50 elk materialized. My head check revealed five bulls, including a nice 4x4 and handsome 5x6! Their leisurely feeding pace indicated no immediate plan to vacate the area, and I was hopeful they would be there come sunrise! Everything seemed to be falling into place very nicely. With nothing more to do than wait for Ike's return with his horses the next morning, I retraced my route to our meeting point to have dinner, purchase some extra supplies and food, and call Lisa to let her know everything was going smoothly at my end. She assured me that all was well with her – a new novel and warm fire filling my void very nicely, thank you! Content that everything was all right, I returned to the cabin and set the alarm for 5 a.m.

I was up in an instant when the clock buzzed me awake at the appointed hour. I poked my head outside the door, felt the chilled air, and decided to wear more than less. Layering works only if you have enough clothes on to take off, and I recalled those times past when I anticipated warming trends that never developed and spent many bone-chilling hours wishing I had started out with those Damarts and down-filled vest! After downing some "O.J." and doughnuts, I gazed through the frosted cabin window awaiting Ike's arrival. He said he'd be there by 6:00 a.m., and I had begun to worry about his oversleeping when he finally pulled up at 6:45. He didn't seem at all doubtful about locating the herd I had spotted, giving me the impression he knew their habits and movement patterns quite well and that we had plenty of time to find them. Ike's nonchalant manner was both comforting and reassuring and conveyed the message, "Everything's under control. There's no need to worry."

After Ike saddled the horses, we rode past the weathered red barn and corral toward the base of the mountain on the eastern end of the ranch's expansive acreage. Ike's strategy was to follow the winding trail to the crest, hitch the horses, then continue on foot to the ridgetop where we could start glassing.

One of my first observations about Ike McBride that morning was the absence of any optics – spotting scope or binoculars! Before I had the chance to ask him if he had forgotten his and might want to borrow mine, I came to realize it was no oversight on his part. The fact was he didn't need either! His eyesight was so keen that he could spot even partially concealed game with his naked eye at distances I could never hope to match. I was constantly amazed at his ability to see elk across distant ridges or in heavily-treed valleys. Of course, he had trained himself from years of guiding to pick out game in their surroundings by looking for horizontal forms against vertical backgrounds, movement, color disparities, the sun's reflection off an antler tine, etc. Not withstanding, Ike McBride had the best eyesight I've ever witnessed. Period!

After an hour's climb, we reached a dense stand of pines where we tied the horses (low and with enough rope to allow them to graze in our absence). We hadn't walked 50 yards when Ike pointed ahead to a cow elk staring at us. We froze, hoping she wasn't the sentinel for a larger group – even possibly the herd I had spotted the previous evening – and initiate a massive exit over the top of the ridge we were near! However, after eyeballing us for a few minutes, she joined another cow and slowly disappeared into the pines. They were 100 yards ahead of us, but we were soon on their trail, anticipating seeing others with antlers adorning their heads!

On the far side of the ridge, Ike spotted a black bear feeding several hundred yards away. While I was preoccupied with that rare sighting, Ike pointed excitedly to a large herd of elk in the valley below, walking hurriedly in single file through thick undergrowth and dense pine groves. My binoculars located two bulls in the group, a large 5x5 or 6x6 and a smaller 4x4 satellite bull. I was certain those were the same ones I had observed the prior evening! However, they seemed to know where they were headed, and the approximate 500-yard distance was widening quickly. We had no time to lose.

Ike suggested we take a diagonal path between us and the elk with the hope of cutting the distance and intercepting them for a closer look and possible shot. He set a fast pace down the ridge and through the dense pines, and for a man past my 50 years, his physical condition certainly defied his age! Another unspoken part of Ike's plan was that the herd would slow down their pace to help us out! Luckily, we were downwind, so our only chance of being detected was via our movement.

The elk paused briefly on a distant hillside, then split into two groups: one included the big bull and soon resumed its unmatchable pace away from us; the other, led by the 4x4, headed to our right over a small ridge. Ike felt we could cut across our ridge location and drastically reduce the distance gap by the time the second group emerged from the valley it had entered. In such situations you have to hang your hat somewhere, and Ike's plan seemed feasible, if not our only hope. Again, the race was on!

Our timing wasn't as good as anticipated, since no elk were visible when we hit the ridgeline. Either they hadn't taken the route we expected or they had already passed through by the time we reached our designated spot! Ike's "never say die" attitude kicked in immediately as he motioned for me to follow him down the ridge and across a grassy field interspersed with pockets of ponderosa pine and small aspen groves to a new observation point several hundred yards to our right. Ike's thinking was that if the elk continued their circular path, we might have another chance to find them. After reaching our destination, I immediately started glassing the narrow ravine and hillside stretching before us 350 yards away. Simultaneously, Ike caught some movement on the hillside, and when I concentrated my search on the area he was pointing to, the 4x4 bull came into focus! He was facing to my left halfway up the hill and staring our way. Ike told me to attempt a shot since the bull had spotted us; otherwise, we'd have to cross the deep ravine in an attempt to get closer. We decided both factors put us at a distinct disadvantage, and that the bull wouldn't hold his position much longer.

It was then a matter of finding a good anchor point and accurately calculating the distance and "drop". With an estimated 350-yard flat trajectory, I held six inches over his back in line with his left foreleg and touched off. We both heard the telltale ***whomp*** of a hit as the bull lurched forward and ran upward to the crest of the hill. I didn't have time for a second shot, but was hopeful I wouldn't need one!

Ike and I scrambled through the ravine and up the hill to the point of impact. Neither of us could find any physical signs of a hit; no hair, no blood, not even the churned-up ground marking the bull's quick getaway! However, we did know the direction he was headed, and a thick stand of saplings approximately 30 yards wide and long was in the path of its flight! Since we had neither seen nor heard him on our approach but assumed he was hit hard, Ike and I concluded that the bull was bedded in that thicket! Ike whispered that he'd circle above the dense growth and, hopefully, push the bull out in a downhill escape route to my waiting gun. He hadn't walked five feet when the bull jumped up from some high weeds short of the thicket and crashed into that temporary patch of security. We knew we had him trapped.

With both of us stooped over and peering into the thick cover, we inched forward, looking for any movement or sign of the downed bull. Perhaps he was storing up his remaining energy for one last flight. I had mental images of that desperate, 800-pound express train with antlers trying to stomp me into the ground as he exploded from cover! However, before that possibility could become a reality, I spotted him lying motionless in the heavy cover 15 yards in front of me. A quick finishing shot ended the chase!

Needless to say, Ike was as pleased with my success as I was with his guiding knowledge and skill. After the usual handshakes, congratulatory comments, and photos, the hard work of gutting and packing began. In our excitement, we hadn't given the slightest thought to the severely dropping temperature, and, by the time Ike pulled out his knife, snow

205

began to fall. It started as a gentle dusting, but soon increased in density, accompanied by a chilling wind. To add to the misery, Ike broke his knife blade trying to cut through the bull's shoulder and had only my four-inch Buck knife to complete the task – no saw, no hatchet!

What happened next still causes me to shiver just thinking about it. Ike was wearing a new shirt, and to keep it from getting bloodied during the gutting chore, he removed it **and** his outer jacket and completed his work with only a T-shirt between him and the elements! He refused my offer to wear my polar fleece jacket as if it were a balmy mid-summer day, and I could only stand by helplessly as he finished dressing out and quartering the entire elk in a driving snowstorm without complaint! I'm not sure if hearty or "nuts" – or both – would properly describe Ike's macho behavior, but I can only say better him than me! As far as I know, he didn't die from pneumonia.

As it turned out, the kill site was at the top of the mountain fronting the ranch, about one mile from my cabin quarters and within a couple of hundred yards from where I first observed the herd the previous afternoon! After what seemed like a 10-mile chase and stalk, we ended up full circle from where it all started! We were then faced with the task of packing out the elk; so, after retrieving the horses, Ike rode back to the ranch to get his mule while I stayed with the elk.

I wish I could report that Ike's mule possessed a greater intelligence and sense of cooperation than those on my Montana elk hunt, but in truth it was **worse** in every respect! Upon Ike's return, I immediately sensed trouble as the mule kept stubbornly pulling back on the lead rope and digging in its hooves with every step. It seemed to know there was work to be done and wanted no part of it. The next problem occurred when Ike led the mule into the thicket to get as close as possible to the elk to ease the loading chore. Ike strained to overcome the mule's resistance and finally got it hitched to a nearby tree. The actual packing and loading went smoothly, and Mr. Mule appeared to accept his role **until** Ike tried to lead it out of the thicket to the trail leading back to the ranch. The stubborn beast seemed to make a spontaneous decision that it didn't like the additional weight and was determined to lighten his load, completely and immediately! The mule started bucking, kicking, and spinning with such reckless force that it became entangled in the saplings and fell to its knees. Ike was given little choice but to completely unpack the mule to enable it to stand up, figuring it would be easier to reload once the mule was led out to the trail clearing. Once again the theory was sound, and after we finished repacking, Ike decided to lead the mule on foot down the severely sloping trail. I was to follow on my horse with Ike's steed in tow.

Without warning, the mule bolted forward, ripped the rope from Ike's grasp, and charged straight downhill on a dead run! I couldn't believe it kept its balance as long as it did, with the full weight of the elk shifting violently to-and-fro with each leap! Dumbfounded, Ike and I watched the spectacle unfold before us for at least 100 yards until our stubborn friend's journey came to an abrupt ending. Whether or not it saw the barbed-wire fence or just couldn't stop due to its speed and load-generated momentum is besides the point. I only know that the mule became airborne, cartwheeled "head over hooves" down the slope, and crashed through trees and whatever else was in its path with enough accompanying noise to scare any remaining elk off the mountain. Finally, there was silence, and the look Ike and I exchanged carried the same message: Ike would soon be in the market for a new mule! I would have bet any amount that nothing could have survived that fall as we wove our way down the mountain to see if there were as many pieces of mule as elk!

To our complete surprise, we found the mule lying on its side breathing heavily with nostrils flaring and sides heaving - but **alive**! A ripped ear was the only physical evidence of its spectacular journey. The meat bags were still attached, and the entire elk was present and accounted for! Unbelievable! I must admit Ike wasn't in a very good mood and was quite unsympathetic about his animal's plight. Less than kind words were used to get the mule upright - only to show its displeasure again by bolting a second time! After what it had been through, I was amazed it could even walk, let alone run! Ike was soon in hot pursuit and eventually caught up with the ill-tempered creature near its corral at the ranch. It was a bizarre conclusion to a wonderful hunt.

The story was complete. I had filled my tag with a fine 4x4 bull, and it took only one day. Not bad for $125! To show my appreciation for his remarkable talent and tireless effort, I gave Ike an additional $50 tip **and** my Buck knife, which he had used so skillfully. I could never hope to duplicate Ike's performance with that little blade, so my decision was an easy one. He was truly an experienced professional and gave the old 1950's political slogan, "I Like Ike", new meaning!

As I packed my car for the trip home, I thought of one other person who would be happy that day – Lisa, for my safe and early return!

Unfortunately for me, the ranch was leased to a group of Nebraska hunters the following year, and my attempt to contact Ike to arrange another hunt with him was unsuccessful. He was no longer with <u>Triple G Outfitters</u> and his whereabouts were unknown – gone, yes, but ***never*** forgotten!

(Above) Ike McBride with his unpredictable, "somersault" mule
(Below) with his very dependable horse!

October 18, 1993: Kim and guide, Ike McBride, pose with
my 4x4 Rocky Mountain bull elk, taken in Eagle, Colorado
with trusty old Remington .30-.06 model 742 Woodsmaster

Chapter 15: Final Hour Mule Deer Buck – Craig, Colorado (1995)

The fellow who took over <u>Triple G Outfitters</u> tried to talk me into an elk hunt on public land for the fall 1994 season, but I couldn't get charged up about paying $1,500 for a hunt on land I could hunt on my own at $0 cost! I also had no way to control the number of other hunters I'd be competing with on that rather small parcel, whether "locals" or others he may have planned to book. It's tough to score when you see more orange vests than orange leaves, so I decided to pass. I certainly wanted to keep my momentum going from 1993, but my "gut" said no. At the very least, it made me determined to plan ahead for the 1995 big-game season!

I applied successfully for my 1995 resident archery licenses for deer and elk, specifically for Game Management Unit #461, which includes the mountain community of Conifer. I'd seen enough of both species on or near my three-acre parcel to feel confident about my chance to score on both, and being within walking distance of my home was an added bonus! As it turned out, I spent many enjoyable mornings and evenings in my tree stand observing several good bulls and bucks, but none close enough for a shot. Just being outdoors during those wonderful late August through late September days - watching the sun rise, listening to the multi-pitched choruses of bugling bulls, and observing foxes and squirrels scampering about - was worth the price of the licenses alone. However, I still wanted to score on a good Colorado mule deer, and since I hadn't scored with the bow, I was eligible to try my hand during rifle season.

The only obstacle I had to overcome was obtaining a license for a promising mule deer area. Luckily, the Colorado Division of Wildlife had a generous number of leftover licenses available for each of the three rifle seasons. They represented "GMUs" with low demand, "GMUs" with a greater number of licenses available versus demand, and for the category that interested me: Private-Land-Only licenses. After reviewing previous season harvest records and picking the brains of Division of Wildlife personnel, I found that "GMUs" #3 and #301 in the extreme northwest corner of the state produced consistently good mule deer numbers. I first had to obtain permission from a landowner before being issued the license, and "DOW" personnel provided me with a landowner list for that area. In response to my request to prioritize the list – whom would **they** call first! – they recommended Shirley Stehle, who, along with her sons John

211

and Jim, owned and operated <u>Colorado Trophy Guides </u>in Craig, Colorado. I called Shirley immediately, was impressed with her answers, and negotiated a three-day hunt for October 14-16 during the first combined rifle season.

Shirley owned 500 acres of good elk and mule deer habitat which she and her deceased husband had purchased years before for the purpose of raising sheep. She was 68 years old, but led an active life and even shared the guiding duties with her sons during hunting season! The Stehles leased another 1,400 acres, and, even though there would be a total of eight hunters "in camp", I felt comfortable there was enough land and game for everyone to have an enjoyable and, hopefully, successful hunt. Four of the hunters were from Kansas, were returning for their second season with the Stehles – always a good sign! – and chose to hunt the ranch on their own, unguided. They felt they knew the acreage's bedding and feeding areas and connecting travel routes well enough to be successful on their own. That left three guides for the remaining four of us, and it worked out perfectly, since another hunter and I both wanted our own guides while the others chose a 2x1 arrangement.

The less than two-week wait from the time I arranged the hunt until it started allowed enough time to prepare and get excited without getting antsy! Since it's a five-hour drive from Conifer to Craig, I got an early start on the 13th in order to get settled at the prearranged rooming house in Craig before making the 15-minute drive to the Stehle Ranch to meet everyone and get organized for the next day.

Shirley was very friendly and gracious, and you could tell she enjoyed the seasonal company. She prepared a home-cooked meal each night for all of us and made our lunches to take into the field. Those hunters staying at the ranch were treated to breakfast as well. However, I found it just as convenient to grab an early bite at a diner in town, then join the others at the ranch by 6 a.m. to discuss the day's hunt and determine our guide and territory assignments.

John and his 11-year-old son, Clifford, were my guides that first day, and the modus operandi was to drive the ranch roads in vehicles, then stalk and shoot when an acceptable trophy was spotted. Within 15 minutes of leaving the ranch house, we saw a respectable 3x3 mule deer buck with two does crossing a meadow. I passed for two reasons: I had set a prehunt goal of at least a 4x4 with good spread and height that would compare favorably to my Montana trophy; and, it was too early in the hunt to settle for less than my goal. We also spotted some does running across an open field heading for their daytime bedding area among some ponderosa pines on a nearby hillside. We drove and looked until we were satisfied that the early morning traffic had found their preferred rest areas, then returned to the ranch to plan the afternoon hunt. In the meantime, Clifford and I became fast friends. His enthusiasm was contagious, and he loved my hunting stories. I could easily relate to his budding love for hunting just as I had as a 12-year-old duck hunter! He insisted on nicknaming my reliable and game-tested .30-.06, "Old Meat"!

We glassed some cut grain fields that afternoon, but saw nothing. I'm sure the weather wasn't helping our situation either. The temperature was in the 80's; hardly conducive to mass game movements! I'm sure they were bedded in the shade waiting for cooler nighttime conditions to move and feed.

There were fewer hunters at the diner the second morning, attesting to opening day successes for some, and perhaps discouragement and early departures for others. I was still optimistic about my chances and was looking forward to working with Jim Stehle, John's older brother, who was considerably shorter and thinner than John, but just as nice. We saw one 5x5 bull elk that day, but were unsuccessful in trying to get close enough for a shot. We also found an unauthorized hunter field dressing a small buck on one of the Stehle leases, and Jim wasn't very empathetic when the fellow said he **thought** he was on public land. Jim took his name to report him for trespassing, which may seem a bit harsh for a first offense, but understandable when one takes into account leasing costs and wanting to fill their own "paying" clients' tags! By the end of that second day, my tags were among the list of those "unfilled"! The weather had continued its unseasonably warm trend, which made it difficult to even get into a hunting mood. However, I had one day remaining, and I intended to make the most of it.

I remember sitting in the diner that third and last morning among an even greater number of empty tables than on Tuesday, contemplating how circumstances and luck might change that day versus the first two. The game would be warier of roving 4WD's, the weather remained warm, and the mule deer rut was still a month away – all factors contributing to a rather dismal outlook. However, the one bright spot that gave me hope was that Shirley would be my guide that day, and if anyone knew the patterns and movement of deer in that area, she was the one. I had to place my full faith in her ability and experience.

213

Shirley was ready to go, complete with orange hat and vest, when I drove up to her ranch home on October 16th. She informed me that four of the hunters had scored on nice bucks, and said she wanted me to be the fifth! The largest of the bucks was still hanging in her son Jim's barn, and we stopped by to see it on our way out. It was a 3x4 big-bodied bruiser that got my adrenaline flowing!

Shirley asked if I would drive my 4WD Blazer for our morning's search while she glassed, and, during the first two hours, we covered nearly every observation point on the ranch hoping to see deer moving to their bedding areas. By 9:30 a.m., we had spotted only a small "forkhorn" buck silhouetted against the sky at the top of a hill several hundred yards away. I told Shirley I had no interest in pursuing it, so we just watched as it trotted away.

By the time we finished a mid-morning cup of coffee at the ranch, the odds for ending my hunt on a positive note were fading fast. With the five-hour drive ahead, I wanted to leave by early afternoon, and with a quick glance at the thermometer showing 80°, I didn't hold out much hope of scoring. Shirley then mentioned taking one last drive into a dead-end draw nearby that served as a favorite midday resting area for the local deer. With nothing to lose, we headed into the protected peninsula of land surrounded on three sides by steep, scrub pine-covered hills. Shirley explained that over the years she had observed a consistent movement of deer heading into that area to bed down midway up the hillside. As we neared our stopping point, she told me to be ready to shoot if deer jumped up when we shut the car doors. She even suggested giving the doors a good slam just for that purpose! I had the clip in my gun, but for safety reasons had not yet chambered a 150-grain cartridge. At first observation, it seemed unlikely that any deer were bedded in the sporadic cover; however, the slamming doors proved otherwise! Immediately, three deer jumped from their beds halfway up the hill directly in front of the car. Shirley identified two bucks and a doe, all of which were heading quickly toward the top. When I anchored my rifle on the sideview mirror and peered through the scope, I could locate only one of the bucks, which had paused momentarily to observe our presence and determine its next move. The other two deer had continued their upward escape through thicker cover.

The sight in my scope was of a young, full-racked mule deer buck. I wasn't sure if he carried 3 or 4 points on each side plus possible brow tines, but I felt with all things considered, he was a trophy I'd be proud to take home. When he resumed his climb, I touched off a smooth shot that I estimated at 250 yards. I held high above his left foreleg to allow for the expected drop over that distance, and it was instantly evident that my calculation was correct. He spun around, stumbled, fell heavily down the hill, and finally came to rest 100 yards below the point of impact. I was relieved to have an easy downhill drag, especially at one o'clock under a hot midday sun. My hourglass had run out, and it was time to go home.

Shirley was delighted with my "eleventh-hour" success and accompanied me on the short, but arduous climb to retrieve the buck. He was a symmetrical 4x4 without brow tines and had a 15-inch inside spread – no monster to be sure, but a satisfactory trophy nevertheless. Remembering that only an hour earlier I was resigned to leaving empty-handed made it that much more gratifying and special! I wonder if my buck qualified Shirley for the *Guinness Book of World Records* as the oldest successful female hunting guide in the United States? Could be!

The one basic hunting rule that was confirmed on my hunt at the Stehle Ranch and which consistently holds true in any hunting situation is that one's luck can change quickly and unexpectedly. Hunters who have learned that, hang in there against all odds and weather conditions and **never give up**!

Don't **EVER** give up

(Above) Shirley Stehle, 68, cook and guide extraordinaire
(Below) Shirley's mobile ranch house and my Blazer "spotting" vehicle

Typical Craig, Colorado mule deer country – rolling and steep hills
dotted with ponderosa pines, open fields, and grassy meadows

The dead-end draw where I jumped my buck, halfway
up the hill in the center of photo

The result of a gamble and a good shot!

Chapter 16: Front Yard Mulie Buck with a Bow (2000)

My book was supposed to end with Chapter # 15, but something new and exciting changed my plans. On September 21, 2000, I harvested my first mule deer with a bow, a sleek 5x5 buck, and only 50 yards from my front door!

Each year since purchasing my Conifer, Colorado home in 1992, I have successfully applied for my either-sex elk and mule deer bow licenses for Game Management Unit# 461. That "GMU" includes my three-acre property, located at the end of a culdesac with no through traffic. At 8,500 feet, it's the highest house in my Conifer Meadows community and is nestled directly below 9,400 foot Riley's Peak in the foothills of the Rocky Mountains.

Due to my home's unique location, I enjoy a wide variety of game sightings and have no need to travel outside my own little compound to hunt. Besides numerous trophy bull elk and mule deer bucks, I have seen black bear, wild turkey, coyote, red and grey fox, and bobcat on numerous occasions in addition to the legions of grey squirrels and chipmunks which regularly visit my feeders and gardens!

Only private land rifle hunting and bowhunting is permitted in GMU# 461. As such, big game is not as heavily hunted and, therefore, not as wary or as easily spooked as those found in more congested public hunting areas. This might explain why the elk and deer feed and meander nonchalantly on my property while I watch and take pictures from my deck within comfortable bow range - a perfect scenario for those hoped-for 30 yard or less shots from tree stands!

Despite the many sightings and "close encounters of a frustrating kind" through the 1999 season, I never filled a bow tag. Seven years without a harvest did serve one very important purpose, however; by hunting from various tree stand locations on my property, I was able to observe the movement and travel routes of deer and elk during both a.m. and p.m. vigils. Those sightings contributed greatly to my eventual tree stand choice and set the stage for my success in the first bow season of the new millenium!

I placed my stand in a large pine tree that happens to be exactly 50 paces from my front door! In fact, as I sit on my living room couch enjoying a warm fire, I can see my portable stand

and seat clearly through the east-facing window! My stand location is so close to the house, in fact, that before leaving in the early morning darkness for "my tree", I make sure all the windows are closed so any approaching game won't be spooked if the telephone rings! And, of course, I'm kidded by my hunting buddies about how many rest stops I have to make while walking to my stand! As they say, jealousy will get you nowhere! I must admit I often think of out-of-state hunters who fly thousands of miles or even in-state hunters who drive hundreds of miles to find a location as promising as mine!

From the deck fronting the house, my "lawn" (if you can call it that) covers a mere 15 yards before sloping upward to a narrow hillside consisting of mature lodgepole pines, spruce, and pockets of aspen. That 30-yard stretch of cover ends at a firebreak access road bulldozed by my neighbor who owns the adjacent 600 acres to the south. A small meadow borders the far side of that overgrown dirt road, and a thick pine forest with a series of ridges continues upward from the meadow to Riley's Peak above.

Both deer and elk feed in the valley meadows 400 yards below me, then work their way up at first light to bed down in the pines between my property and the summit. In the evening, they reverse the process. Well-worn trails mark those journeys, and one such route actually bisects my two-car garage and archery target positioned 20 yards away! I have my mental "notebook" filled with sightings of individual, groups, and even herds of elk that have used that path, crossed my driveway, jumped the embankment, and continued through the protective growth on the hillside to the meadow and beyond!

Looking south from my front deck, the access road at the top of the hill slopes downward toward the east, then continues on a relatively straight course for about 300 yards before taking a more severe dropoff north. I have observed many deer - but no elk - appear from the eastern end of that road. By compiling and reviewing all my game observation data, it was easy to finally choose the "stand" tree that I did. I first used it during the 1999 bow season, and from my perch 18 feet above the ground, I saw four 4x4 or better bucks, two 5x5 bulls, and one 6x6 bull, all within 60 yards. I did have one unsuccessful shot at a nice 5x5 buck; otherwise, no others approached within the shooting "circle" I had created by placing eight small marker flags equally spaced in a 20-yard radius around my stand. Such yardage indicators make it easy to determine the correct bowsight pin choice and alignment when an animal comes within range.

Raising or lowering my 10, 20, or 30-yard pin in relation to where the elk or deer is standing vis-à-vis one of the nearby 20-yard flags, takes away the guesswork at the moment of truth and promotes more accurate shots and clean kills - what every bowhunter desires. Though I didn't confirm the effectiveness of my system during the 1999 season, I felt confident it would eventually help me achieve success.

With the 2000 bow season set for August 26-September 24, I had my stand set up well in advance, with fresh pine boughs nailed in place to conceal my "workspace". It was undetectable from every angle, and my confidence soared as I began the countdown to opening day. Intervening time was spent tuning my bow (which I found shot consistently high and to the right from its one year of inactivity), replacing fletching, inserting new 125-grain, three-bladed Thunderhead broadheads, and purchasing new cow elk urine attractor lure and earth scent masking spray. I also replaced the two hay bales in my practice target and was pleased that my groupings out to 25 yards continued to narrow as the season neared!

The weather on the August 26 opener was hot - one of the state's summer record sixty-two 90 degree plus days - and besides no game sightings, it didn't even **feel** like a hunting day! I hunted only one other day before leaving for a family wedding/vacation back East from 8/31-9/6. While away, I was praying for cooler weather on my return. However, the summerlike temperatures continued as I forced myself into manning my station just in case an in-the-velvet buck or bull showed up. Although I did see enough game - some mulie does, one with her two fawns, a fluffy-coated red fox, a cautious bobcat, and a beautiful male coyote with its multi-colored rust/brown, gray, and black coat - to keep me alert and interested, a decision not to take my stand for one late afternoon watch proved costly.

I had hunted the morning of Friday, September 8 without success. I planned to be on stand that afternoon as well, but I got involved with chores and phone calls, and by the time all was said and done, it was 6:30 p.m. There was still good shooting light until 7:30, but I decided to "pass" and resume the pursuit in the morning. I had made a similar decision during the 1999 season and, while "sitting it out", watched helplessly from my front door as a 5x5 bull elk followed two cows directly beneath my stand! That was at two o'clock, and I had been vascilating back and forth about whether to hunt earlier than later due to the promising weather, but I didn't, with the above result! Right then, I vowed to follow my instincts better in the future and not let another slam dunk opportunity slip by.

Fast forward to the afternoon of September 8, 2000, as I kept second-guessing my "no hunt" decision and became increasingly nervous as I thought about my ill-fated decision of the previous season. Every 10 minutes I went to the front door to check the nearby hillside, hoping and praying that no shootable trophy would make an appearance. My prayers were answered.....**until** 7:20, when my look was greeted with the image of a monster 30-inch plus buck with at least six points per side staring at me 25 yards away! To say my heart sank is not only an understatement, but a poor substitute for the mental butt-kicking I subjected myself to! To make matters worse, that gigantic specimen was flanked by two lesser, but definitely "keeper" bucks. My mouth dropped open at the sight, but the only thing left to do was to try to capture on film what I wouldn't have the opportunity to hang on my wall! I did manage to ease outside without them running off, but the fading light prevented me from capturing the magnificent image that filled the lens of my 35mm Canon EOS 650. Wouldn't you know it! Of course, by the time I went back inside to get my flash unit, the triumverate had departed, leaving me to wonder if what I had just seen was imagined. I wish it were! At times like that, you can only try to convince yourself that it "wasn't meant to be" (or some similar empty rationalization!) to keep from going *CRAZY,* and move on. I had only myself to blame and, once again, realized that if I wanted to score, I had to be in my tree stand, not my house! Needless to say, I promised myself not to squander any more opportunities for the rest of the season.

Being aware that mature big-game animals can pattern a hunter who either hunts the same stand when the wind is unfavorable or who has been seen climbing into or down from a stand, I am ultra-careful not to be detected by either sight or smell each time I hunt my "front yard" stand. In the morning, I set my alarm for 5:00 a.m. and am settled on stand by 5:45, a full hour before sunrise. Even though it is only a short walk, I never fail to apply fresh cow elk urine to the felt scent pads fastened to my low-cut rubber-bottomed L.L. Bean boots or spray my clothing with earth scent spray. I also have a piece of thread attached to my bowstring to be ever-mindful of wind direction, and additional elk or mule deer cover scent and my traditional green, tan, and black patterned camo suit (kept in a plastic bag filled with pine boughs and rich smelling earth between hunts) all contribute to the non-detection goal. I always try to get as many factors as possible in my favor, having learned over the years from many mistakes that cutting corners or being in a hurry will more often than not turn the tables in the animals' favor. There are so many things that can go wrong that it pays to be thorough and detail oriented before **and** during every hunt!

Warm weather continued, and though I spent countless hours on stand, I had yet to see a buck or bull, let alone have one come within range. It was September 20th, and only four days remained in the season. I was beginning to think another non-harvest bow season was at hand.

On Thursday morning, the 21st, I decided to hunt a little longer than my usual 8:30 quitting time, since I had a busy schedule that day and wasn't sure if I'd get home in time to hunt that evening. I saw only the handsome coyote previously mentioned and tried to lure him in by using my cow elk call as an impromptu distressed rabbit call. Didn't work! He paused briefly, then disappeared down the access road. I was back in the house by 9:15.

Luckily, my day's chores and activities went smoothly, and when I glanced at my watch, it was only 4:30 - plenty of time to get home and up in my tree.

The weather forecast had called for sunshine early, wind picking up in the afternoon, and a 10% chance of rain. In reality, a clear morning soon turned to overcast skies and a light drizzle in the early afternoon. When I arrived home, dark thunderclouds loomed overhead, but I was determined to hunt, regardless of the weather. By the time I changed into my hunting clothes, applied my camo makeup, and checked my bow and other equipment, it was raining much harder. Lightening bolts could be seen and rolls of thunder could be heard as I stepped from the protection of my garage and headed for the stand. It was 5:30 p.m.

At first I wasn't concerned about the rain, since the canopy of thick pine boughs offered good protection. However, the weather gods decided to turn things up a notch, and, before I knew it, I was caught in a full-fledged thunderstorm. By 6:30, I was soaked to the skin. My rational brain told me to head for the house, but my **hunting** brain overruled, especially with the two "absentee misses" in mind, and I decided to stick it out. By 6:45, the rain had let up, but I knew there was only a half hour of good shooting light remaining due to the ominous cloud cover. Darkness would come earlier than under clear conditions.

223

The rain had dampened the forest floor, and I knew any approaching game would appear like ghosts, without warning and suddenly present where only seconds before there was nothing! It's uncanny, but every serious hunter has experienced such phenomena! I soon realized I'd have to rely on my eyes versus ears to detect any buck or bull that evening. I always make a concerted effort while on stand to keep as still as possible, sitting on my seat with bow hanging within easy reach, and searching the expanse below with more eye movement than head movement. I know my predetermined shooting lanes and anticipate and visualize shots from each, both sitting and standing, depending on how and where the game will approach, their body angle, distance, etc. On that evening of September 21st I was sitting straight forward, facing my house and relying on my peripheral vision to pick up any movement. I was also playing the percentages of a buck or bull approaching from my left, angling toward me in a downward direction from the pines on the stand side of my driveway. That is their typical pattern in the evenings.

At 7:05, with shooting time running out, I caught movement to my left through a small opening in the pine branch hanging directly overhead. Within seconds, the brisket and front legs of a deer appeared! I couldn't tell if it was a buck or doe, or whether it was traveling alone, but I did know it was quickly approaching the shooting lane directly in front of me and perfectly in line with my front door only a short distance away!

I instinctively gripped my bow and quietly lifted it from the bow hanger screwed into the limb above. I simultaniously raised the arrow from the moleskin-covered handle riser to its ready position on the arrow rest prongs. At the same time, I pulled my feet under my seat, stood up, and turned to the right to get into a good shooting position. All the while I kept one eye on the deer, which inched slowly ahead toward the selected opening. And, then, I saw what I had hoped for - *antlers* emerging from behind a small pine tree just beyond one of my 20-yard markers! I locked him into my preshot computer at 22 yards, which would put my 20-yard pin slightly above his lung area behind the right shoulder. He had a nice rack, too, with at least four points per side, and as he turned his head to the left, I noted a good spread that outweighed its average height; not the true trophy I had seen from the other side of my door a couple of weeks earlier, but a very nice young buck that I'd be proud to claim as my first mule deer via bow. I immediately put such post-kill thoughts aside and concentrated on the task at hand. He was completely unaware of my presence, and a light breeze was, thankfully, in my face. I felt relaxed and confident due to a good practice session the previous afternoon, and I only needed for him to take two more steps forward into my "lane" to put my shooting prowess to the ultimate test. I slowly came to full draw, with my Easton XX75 aluminum 2315 shaft sliding silently to its full 29-inch length, and found my anchor point with right thumb extending under my jawbone and nose touching the string.

Within seconds, the young buck entered the clearing, offering a downward quartering-away shot - perfect for double-lung penetration. My release was smooth, and a split second later I heard the telltale sound of a successful shot hitting its mark. At impact, the buck bolted to my right, circled below, dashed down the sloping terrain, and disappeared into the pines. I heard a loud crashing sound, as if he had stumbled over a log or blowdown, soon followed by dead silence! A quick review of the event that had just transpired left me with a positive feeling that I had made a good, fatal shot. I didn't expect a long search, but I was a bit concerned about the continuing rain obliterating whatever blood trail he might leave. Darkness was only minutes away as I climbed down to start the tracking process. I wanted to find him as quickly as possible, not only to keep the meat from spoiling in the warm weather, but also because I didn't want him to become the next meal of a coyote or mountain lion!

I immediately went to the house to get my heavy duty Mag-Lite, rope, and Buck knife, then returned to the impact point to search for the blood trail. However, by the time I reached his entry point in the pines, I had found neither blood nor my arrow. I reasoned that the lack of blood could have been caused by the arrow plugging the entry wound, and, with no exit wound, all the blood was filling his chest cavity. Good theory or not, I still had to find the buck, and I knew then my only hope was to spot him with my flashlight. I proceeded slowly, shining the beam left and right to cover every bush, depression, and thicket hoping to catch either white belly hair, the green iridescent glow from his eyes, or antler tines protruding above the ground cover.

I gradually turned left and headed downhill approximately 30 yards below the access road on my right. I had gone perhaps 75 yards when I came to an opening on the hillside. When I cast my light toward a brush pile on the right, the welcome sight of my downed deer appeared! The buck's body was facing me, lying motionless 15 yards away. I still approached with caution and touched his rump with a stick to be sure I wouldn't catch a face full of antlers if he had a final burst left in him. But he was dead, and my first bow-killed Rocky Mountain mule deer buck was in the books!

A closer examination of his symetrical 4x4 bifurcated antlers revealed two small brow tines, which immediately elevated him to a 5x5! I was delighted and proud of myself for a well-placed shot that entered mid-body below the spine and angled forward into his lungs. As predicted, the arrow was still in place, and I removed it during the gutting process to save as a souvenir from another successful hunt.

Having finally reached one of the bowhunting goals I had set for myself when I moved to Colorado, I am now looking forward to adding a nice bull elk to that list or, perhaps, getting a second chance at that monster 30-inch mulie buck. One thing's for sure: I'll be in my "front yard" tree stand as often as possible!

Author's Note: Shortly after penning this final chapter, the author sold his Conifer home and moved back East for a brief time. He returned to Colorado in January, 2002, settled in Evergreen, and resumed his hunting adventures in the fall of 2003.

My 2000 "front yard" 5x5 mulie buck

My 1999 missed opportunity....Ouch!

(left) looking back at "my tree" and stand (upper center) from spot where I shot my buck

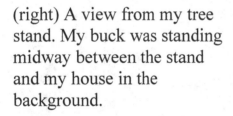

(right) A view from my tree stand. My buck was standing midway between the stand and my house in the background.

Conclusion

Hunting has provided many thrills and been the source of tremendous adventure and enjoyment throughout my life. I feel a wonderful sense of exhilaration every time I venture afield in anticipation of the unknown events that lie ahead. Such drama and suspense more often than not have ended in failure, but the occasional successful harvests keep me going back. More importantly, it's "the thrill of the hunt" and **not** the kill that makes me look forward to each new season and puts every nerve ending on alert as opening day approaches.

It was my Dad who got me started, and his last letter to me contained the following comments about our shared love for the sport: "You're my hunter, and I'm so glad it stuck—to enjoy nature, and the satisfaction of a hunt (especially a successful one). When you look at the trophies on the wall, many good memories return." I'll always be grateful for his introduction and encouragement.

I still look forward to each hunting season with the same high level of excitement, interest, and passion I had as a 12-year old awaiting that first Delaware duck hunt! The day those feelings are no longer present is the day I'll shut off the early a.m. alarm and go back to sleep!

Printed in the United States
By Bookmasters